SECRETS OF S[...]
By Stacey

Copyright 2012 by Stacey Coverstone

t:

.com

mes,
are either
ation or are
ance to
iness
, is

of this
any manner
ion of the

Dedication

To my husband and best friend, Paul

Acknowledgements

A huge thank you goes to Kelly Schaub for professionally editing this book.

And thanks to Sue Billings and Melissa Blue for reading this story and providing invaluable comments and suggestions.

CCBC
AMAZON
/01/15

Praise for Stacey Coverstone Novels

"A suspenseful, intriguing and heartfelt story!"
-Sue Billings on *Secrets of Seacliff House*

"5 Angels! *Tularosa Moon* is a whirlwind of a tale. Stacey Coverstone always creates magnificent magic when she composes a story. She weaves in chemistry to create a beautiful simmering romance, with a touch of mystery and suspense, to keep the reader edged on their seats. This gripping tale combines great dialogue, along with a grand plot and robust characters to make this a winner."
-Linda L. at Fallen Angel Reviews

"Stacey Coverstone delivers a heady mixture of mystery and romance, and pulse-pounding suspense."
-Michelle Black, Award-winning author of Victorian suspense

"5 Hearts for *Big Sky*! I dearly loved this book. The characters were wonderful, well drawn and diverse. The attraction between Brett and Taylor is strong and realistic. The love scenes were beautiful. I also really liked the ghost, Jamie, especially since she somehow managed to get forgiveness from beyond the grave. The reuniting of the sisters in this unusual way was poignant and brought tears to my eyes. The setting was quite descriptive and enjoyable, and the emotions

well done. It's a well-done mystery with plenty of red herrings. I kept changing my mind on the identity of the guilty party, all the way up to the very logical ending. I will most definitely read more by this author."
　　-Jaye Leyel at The Romance Studio

　　"Unraveling a mystery in a haunted saloon has never been more romantic."
　　-Publishers Weekly on *A Haunted Twist of Fate*

Chapter One

When Kayla Grayson heard the ding that indicated her mother had received an email message, she glanced quickly at the nightstand where the laptop sat and then at her mother, who was sitting upright in her bed. The private nurse wrapped a blood pressure cuff around Suzanne's arm, placed the stethoscope in her ears, and began to pump.

Ever since Kayla could remember, her mother had suffered from periodic panic attacks. But in the past few years, Suzanne had begun to experience rising levels of anxiety. Each episode had become more serious in nature. This last bout a couple of months ago had unfortunately landed her in the hospital, with a psychologist diagnosing her with agoraphobia. Kayla had studied the disease in her college psychology class. In layman's terms, her mom suffered from a debilitating fear of open spaces, crowds, and unfamiliar surroundings.

Kayla stared at her mother and wondered for the umpteenth time how they could be related. Suzanne was a slim and petite five-foot-three with no hips, while Kayla filled out a curvaceous five-foot-seven frame. At fifty-eight, Suzanne's hair was still ash blonde and as smooth and shiny as silk, whereas Kayla's auburn hair was thick and naturally wavy. As a teenager, she'd hated when it rained or the weather was humid, because her hair would turn into a wild uncontrollable mass of frizz. It wasn't much better these days, but at least she earned a good living as a graphic designer and children's book author. She could afford expensive haircuts and the best styling products to keep her mane manageable.

As far as their personalities went, Suzanne was quiet and reserved, almost to the point of being standoffish. The few friends she'd had when Kayla was growing up had dropped away due to her increasing inability to socialize. Completely opposite, Kayla liked to laugh, make new friends, and speak her mind. She intended to experience life to its fullest, and so far, she'd done just that.

"Your blood pressure is normal, Mrs. Grayson," the nurse said. "Let's check your pulse now."

Kayla's gaze remained glued to her mom, who extended her arm to the nurse. Suzanne rested her head on her pillow and closed her eyes, ignoring the waiting message that blinked on the computer screen. Kayla couldn't help but wonder who would be emailing her mother. It was probably spam. But what if it wasn't? What if it was from the mystery person?

Like clockwork for the past ten years, Suzanne had received an email every year on her birthday. Before that, a card had come in the mail. From whom, Kayla had no idea. She only knew that Suzanne would read the card privately in her room, and Kayla was never allowed to see the envelope, which had a return address printed in the corner. It was the same routine once Suzanne began using a computer and the emails started arriving. She'd read the email in private. Later, Kayla would see that she'd been crying and her mouth would be set in a tight line, warning Kayla not to ask questions. Her mom's pain was obvious, but she'd learned early on to keep silent.

Suzanne had always had her secrets. As

Kayla grew older, she became increasingly more resentful of them. She'd never been able to convince her mother that the things she held onto deep inside also concerned her.

"Your pulse is fine," reported the nurse. "I'll go get a glass of water for you. Be right back." She exited the room. Suzanne's eyes remained closed.

Kayla glanced out the screened window next to her. She could hear the muffled sounds of downtown traffic and smell the sweet fragrance of freshly mowed grass next door. It was early summer in Staunton, Virginia, a small town in the Shenandoah Mountains known for the birthplace of Woodrow Wilson and the home of historic Mary Baldwin College. It was where she and Suzanne had always lived. Although Kayla had grown up with the culture and history of Virginia as a part of her life, she'd never been completely sure whether or not she'd been Virginia-born.

While she'd gone to school here and had friends, her growing up memories were both pleasant and disturbing. Even as a child, she'd recognized that most families consisted of a mother and father, grandparents, and aunts, uncles and cousins. Even if some of the kids' parents were divorced, they usually knew something about their father—and even visited him on weekends. Her friends felt sorry for her when Thanksgiving, Christmas and Easter rolled around and family celebrations abounded.

Kayla had only her mother, and never an explanation for their lack of family.

The thing that increasingly nagged at her was the secrets. She was a sensible, mature, twenty-seven-year-old woman who needed to know who she was, and where she came from. If her mother believed she was protecting her from something—or someone—she was wrong. Kayla had a right to know her birthright. After all, how bad could her father, his family, and her mother's family have been?

Wild fantasies had filled her thoughts for years. But it was apparent *someone* knew how to reach her mother—the author of the annual emails. However, today wasn't her mom's birthday, which aroused Kayla's suspicions.

"Sounds like you have a message, Mom," she said nonchalantly, rousing Suzanne. "Do you want me to put the computer on your lap?"

The nurse returned to the room at that moment and handed Suzanne her pills and a glass of water. Suzanne swallowed the pills and drained the glass.

"I'll be going now," the nurse said, packing up her medical bag. "See you tomorrow, ladies. Call if you need me before then."

Once she'd retreated, Suzanne motioned for Kayla to hand her the laptop. "I don't know who'd be sending me an email, but I'll check it out. Maybe it's a notice about a bid I recently made on e-Bay."

Kayla rolled her eyes playfully. That was her mom's new interest—e-Bay. At least, it distracted her from her illness and gave her something to do to pass the time.

As soon as Suzanne began to read, Kayla noticed her hand was trembling.

"What is it, Mom?" she asked, leaning forward. A gray look tinged her mother's pallor, and Kayla wondered if she might pass out. "Shall I call the nurse back?"

Suzanne shook her head, inhaled a deep breath, and squeezed her eyes shut. When she opened them a moment later, a mixture of conflicted emotions flashed across her unlined face. It was as if she were trying to make a decision. Suddenly, she thrust the laptop toward Kayla and then laid her hands limply in her lap.

She cleared her throat. "Go ahead. Read the email. It's open on the screen."

What was in the email that had so shaken her mother? "Are you sure you want me to?" she asked. Her mother had always been such a private person.

"Yes," Suzanne answered.

Kayla placed the computer on her thighs. As she read the words on the screen, a twinge of alarm surged through her. "You have a cousin named Kitty who lives in Maryland?"

Suzanne nodded.

"Is she the person who used to send cards on your birthday?"

"Yes. Now she emails a greeting."

"Your mother is still alive?" Kayla jerked her gaze toward Suzanne and saw her cringe. A string of questions filled Kayla's mind, but she remained quiet and continued reading.

The cousin, Kitty, was pleading for Suzanne to return home to Harmony Beach, because of some man who had come back to town. She then went on to mention how she'd loved both Suzanne and little Kayla, how Suzanne had always been the strong one, and how Kitty was not only confused, she was afraid.

Afraid? Kayla's heart flew into her throat. *Afraid of what? Or of whom? The man?*

At that moment, Suzanne wailed in distress, and Kayla's gaze shot in her direction. Her mother had covered her face with her hands.

"I can't go! I'm sick. And even if I weren't, I would never go back there, not after what happened. Kitty doesn't know what she's asking of me!"

Kayla set the computer aside and perched on the edge of her mom's bed. She took her quivering hand in her own and then wiped the tears that had trailed down her cheeks. "Of course she doesn't understand, Mom, or she never would have made this request."

Kayla's mind raced. Who was the man that had returned to Harmony Beach? Did he have something to do with Suzanne having left her home and family?

After Suzanne quieted and her staccato breathing returned to normal, Kayla dared asked the questions that her mom could no longer deny answering.

"Mom, who is this cousin of yours?"

Suzanne's voice came out in a whisper so faint Kayla could barely hear her. "Her name is Kitty Chandler. Her father and my father were brothers. She and I were very close growing up. I was raised in Maryland. You lived there, too, for a while."

"For how long?"

"We left when you were three." She cut a quick glance toward Kayla and then her gaze dropped to her hands. "I sent our mailing address to Kitty once I got us settled here in Virginia, and then later, my email address. She's the only family member I trusted."

"I can't believe it. We lived in Maryland." Kayla's suspicions about not being Virginia born hit her in the middle of the chest like a brick. "Is your father still alive?" she asked, wanting to know about her mother's family.

Suzanne shook her head. "No. I never

knew him. He abandoned my mother and me before I was born."

The breath caught in Kayla's throat. They had something in common after all—absentee fathers. "But your mother is still alive and living in Maryland?" she asked, still finding the news bewildering.

Suzanne pursed her lips and spat, "Yes. In the house I grew up in. Seacliff House. I haven't spoken to her in twenty-four years."

Kayla couldn't believe what was happening. After a lifetime of wondering, she'd discovered in a matter of moments that she had family, and not so far away, either.

Seacliff House. The name conjured up dreams of romance—something Kayla didn't have much experience with. Having no current boyfriend, relationships had been few and far between, what with college and then work and her writing, and taking care of Mom. Besides, guys raised in a southern community where bloodlines are important tended to shy away from a woman who couldn't hold claim to any relatives, or a father. Even a deadbeat one.

She swallowed hard before asking the most important question. "Mom, your cousin Kitty says a man has returned to Harmony Beach. Could he be my dad?"

Suzanne's eyes widened. "No! Of course not! Your father is dead."

Kayla's heart sank. Suzanne had never told her that. She'd never said anything about him. Not his first name. What he looked like. Kayla had never even been shown a photo of him.

Her mother tilted her head and added, "At least I've always hoped Matt was dead."

She'd hoped her husband had died? Kayla didn't understand the strange comment. But at least she had a name. Finally! Matt. Her father's name was Matt.

Suzanne continued. "His jacket was found washed up on the beach. We thought he'd drowned. It was easier for me to accept that scenario than the one I believed in my heart to be true."

Still uncomprehending, Kayla said, "What do you mean?"

Suzanne's gaze held her in an iron grip. "All these years, I've believed my mother ran my husband—your father—out of town. According to Kitty's email, it appears I was right."

Kayla gasped. "So you *do* think the man she saw *is* my dad?"

Her mother didn't answer, only stared at her hands, apparently confused and lost in thought.

"Why would my grandmother do such a thing?" Kayla wanted to know. "What did he do that was so wrong?"

Suzanne's head snapped up. "He did plenty! Your father was not a nice man. And I have no desire to find out whether he's returned from the dead or not. I said goodbye and good riddance to him a long time ago. And to Seacliff House, too."

Stunned by her mom's bitter outburst, Kayla was struck speechless for a moment. She hadn't heard so much passion in Suzanne's voice in years. The moment passed, however, and anger boiled to the surface of her rippling emotions. How dare her mother! She'd had no right to shelter Kayla from the truth.

Kayla's voice cracked with emotion. "You can do, or not do, whatever you want, Mom. But I intend to find out if that man is my father. As well as meet my grandmother and

12

any other relatives you've kept from me all my life."

Her mother's face crumpled, and she reached for Kayla's hand. "I'm sorry, darling. In the beginning I only wanted to protect you. I didn't want what happened there to scar your life. Your father did some very bad things. Your grandmother did, too. It's best to forget you ever read this email or heard of Harmony Beach."

Kayla heard the sorrow in her voice, but she wasn't to be deterred. "It's too late. Not knowing them, or where I came from, has scarred me in ways you don't even understand."

Her crushing admission started the tears rolling down Suzanne's cheeks again. Then Suzanne's face sobered, and she turned her head and crossed her arms over her bosom, shutting Kayla out.

There were so many questions Kayla had, but it was obvious she wasn't going to get them answered this evening. Standing up, her spine grew rigid. She announced, "I'm going to Maryland, Mom. I have vacation time due me. You can come with me if you'd like. After all, you're the one Kitty has asked for."

"I can't leave here," Suzanne cried, swiping at her reddened eyes. "You know how it is."

Kayla nodded and then remembered what Kitty had said about her in the email. "Mom, you weren't always like this, were you? Your cousin remembers you as a happy, courageous and independent person. What happened to that woman?"

Suzanne sighed heavily. "She died the day I left Seacliff House."

Kayla's heart pounded. What had happened

to her mother? What had caused her to flee
with her and leave home never to return? What
terrible thing had Kayla's father done? If
the man who'd returned was him, where had he
been all these years? And what role did her
grandmother play in the dramatic saga that
took place twenty-four years ago?

A sudden stirring of excitement pulsed
through Kayla's body at the realization she
really did have a family. From all accounts,
her father was alive and well in a beach town
on the coast of Maryland. Come hell or high
water, she was going to find him.

She pulled up MapQuest on the computer
and discovered Harmony Beach to be only a six-
hour drive from Staunton. Her brain could
hardly comprehend she'd been so close in
proximity to relatives all this time and never
knew.

"Please don't go," Suzanne begged,
tugging on her arm.

"I *need* to, Mom. I'm calling my boss now
and requesting a week or two off."

"A week or two? Why so long? What do
you hope to accomplish?" Her face twisted into
a mask of desperation.

Kayla had no intention of coming home
until she learned all she could about the past
as it concerned her. But she didn't tell
Suzanne that. She took a deep breath. "If
you don't feel comfortable being alone, I'll
call your nurse and pay her extra to come stay
in the house with you until I return. I'm
going to pack. In the meantime, you might
want to reply to Kitty's email and tell her
I'm on my way in your stead."

Even though it was last minute, Kayla's
boss granted her the vacation time. So it was
settled, whether Suzanne approved or not. The

next morning, Kayla would drive northeast to
Maryland and whatever awaited her at Seacliff
House.

Chapter Two

Although the drive took less time than working a full day, Harmony Beach might as well have been a thousand miles away. The scenery changed gradually, but drastically, once Kayla left the comfort of the mountains. With each mile closer to Maryland, she felt she was driving into another world. When she finally parked her car on the street a block from the bed and breakfast owned by her mother's cousin, something magical happened.

The moment she stepped out of her vehicle, a soft breeze carrying the scent of salt and sea water wafted into her nostrils. Squawking seagulls drifted through the air above her head. And the sounds of waves crashing and people playing on the beach invaded her ears.

Her tense muscles relaxed, and a smile filled her face. This was where she'd been born! No wonder she'd grown up loving the water and swimming so much. Not that she'd ever been to the beach or seen the ocean. The community pool had been the closest thing.

This was her true home, she thought, moving toward the water as if being pulled by an invisible string. She walked up a ramp and stood on the wooden boardwalk that was elevated above the sand. She glanced around. The ocean view was breathtaking, and the beach stretched out for at least one mile in both directions. In front of her, teenagers played volleyball, flew kites, and little children built sand castles. Along the shore, people walked their dogs, collected seashells, and lounged in beach chairs watching the rolling surf and worshipping the sun. Happy vacationers played in the waves.

A flurry of activity took place there on the boardwalk as well, including wall-to-wall people walking and jogging, and bicycles and trams whisking by. Combinations of sweet and savory smells from nearby restaurants filled the air. Shop owners called out their T-shirt and knick-knack deals to everyone passing by.

Kicking off her shoes, Kayla stepped into the hot sand and relished the grit between her toes. An overpowering sense of joy made her heart feel like it was going to explode.

The closing of a door behind her caught her attention. She craned her head over her shoulder and saw several people exiting a blue clapboard-sided cottage with white shutters. According to her GPS, this was Kitty Chandler's bed and breakfast. On the front porch sat several wicker rockers and two round dining tables with chairs. Pots of summer flowers were scattered about. At the bottom of the porch steps was a small patio set with lounge chairs. The area was enclosed by a white picket fence. The name printed on a sign at the deck entrance assured her this was Kitty's place. The sign said it was the only oceanfront B&B in Harmony Beach.

Kayla drew a heavy dose of salty air into her lungs. Suddenly, her stomach began to roll like one of the waves far beyond. Was she ready to meet Kitty? The woman was a relative, but also a stranger. And she'd asked for Suzanne. Kayla hoped her mother had replied back to the email, so Kitty would know to expect her instead of Suzanne.

The long drive had given Kayla plenty of time to think about what she was going to say when they met. But now that the moment had arrived, her mouth felt as dry as sawdust. When the front door opened again and a heavyset woman stepped onto the porch carrying a watering can, Kayla ducked, slipped on her shoes, and hurriedly started down the boardwalk.

The answer was no. She wasn't ready to face Kitty yet.

Before long, she'd walked the length of the southern half of the boardwalk and ended up at a small amusement park. Her mouth watered as she eyed the carts of taffy, caramel popcorn, funnel cakes, cotton candy, and ice cream that were parked between arcades. After watching kids play games for a few minutes, her gaze moved to the rides.

She chuckled at the youngsters who were screaming with delight on the roller coaster, and then her gaze lifted to the Ferris wheel that was circling high in the blue sky. No doubt there was a spectacular view from the top. It had been years since she'd gone to the county fair back home.

A beautiful carousel of carved animals and gilt ornateness was obviously the small park's center of attraction, and quite the showpiece. A historic marker nearby stated that the merry-go-round had been built in 1902 in New York and moved here in parts in 1907. It consisted of forty-five animals, three chariots and one rocking chair. At the time, it had been driven by a steam engine, and each ride had originally cost a nickel.

A voice from behind Kayla spoke, startling her. "It's magnificent, isn't it?"

She turned to face a man a few inches taller than herself. His dirty blond hair touched his collar, and his eyes were a caramel color, like toffee. He looked to be around her age. His smile was friendly, and since she was a friendly person, she smiled back.

"The land most of the town of Harmony Beach was built on was originally owned by an Englishman named Tillman. In 1894, his daughter-in-law, Maude, built the first beachside cottage to receive guests. Apparently, her husband had no initiative about such endeavors, but she was a tough and formidable businesswoman. In a short time, she became successful beyond her wildest dreams, and transformed a drowsy fishing village into a million dollar resort. Maude and her husband became the wealthiest people in Harmony Beach."

Kayla chuckled. She hadn't asked for a history lesson, but had gotten one free of charge.

He pointed past the amusement park to where the boardwalk ended and an isolated stretch of beach began. That's when she noticed the armband tattoo encircling his bicep just below the sleeve of his T-shirt. A glance at his other arm revealed another more intricate design that covered the entire lower part of his arm.

Although it seemed every other person on the street was tattooed these days, her opinion as to why people inked their bodies was old fashioned. In her mind, it was all about seeking attention. Being an artist herself, she could appreciate the creativity of a tattoo artist, and she could also understand an individual wanting to express her or himself. What she couldn't comprehend was why a person would willingly experience the pain associated with the needles. Even as she wondered about this guy's reasons for tattooing his body, she couldn't help but notice the muscle bulging in his arm.

Curiously, she speculated whether there were more tats on his back or chest. She felt his gaze on her and realized she'd been daydreaming for a second. Her gaze followed to where he pointed. Jutting up in the distance were rocky cliffs, with waves crashing upon the boulders below them.

"See there, on top of that mesa?" the man asked.

Kayla squinted. Perched on top of the cliffs was a three-story Victorian-style house.

"That's the house Maude built with her riches."

Her mouth dropped open. "Wow. She was a real entrepreneur. That's something for a woman to have achieved all that back in those days." She turned her attention back to him. Her gaze perused him from his funny T-shirt that read *Maine: We're really cold but we have cheap lobster* to his faded blue jeans on down to his tennis shoes. Mom had always told her you could judge a man by the quality of his shoes. Although this guy's shoes appeared to be comfortably worn in, they weren't ratty looking nor did they have any holes or a lot of wear or tear on them.

"You know a lot about the history of Harmony Beach. You must be a local," Kayla said.

"No. I'm from Maine. Hence, the shirt." He stubbed a finger into his chest and grinned.

"Of course." Feeling foolish, she rolled her eyes playfully, while noticing the sun glinted off his white teeth. "Have you come here to work as a tour guide for the summer?"

"No. I'm here doing some research," he explained.

Her head tilted in question.

"I'm a journalist. I have a degree in journalism, but technically, I'm a reporter for a small-town newspaper back home in Boothbay Harbor. I plan to be the editor one day."

Kayla liked his confidence. She found herself drawn into the depths of his eyes, which sparkled with good humor. "I've never met anyone from Maine. What kind of article will you be writing?"

"It's not for the paper. I'm looking for a story, but it's personal in nature."

"Oh." That sounded intriguing and mysterious. But he wasn't saying more, and she knew better than to pry. It wasn't polite.

"I'm Tanner Bishop." He stuck his hand out to shake.

His clasp was strong and firm, but brief, presuming nothing. "My name is Kayla Grayson. Nice to meet you."

"Same here."

The pause that lingered between them was awkward, so Kayla smiled again and said, "I hope you find what you're looking for. Enjoy your stay." When she turned to depart, his hand shot out and landed on her arm.

"I just got to town and it's time for lunch." He patted his stomach. "I'm starving. Have you had lunch yet?"

She hadn't realized the time, but suddenly, as if on cue, her stomach began to grumble. "No, I haven't."

"I don't know anyone here. Would you like to join me? Unless, that is, you're meeting someone." He gazed around her shoulders as if someone might pop up behind her.

"I'm not meeting anyone." He was pleasant and interesting, and quite attractive. They were both newcomers to Harmony Beach. What harm could it do to grab a quick bite with him? "There are several restaurants back that way where we could eat with a view of the ocean." She motioned north, the way she'd come.

"Sounds like a plan."

They walked up the boardwalk and chose an Irish pub where they were shown to an outside booth. Once they'd perused the menu and ordered, Kayla gazed out at the ocean and said, "The water is so beautiful. I can't stop looking at it. People who can afford to live on the beach are so lucky."

"Where are you from?" Tanner asked.

"A small town in Virginia called Staunton. We're surrounded by mountains, which I love. But there's something mesmerizing about the water. Don't you think?"

The waitress set their drinks in front of them, lemonade for her and iced tea for him.

"It's old hat to me. Boothbay Harbor is on the water," Tanner answered. My grandfather was a fisherman, and his father before him, as was *his* father. It's a dangerous occupation. My great-great grandfather was lost at sea. Dad broke the cycle by becoming an architectural engineer."

"And then you became a journalist." Kayla sipped the lemonade and was amazed that this lemonade tasted sweeter than anywhere else she'd drunk it. Being near the ocean lifted her spirits and seemed to make everything look, taste and feel better.

Tanner nodded. "Yes. But we Bishops still love our lobster and shrimp. We just let others catch it for us now."

Kayla smiled and decided to pick his brain. She knew nothing about Maryland, yet it had been where her mother had been raised and she'd been born. What a fortunate coincidence that she'd met Tanner. He seemed to know something about the area.

"What else have you learned about Harmony Beach so far?" she asked.

"Not much. I know that in the early days, people arrived by stagecoach and ferry. They came to fish off the shore and to enjoy the natural beauty of the Atlantic Ocean. After the area started becoming a popular vacation destination, Maude Tillman had a pavilion built with a ballroom where dances were held. Did you see it? It's located farther down on the northern end of the boardwalk elevated above the sand and sea. You get to it by walking across a wooden pier."

Kayla shook her head. "I only just arrived. I haven't investigated the other end of the beach."

"Mrs. Tillman also established a casino for the gambling crowd. It's also down that way. And as I understand it, she eventually built the largest hotel on the beach, which, unfortunately, burned to the ground in the 1960s long after she'd passed away."

Maude Tillman had been an enterprising woman. Kayla twisted in her seat hoping to catch another glimpse of the beautiful Victorian house above the cliffs, but she couldn't see either the house or the cliffs from this distance or vantage point. "Who lives in the Tillman house now?" she asked.

"I don't know."

His answer was short, and he lowered his

gaze, but not before she caught the furrowing of his brow. Although her lunch companion seemed to know a lot about the Tillman matriarch, Kayla got the distinct feeling he didn't want to talk about her anymore. Was he someone else with secrets? Kayla knew when to stop asking questions. She'd had lots of experience in that department.

Their meals were delivered, and the two of them ate as heartily as if it was their last supper. When they were finished and the bill was laid on the table, Kayla reached for it so she could pay her share. Tanner's large and warm hand covered hers, and for longer than was necessary, she noticed. Goosebumps prickled her skin when a grin quirked his mouth.

"I'll be glad to get it," he said.

"I wouldn't dream of it. I'll pay for my own." Even though he'd been the one to suggest lunch, he was a stranger. Her hand slipped out from underneath his, and she dug into her purse for cash.

Apparently realizing there would be no negotiating with her, Tanner pulled out his wallet and retrieved some folded bills to pay for his meal. Both of them left the waitress a nice tip, which she thanked them for before they left.

"It was a pleasure," Kayla said, once they stepped onto the boardwalk. Tanner had been a congenial person to become acquainted with, but she was not here to meet a man. There was a mission to be accomplished. Apparently, he had his own objectives to achieve, as well.

"Goodbye, Miss Grayson. It *is* Miss, isn't it? I didn't think to ask before." His eyebrow arched in question.

"Yes," she said. "But there's no need for formality. I'm just plain Kayla. Goodbye. Good luck with your research."

When they both began walking in the same direction, Kayla halted her footsteps, suddenly worried she might have a stalker on her hands. "Are you following me?"

"No," he chuckled. "This is the way to the bed and breakfast I'm staying at."

Bed and breakfast? From the sign at Kitty's, she knew there was only one of those on the beach. When she mentioned the name of Kitty's establishment, Tanner grinned again.

"Have you got reservations there, too?" he asked.

She shook her head. "Not yet."

He started them walking again. "At breakfast, I heard the proprietress mention to another guest that she'd just had a cancellation this morning. I'll bet you can snag that room. Let's hurry." He looped his arm through hers and began dragging her along the boardwalk before she could utter a refusal.

Chapter Three

The porch was empty of guests when they arrived at the B&B. Tanner opened the unlocked front door and gestured Kayla inside. "Ms. Chandler is probably in the kitchen," he said, leading the way through a parlor that was decorated with cozy overstuffed furniture, antiques, and oil paintings of boats and the sea.

Kayla followed him with hesitant steps, still uncertain of what she was going to say or do when she met Kitty. Usually daring and unafraid of taking action in any situation, she now felt like a child, with all of a child's uncertainties. Glancing around and smelling a sweet and spicy fragrance in the air that reminded her of gingersnap cookies, she wondered if she'd been in this house when she was small. Had her mother visited her cousin here and brought her along?

"She's not in the kitchen," Tanner said, glancing over the counter. He rang a small bell, and Kayla's chest began to quicken.

The same woman she'd seen earlier on the porch with the watering can appeared in the hallway. "Hello. How can I help you?" she asked. Apparently recognizing the man beside Kayla as one of her guests, she nodded hello to him and directed her attention to Kayla.

Although they'd never met before, Kayla experienced an immediate sense of recognition. Remembering Kitty's statement in the email that she'd loved both Suzanne *and* her daughter, all of Kayla's fears disappeared. For a second, she had the silly desire to run and throw herself into the woman's arms. Instead, she remembered her upbringing and merely stood there looking at her.

Kitty's short hair was brown, with streaks of gray running through it, and despite wearing too much makeup, her round face was still youthful. Kayla noticed her fingernails were painted a bright red. She wasn't beautiful, like her mother, but Kitty had aged well and appeared cheerful and welcoming.

Tanner began the introductions. "Ms. Chandler, I just met this young lady, and she mentioned needing a place to stay. I thought you might have an available room."

Kitty's friendliness turned to Kayla. "As a matter of fact, I had a cancellation just this morning. The one room that faces the ocean is free. It's here on the main level and has French doors leading onto your own private section of the porch. I'd be glad to put you there. It's two hundred twenty dollars per night." She stared, waiting for Kayla's response.

Although the rate was higher than she'd expected to pay while she was here, Kayla couldn't turn down the opportunity. She had a credit card with a low balance. "I'll take it," she said, pulling out her wallet.

Kitty disappeared around the corner and stepped into the kitchen, which evidently served as her office, too. She pulled out the guest registry. "Please provide your name and address, as well as the make and model of your vehicle. I'll give you a sticker for your window. We have several parking spots behind the house."

The moment of truth had come. With trembling hands, Kayla handed Kitty her credit card and then signed her name in the registry.

"Your name is…"

Upon hearing the rise in Kitty's voice, Kayla glanced up to see her staring at the credit card. Their gazes connected briefly, and then Kitty turned the registry toward her. Her eyes grew wide.

"No! You can't be! I asked Suzanne to come. I never dreamed..."

Her mom hadn't replied to the email. From the corner of her eye, Kayla saw Tanner's confused expression.

Kayla let out the breath she'd unconsciously been holding. "I'm sorry," she blurted. "My mother is ill. I came in her place. I hope you don't mind."

Kitty stood staring at her, with her palm at her heart. Then she darted out of the kitchen and appeared at Kayla's side. Her hands reached out to Kayla as tears filled her eyes.

"Little Kayla! I've thought of you so often through the years. And here you are in front of me, my own flesh and blood. I can hardly believe it!"

Kitty swept her into a warm cushiony embrace, and a profound sensation of familiarity moved through Kayla's body. Over Kitty's shoulder, she saw Tanner staring at her as if the joke was on him. She threw him an apologetic look. She hadn't planned on her first meeting with Kitty to take place in front of a perfect stranger.

"I'm not so little now," she said, once Kitty had released her. "I didn't know anything about you or Harmony Beach until your email came yesterday and my mother let me read it."

Kitty dabbed at her eyes with a tissue pulled from her pocket. Tanner gently broke in and asked, "What's going on here? Is this a family reunion?"

"You could say that," Kitty answered through happy sniffles. "The last time I saw Kayla she was three years old. That was twenty-four years ago." She blubbered again and then calmed when Kayla touched her arm. "If you'll both excuse my tears, I'm a bit overcome."

"That's understandable," Tanner said, smiling at Kitty. He cocked his head in question when his gaze met Kayla's.

"I think I've handled this wrong," she said. "I didn't mean to upset you, Kitty."

"You haven't upset me, child," Kitty replied, palming Kayla's cheek with her hand.

"You seem to have handled everything perfectly," Tanner said to Kayla. There was a slight edge to his tone. "You came here to find Ms. Chandler, and you've managed to move into her house within hours of your arrival. I'm not sure why you simply didn't tell me about your connection when I mentioned her name."

Suddenly, something about his attitude didn't set right with her. But it didn't matter what he thought. He was no one to her. The complicated details of her mother's life and the secrets Harmony Beach held weren't any of his business.

"Kayla is my cousin's daughter, Mr. Bishop," Kitty clarified.

"We don't need to explain to him," Kayla said, tossing a *mind your own business look* Tanner's way. "Can we go somewhere private to talk?" she asked Kitty.

"Yes, dear. I'll show you to your room. We can talk there. I won't be needing this." She handed Kayla her credit card and left her and Tanner alone for a moment while returning to the kitchen to snatch a key off a hook on the wall.

"Sorry if I offended you," Tanner whispered. "But I find it strange that you didn't say you were related to this woman when I suggested the B&B."

"What *I* find strange is that you're so interested in my personal life." Kayla's gaze was bold and unwavering. Any appeal he held for her earlier suddenly vanished.

"Follow me," Kitty interrupted, placing her hand on the square of Kayla's back. "Will there be anything else I can do for you, Mr. Bishop?" she asked Tanner. She obviously noticed he hadn't excused himself.

"No, I don't need anything, Ms. Chandler. And please, all my friends call me Tanner. I'm going to be here for a while, and I'm not into formality."

Kitty nodded. "All right. Tanner, it is."

"See you later," he said. "Goodbye, Kayla. Nice to have met you."

She glanced over her shoulder and offered him a polite smile. "Goodbye, *Mr.* Bishop."

* * * *

Tanner climbed the wooden stairs to his second floor room. "That one's a little spitfire," he chuckled under his breath. It felt like someone had just injected him with a shot of adrenaline. Since he was here to learn more about Seacliff House, it was an incredible coincidence to have met Miss Grayson and discover she was a Chandler by blood.

Once he'd closed the door behind him, he removed the diary belonging to Vivien Bishop from the zippered pocket of his suitcase and flopped onto the bed. Even though he'd read it cover to cover, twice, after initially finding it in his grandfather's things, the story had become more real now that he was in Maryland. He opened the small leather journal and carefully thumbed through the pages until he reached the entry that had been the driving force behind his traveling to Harmony Beach. By now he was familiar with Vivien's slanted handwriting. He read the entry aloud once again.

May tenth, nineteen fifty-eight. That young trollop, Pearl, has been gone for more than a month now. My poor brother still believes she will return. But Vince is a fool. He was a fool to have taken up with the girl in the first place. And he was an even bigger fool to have allowed her to seduce him.

Now he has her child to raise on his own. Pearl is not coming back. How do I know? Because I was the one to find the letter she'd written before abandoning him and their son. In it, she thanked him for offering to marry her, but that she didn't love him. Didn't love him? The nerve of her! She's a girl from the wrong side of the tracks. She would be lucky to have a man like my brother. Who does she think she is, anyway?

Imagine how our sweet, gentle Vince would have been crushed to read such heartless words. I don't know why, but Pearl meant everything to him. That's why I destroyed the letter. She'd already created a scandal by getting pregnant and breaking his heart by leaving him and their baby behind. I couldn't—wouldn't allow her to hurt him any further.

Just yesterday, a friend of mine

overheard Pearl's sister tell a woman at the
market that she'd gone to the Maryland coast
to try to find work in a resort town called
Harmony Beach. A cousin lives there and knows
of a wealthy family living in a mansion called
Seacliff House where Pearl might find work.

Good riddance to the little tramp, I say!

I'll do whatever it takes to keep that
information from my brother. He and the baby,
Arlan, are doing just fine without Pearl.
It's difficult, a man raising a child alone,
but Vince is a good father. Mama and I help,
but Vince shoulders the bulk of care. He does
seem to love the little tike. The boy is
Vince's priority now. Eventually, he will
forget all about Pearl. She will become only
a distant memory to him, and nothing but a
forgotten name to his son. At least, that is
my fervent prayer.

Tanner closed the diary. He slipped his
cell phone out of his back pocket, pushed a
number on his contact list, and scooted
against the headboard. When no one answered
he left a message.

"Hi, Dad. Just checking in. I haven't
learned much yet. Still getting the lay of the
land and doing some research before I make any
personal contacts. It's nice here. The
weather is great and the beach is beautiful.
First time I've stayed in a B&B. It's a heck
of a lot better than the fleabag motels I've
gotten stuck in when I've had to travel for a
story. Tell Grandma Mary Ann thanks for
recommending I try this one. Well, take care,
Dad. I'll call you again in a couple of
days."

As soon as Tanner signed off, his phone
rang. A low growl escaped his lips upon
seeing the number on the screen. For a

moment, he debated whether he should answer or not. If he did, she'd cry and beg him to rethink his decision. If he didn't pick up, she'd leave a long, rambling message and try to manipulate him through guilt. Either way, he was bound to develop a headache.

Tanner inhaled a deep breath and hit the answer button. "Hello, Whitney." He listened quietly for a couple of minutes, but when the crying began, he rubbed the back of his neck and said, "I'm sorry if you feel hurt, but I've apologized over and over. I don't understand why this has been so hard on you. You've acknowledged we don't have similar goals and dreams. We don't think about life the same way. It's simple. We're not a good match. It's nothing personal."

He listened another minute before firmly stating, "You've really got to stop calling. If you're not careful, you'll be moving into stalker territory soon." Although he chuckled to ease the tension between them, the sentiment was very real. Enough was enough. They'd only dated four months.

"I have to go, Whitney. Please, for your own sake move on. There's someone out there better suited for you than me. Goodbye."

Before she could respond, he pressed the disconnect button on his phone. And before she could call back, he turned it off and laid it on the dresser.

On top of the dresser lay the hardcover book written about the history of Harmony Beach that he'd purchased at the local bookstore when he'd arrived. On the cover was a photo of the elegant and grand Seacliff House.

Tanner picked up the book and returned to the chapter where he'd last left off. This was the information he was most anxious to learn about. As he started to read about life at Seacliff House in the 1950s, he could imagine the young woman from Maine working there. But in what capacity had Pearl worked? As a nanny? A housekeeper? Perhaps a cook's apprentice. Or maybe a laundress.

How long had she been employed there? That information was sketchy. Had she left it for other employment? Had Pearl ever married and had more children?

In another diary written years later that Tanner had also read, Vivien had stated that Pearl never returned to Maine. She'd never made contact with Vince or their child. Her cousin in Maryland had not known where she'd gone, either. It was as if she'd disappeared off the face of the earth. What had happened to Pearl?

The journalist in Tanner wanted to know. But as her great grandson, he *needed* to know.

Chapter Four

"Was I in this house when I was little?" Kayla asked. She was sitting cross-legged on the bed, and Kitty looked uncomfortably squished into a small chair that sat next to the French doors. Kayla gazed around trying to recapture a memory, any kind of distant happiness.

"No. I went through a divorce fifteen years ago and bought the B&B then." Kitty sighed. "You were so small when you left Harmony Beach. I doubt you have any memories at all."

They were both silent for a moment. There were so many unanswered questions. Where was Kayla to start?

"Please tell me why you emailed my mother yesterday," she began. "Why did you want her to come?"

"I shouldn't have written that email. It was sent out of my own weakness. Though I'm not sorry it brought you home." Kitty reached for Kayla's hand and squeezed.

Kayla got straight to the point. "Kitty, you told my mother that *he* has returned. Who is the man you spoke of?"

Kitty stared at her hands in her lap. She wrung them like they were wet dishcloths. "Let's not get into all that. Let me show you the rest of my house." When she stood up, Kayla's pleading gaze forced her down again.

"I asked my mother if the man could be my father," Kayla said. "She said it's not possible, because my father is dead."

Kitty nibbled her lower lip. It took her several long moments before answering. "We all thought so. At least, *I* thought he'd drowned. Maybe your mother knew the truth all along."

Kayla's heart began to pound with an insane rhythm. "Are you saying the man you saw *is* my father?"

Kitty nodded. "I'm pretty certain. He's much older, of course. And he has a beard now. But I'd know those pale gray eyes anywhere."

Feeling as if she'd been delivered a fist to the stomach, Kayla closed her eyes to let the news sink in. When she opened them again, the questions shot from her mouth like bullets from a gun.

"Where is he now? How can I find him? When can I visit Seacliff House and meet my grandmother?"

"Slow down," Kitty said.

"I can't slow down. I don't know anything about my family. I only just found out that my mother ran away from here twenty-four years ago. I don't know why, and I'm confused as to why she, and you, thought my father had drowned. I never knew I had a grandmother. You can't imagine how alone I've felt all my life."

Kitty stared at her. "Your mother never told you *anything* about Harmony Beach or Seacliff House?"

"No. I know nothing about her life here. Or mine. She never even showed me a photo of my dad. I'm twenty-seven years old. I deserve to know about him and what happened between them. It's my right to meet my father and my grandmother."

Tears gathered in the corners of Kitty's eyes. "But, Kayla, some things are better left in the past."

"No!" She hadn't come all this way to be kept in the dark. Now that she knew the man who had returned *was* her father, there was no way she was not going to contact him. She didn't want to threaten Kitty, but her nerves were raw. "I'll learn the truth, one way or another, with or without your help."

Her legs unknotted. When she jumped up from the bed, Kitty stood, too, and put her arms around her. Kayla slumped into Kitty's warm embrace and breathed in her flowery scent. "I have a right," she said quietly.

They separated, and Kitty nodded for her to sit down again. "You're absolutely right. You should know what happened, although it's a difficult story to tell, because of the complicated emotions involved. I don't know where to begin."

"Why not start with my father?"

"All right. His name is Matt Grayson. He didn't grow up in Harmony Beach. He and his father bought the Beach Club and Casino on the other end of the boardwalk back in 1984. Matt and Suzanne met quite by accident one day. She was hitting all the businesses in town to secure promotion and advertising for some event the Ladies League was holding. If it hadn't been for that chance encounter, your parents probably never would have met. You see, they didn't run in the same circles, if you know what I mean."

Kayla thought she understood, given Kitty had mentioned the casino. "My father was a boy from the wrong side of the tracks."

"You could put it that way. More importantly, Suzanne was a Chandler. The Chandlers were a very prominent family in Harmony Beach at the time. They didn't mix with the likes of gamblers and casino owners."

"But my mother didn't care about such pretenses, right? I remember your email saying she used to be the strong one. She was the only person who could stand up to her mother."

Kitty nodded, and she gazed into the air behind Kayla, probably remembering the past. "Yes. That was your mother. She had nerves of steel, and so much passion for life. It was love at first sight for Suzanne when she met Matt. She fell hard and fast for him. When he asked her to marry him a few months later, there was no hesitation on her part. Your grandmother was less than pleased."

"Did she think he wasn't good enough for my mom?"

"That and she didn't like the fact that Matt was a younger man. He was a very handsome and charming fellow. Sonora felt he was using Suzanne and was after the Chandler money."

It was the first time Kayla had heard her grandmother's name, and anything at all about her father. *Sonora*. The name hovered on the tip of her tongue.

"How much younger was he?" she asked.

"Matt was twenty-six. Your mother had just turned thirty-two."

Kayla had no idea. "Was my mom considered a spinster, or something?"

Kitty chuckled and stood up to adjust a picture frame above the bed that was hanging crooked. "Suzanne was particular when it came to men. She had plenty of boyfriends through the years, but none of them set her heart on fire like your father. And, of course, Sonora always did her best to ruin any relationship of Suzanne's that was headed anywhere serious." She gritted her teeth, showing her displeasure, and returned to the chair.

"Didn't my grandmother want her daughter to be happy?" Kayla asked.

"I don't know what Sonora's problem was. She's never been a happy person herself. I suppose she didn't want anyone else to be happy either, including her own daughter."

"Sad," Kayla said. "Poor Mom. What a way to grow up."

"Yes, but Suzanne wasn't to be dissuaded from finding her own happiness. She and your dad eloped, and you were born nine months later."

"Wow. What did Sonora—my grandmother—do when she found out?"

"Threw a fit, like usual. And she threatened to take Suzanne out of her will. But your mother could have cared less about the Chandler money. She told Sonora to do whatever she felt she needed to do. Of course, Sonora didn't make good on her threat. But she made life hell for Matt."

Kayla shook her head. "Why did she dislike him so much? Surely, it couldn't have been simply because he was part owner of a club?"

"I'm afraid not." Kitty's brow furrowed. "How much do you want to hear?"

"All of it. I have a strong backbone. I can handle whatever the truth is." She remembered her mom saying her father had done some bad things. She had a feeling she was about to hear what they were.

"Well, your dad was what, in those days, we called a playboy. With that thick hair and those pale, mysterious eyes, his looks rivaled any movie star's. He was tall and had muscles to boot. And he was very good at talking the pants off of any girl. Literally." She waited until Kayla grasped her meaning.

"My dad was unfaithful to Mom?"

"I'm afraid so, honey. When your grandmother found out and confronted Suzanne, Suzanne didn't want to believe her. She thought it was just another one of Sonora's ploys to break up her family. But I saw Matt with another woman myself. It was all true." She lowered her gaze.

"What happened then?"

"Your mom and Sonora had a big argument. Then, your mom and your dad fought. Suzanne told me Matt admitted his indiscretions and left the house. He'd been missing for two days when his jacket was found washed up on the beach below Seacliff House. Everyone assumed he'd drowned, either from an accident, or from suicide. His body was never found."

Kayla remembered what her mom had told her yesterday. "My mom thought my grandmother ran him out of town."

"If that was Suzanne's impression, she never shared it with me. I assumed Suzanne believed Matt had killed himself out of guilt. The next thing I knew, she'd packed you up, and the two of you were gone from our lives."

"Why did she leave the only home she'd known?"

Kitty shrugged. "She didn't want to face the whispering behind hands that comes with a scandal in this town, I suppose. And whatever bond she'd had with her mother was irretrievably broken by that time, anyway."

"And now my father has returned to Harmony Beach," Kayla said. "He didn't drown that day."

"It appears not."

Kayla turned it all over in her mind for a couple of minutes. The story was remarkable, but there was still something she didn't understand. "Your email said you're afraid, Kitty. What are you afraid of? My father?"

"I'm not sure, exactly," she admitted.

"I think I'm afraid of what's going to happen when Sonora learns Matt is alive and has come back." Her voice lowered to a warning whisper. "You don't know anything about your grandmother, Kayla. She's not a nice woman."

"That's what Mom told me. But I'll never know for sure until I meet her myself, will I?"

Kitty shook her head. "You don't want to do that. Believe me. You're better off going back to Virginia and forgetting you have family here. Suzanne was right to take you away. It was a mistake for me to email Suzanne."

With her chin jutting out in defiance, Kayla said, "I don't mean to be rude, Kitty, but that is not going to happen. I intend on meeting both my dad and my grandmother. My entire life has been shrouded in secrets. And I'm sick of it."

"I can understand," Kitty sighed. "I'm curious. Why didn't Suzanne come?"

"She's sick."

"With what? The flu? A migraine?"

"No. My mother has recently been diagnosed with agoraphobia. She's suffered from panic attacks ever since I can remember. But she's gotten to the point where she can't leave the house anymore. I hired a nurse to stay with her while I'm here."

The expression that crossed Kitty's face was one of shock and disbelief. "Suzanne? An agoraphobic? I don't believe it."

"Well, it's true, whether you want to believe it or not. I've taken care of her most of my life."

"Oh, Kayla. I'm so sorry." Kitty's shoulders slumped. Seemed their talk and the news about Suzanne had taken the wind out of her.

Just then, the bell on the kitchen counter tinkled. Kitty rose. "Would you excuse me, dear?"

"Of course."

"We'll continue talking later. Will you join me for dinner tonight?"

Kayla smiled. "I'd love to." When Kitty headed for the door, Kayla stopped her and gave her another hug. "Thank you for telling me about my father, and how he and Mom met. It's more than I've learned in twenty-seven years."

Kitty appeared exhausted. "You're welcome, Kayla. I'll see you later."

Once she'd exited the room, Kayla stared into the mirror on the wall. Finally, she understood from whom she'd inherited her gray eyes. She must have gotten her thick hair from her dad, too. She paced the floor for a while, trying to decide her next move. She hadn't come here to sit in a bed and breakfast and *think* about her family. She'd come to meet them. But where should she start?

Should I try to find my father first? Or go to Seacliff House unannounced and surprise my grandmother?

That was probably not a good idea. Sonora Chandler had to be in her late seventies or early eighties. A shock such as seeing her granddaughter after twenty-four years could give her a heart attack.

Kayla decided to stroll along the boardwalk. She'd go north this time and find the casino. Maybe her grandfather Grayson still owned the place. She hadn't even thought about him or her father's side of the family until now! Maybe the Chandlers weren't the only relatives she had in Harmony Beach.

But first, she should call Mom. When no one answered the house phone, Kayla left a message saying she'd made it safely and that she'd call again later.

With renewed energy, she grabbed her purse and locked the door to the room. As she walked through the dining room, she heard Kitty speaking with some guests in the kitchen. Kayla squeaked open the screen door and stepped onto the porch. As she jaunted down the steps, a familiar voice caused her to stop in her tracks.

"Where are you going in such a hurry?"

Her head turned to see Tanner rocking in one of the wicker chairs. Kayla's mind had been on the task at hand, and she hadn't noticed him when she'd crossed the porch. When he smiled, something stirred inside her. He seemed like the kind of person you couldn't be annoyed with for long.

"I'm going for a walk," she answered.

He jumped up from the rocker. "I was about to take a walk myself. Mind if I join you?"

How could she refuse? He was already at her side, with his hand on her arm, escorting her down the steps.

Chapter Five

"I'm going this way," Kayla said, turning left after they walked through the gate and stepped onto the boardwalk.

"That's convenient. I'm headed in the same direction."

Tanner would have gone wherever she was going. That little nugget of information regarding her family intrigued him, journalistically speaking. Seeing how she was a member of the Chandler family with a connection to Seacliff House, getting to know her would definitely play to his advantage in a personal way. Although he was a good talker, he hadn't figured out exactly how he was going to get inside the Victorian house above the cliffs…until now. What a stroke of luck.

Anyway, befriending her to garner facts about the Chandlers wouldn't be torture. Miss Grayson was pretty and personable. There'd been many situations in which employing his charm and wit meant the difference between getting a story or not. There was no reason why the same approach shouldn't work on her. But when he flashed her his biggest and most sincere grin, Kayla rolled her eyes and took off like a power walker.

"Hey, slow down," he said, jogging to catch up and matching her strides. It was possible she was going to be a harder nut to crack than he'd thought.

Never one to hide his cards under the table, so to speak, he openly assessed her as they walked. She had a nice body, with plenty of curves, which he liked in a woman. Although her skin was fair, it was flawless, except for the smattering of freckles across her nose, which he found cute. He'd been partial to redheads since that crush on Sallie Martin in the fifth grade. And those eyes…

Kayla turned to look at him right then, as if she could read his thoughts. Her eyes reminded him of storm clouds gathering over a tempestuous sea.

"What are you looking at?" she asked, halting their steps. Her gaze was razor sharp.

"Uh. You." Tanner was also honest to a fault.

Her gaze narrowed. "Well, I'd appreciate it if you'd stop. Better yet, why don't you go your way and I'll go mine." She gestured with her hand for him to move ahead of her. "Sorry to be rude, but I don't have time for socializing. There's some business I have to take care of."

"Family business?"

"You're direct, aren't you? And nosy."

"I'm a journalist. I know no other way to be."

"Well, my business is none of yours, Mr. Journalist."

"Call me Tanner. Mr. Journalist is way too proper."

Snubbing his attempt at being witty, Kayla took up her fast pace again. He fell into step beside her. "It must be exciting to meet Ms. Chandler. She's your mother's cousin, right? If I'm recalling correctly, she said it's been *twenty-four years* since the two of you have seen each other. Wow. How the heck did that happen?"

Kayla stared straight ahead, progressing down the boardwalk at a steady speed. Tanner was used to being ignored, especially when he was trying to interview people who didn't want to be bothered. Not one to give up when he wanted something, however, he decided to try another tactic. He balled his fist into a pretend microphone and thrust it in her face.

Using his most serious announcer voice, he said, "Miss Grayson, can you tell me how it feels to finally meet a relative you didn't know you had and haven't seen since you were a child?"

Kayla stopped. Tanner saw her lips tremble and her back grow rigid. Suddenly, her eyes filled with tears. His heart crawled into his throat. What had he done?

He placed his palm at her back and steered her to an empty bench. They sat down. Kayla sniffled.

"It feels great and scary at the same time," she said, softly and courteously answering his question. "I just found out my father, whom I know nothing about and whom my mother thought was dead, is alive—and he's here in Harmony Beach. And I have a grandmother I don't remember. I may have other relatives I've never been told about, too. To be honest, it's overwhelming. That's how it feels."

When their gazes fused, he had the strongest desire to wipe her tears away with his fingertips. Instead, he reached into his back pocket and pulled out a cloth handkerchief and offered it to her.

"Thank you," she squeaked. After she'd dried her eyes and blew her nose, the corner of her mouth twitched in a small smile. "I've never known anyone our age that carried a hankie in his pocket. It's old fashioned. But sweet."

"That comes from my grandpa. Men of his generation were never without a hankie. We spent a lot of time together. I guess a lot of his customs rubbed off on me."

She pushed a strand of flyaway hair behind her ear. "Is your grandpa in Maine?"

Tanner's stomach twisted with pain that was still as raw as a fresh wound. "Yes, he is."

"You must be close." Her eyes twinkled with glistening tears.

"We were. He passed away recently."

A breath of air escaped her throat, and her hand covered his. "I'm sorry."

"Thank you."

The warmth of her touch radiated through him, jolting him like an electrical current and setting his skin afire. He felt his body hum with a yearning he hadn't felt in a long time. When he stared at her hand, Kayla's gaze followed his, and a lovely pink color flooded her face. Her hand jerked away as if she'd been burnt on a hot stove. She thrust the used hankie toward him.

"Uh. You can keep it," Tanner chuckled. "I have others."

This time, she graced him with a genuine smile, and her gentle laugh filled his ears. "I'll wash it and return it to you later."

"No rush." He turned his head and stared at the ocean for a few seconds, allowing her time to recover from her mini breakdown. "If you feel okay and want to continue walking, let's continue north," he suggested. "I read about the pavilion that Maude Tillman had built. I'd like to see it. Would you?"

She nodded. "Sure. I'm good now."

Satisfied that he'd made a breakthrough with Kayla, Tanner released a sigh of relief. They resumed their stroll.

"Look at that," she said, pointing as they approached a wooden pier that was elevated above the sand. It extended more than one hundred feet out. Perched on heavy-duty wooden posts over the water at the end of the pier was the octagonal building that had been built in the year 1900 for ballroom dancing. With eight bays, the pavilion had an arched roof with large, round-arched windows in each bay, for allowing sea breezes to blow in on hot summer nights. Tanner also knew from reading the book on Harmony Beach that the windows, as well as the hardwood floors inside, were original.

"Can we look inside?" Kayla asked, already stepping onto the pier.

"I don't see why not. There are other people going in and out."

Once they entered the building, Kayla strode around the large open room with her eyes widening with delight. She raised her gaze to the high ceiling and then ran it over the plastered walls. Although the building had lost much of its luster through the years, the painted murals of seascapes that still adorned the walls were artistic masterpieces.

Kayla glided to the elevated stage in the corner where musicians had once sat. Watching her was like seeing a kid in a candy store for the first time. Her innocent joyfulness was contagious. Tanner felt his chest heaving with pleasure as she strolled from bay to bay, perhaps lost in daydreams of yesteryear. His own daydreams invaded his mind. The vision of her in a long, green, low-cut dress flashed through his head in a dizzying swirl.

He found her nearness to be comforting. There was something softly reminiscent about the sound of her voice and the scent of mango that drifted up from her hair. He recognized the feeling for what it was—the first faint stirring of attraction.

Her lilting voice snapped him out of his reverie. "Isn't this place wonderful, Tanner? I can picture an orchestra playing, and the ladies and gentlemen in their tuxedos and gowns dancing in here. Can't you?"

Yes, he could. Flying like lightning to her side, he caught her wrist between his fingers. "May I have this dance, Miss Grayson?"

Kayla glanced around at the other people in the pavilion, who suddenly stopped their conversations and stared. Giggling, she said, "There's no music, Tanner."

"You are mistaken, my lady." He cleared his throat. Then he clasped her left hand in his right and wrapped his other arm around her back and began awkwardly swinging her around the floor while singing *My Favorite Things* from *The Sound of Music*. Having recently watched the movie with his five-year old goddaughter, it was the first song that came to mind.

Knowing he couldn't carry a tune in a bucket, Tanner wasn't offended when Kayla burst out laughing. But moments later, his pride was hurt. They'd barely sashayed around the dance floor one time when he accidentally stepped on her foot.

"Ouch!" Kayla untangled herself from his arms and hopped up and down on the foot that he hadn't mashed.

He wasn't Fred Astaire, but he'd busted a few good moves in his time, so this was really embarrassing. Tanner shrugged his shoulders when the spectators around them laughed.

"I'm sorry," he apologized to Kayla, giving her his arm to lean on. "I'm worse than a bull in a china shop."

"You can say that again." Her coppery mane of hair tumbled into her face as she leaned over and examined her foot. "It's not broken. I think I'll survive," she announced, straightening, but grimacing. "That's enough dancing for me for one day. However, I suggest *you* give it up for good, Tanner." She lightly punched him on the arm and limped toward the door.

Like a whipped dog, he silently followed her outside and down the pier. "I have an idea," he said, once they reached the boardwalk. "There's this place called the Beach Club and Casino. It's located at the intersection of Ninth Street and the boardwalk. From the 1930s until the late 1980s, it was the place for vacationers and locals to go to gamble and party. It had slot machines and blackjack tables, and in the forties and fifties, it featured big band music. Should we check it out?"

Kayla's mouth dropped open. "How do you know about the casino?"

"There's an entire chapter devoted to it in the book I bought on Harmony Beach history. The building is a historic landmark now, but apparently, it was one of the hot spots in town, back in its heyday."

"Did you say it closed down in the late 1980s?" Kayla asked. Her curious gaze eagerly searched his face.

"That's what the book said."

"Did the book say why it closed down?"

"I don't recall." Tanner thought a minute. "I don't think so."

Without waiting for him, Kayla darted like a jackrabbit ahead of him. Obviously, her foot didn't hurt as bad as she'd led on. For the second time, he had to jog to catch up to her.

Chapter Six

What a coincidence it was that Tanner had
read about the Beach Club and Casino, Kayla
thought. He couldn't possibly know her dad
and grandfather Grayson had owned the business
at one time. The book must not have mentioned
their names, or he would have said.

With each street sign she passed, Kayla's
anticipation grew stronger. Perhaps her
grandfather was still involved with the casino
in some way. As the street numbers decreased
along the boardwalk, a thrill raced up her
spine, and her strides became larger. When,
at last, she arrived at Ninth Street, the tang
of salt and seaweed clung robustly in the air.

She gazed to her right to see a series of
sand dunes next to the boardwalk. Between the
dunes were puddles of stagnant water.

Slowly, she gazed to her left. There
stood a large, warehouse-type building with
board and batten siding. From above the front
door, twelve windows allowed light to filter
into the building. The windows were grouped in
sets of three, with six small panes in each.
Green shutters flanked each set of windows.
Although the place was obviously closed, a
wooden patio still welcomed visitors to the
front door, over which hung a large sign with
the words *Beach Club and Casino* printed on it.

"We found it."

Startled, Kayla turned, having
momentarily forgotten about Tanner. "Yes, we
did," she said. Her gaze was riveted to the
building. This was where her mother had met
her father. The place her dad had co-owned.
He'd touched the doorknob and might have swept
the deck and cleaned those windows. This was
probably one of the first places he'd come to

when he returned to town—from wherever he'd been.

Sudden disappointment seeped into her bones. How would she find him, or her grandfather? From the looks of it, this building had been abandoned years ago. Then an idea occurred to her. If her grandpa Grayson still lived in Harmony Beach, he'd most likely have a telephone. She'd look him up in the phone book. Surely, if he were still alive, her dad would be staying with him. That thought cheered her. It might be simpler than she'd thought to find Matt.

Tanner roused her from her thoughts. "Would you like to go closer?" he asked.

She nodded.

Standing on her tiptoes, Kayla peeked through the window of the front door. The interior was a big open room with a high ceiling, reminding her of the community hall back home where her first book signing had taken place. Shadows abounded about the space, but because of the light streaming in from the windows, she was able to make out the bar running along the length of one wall. Old slot machines and blackjack tables were still situated all around the room. At the back was a stage.

She could imagine the band music rolling onto the boardwalk to draw in the crowds, and the energy and raucous feeling that had emanated from the club. What a glorious time it must have been.

When Kayla stepped away from the door, a strange feeling came over her. A shiver racked her body. It felt like someone was watching her.

Tanner must have noticed the expression on her face change. "Are you all right?" he

asked, gently swinging her toward him.
"What's wrong?"

An eerie sensation crept up her arms and
tingled over her neck. Was her father here
now? Something hinted he was. Goose flesh
peppered her skin.

Kayla twirled. Her gaze darted in all
directions. No one in the crowd of vacationers
walking along the boardwalk stood out,
matching the vague description of her dad
Kitty had given her.

"What is it?" Tanner repeated.

It was then that she saw him. A man
wearing jeans and a white polo shirt stepped
from around the corner of the casino. He was
talking into a cell phone. Tanned and looking
fit, his thick salt and pepper hair and neatly
trimmed beard set off his handsome face. His
conversation halted, and his footfalls stopped
in mid-stride.

Kayla was disconcerted when his gray eyes
met hers in a look that was alarmingly direct.
His mouth parted, and for a brief moment, she
thought she saw a glimmer of recognition in
his gaze. He snapped the cell phone shut. They
stared at one another.

Her heart thumped so wildly inside her
chest, she imagined Tanner could hear the
beats. It seemed impossible, but she knew the
man was Matt Grayson—her father!

With a lump in her throat, she took a
step forward. Like a deer caught in
headlights, the man's eyes grew as large as
saucers. Then he bolted. In the blink of an
eye he was gone, sprinting around the corner
the way he'd come.

"Wait!" Kayla screamed. "Please don't
go!" She took off like lightning. But when
she sailed around the corner, he was nowhere

to be seen. She ran to the parking lot behind the casino and gazed around. A set of stairs led to the second floor of the building. But if he'd darted up the stairs, she would have heard the noise. He must have disappeared into the alley.

With gravel crunching under his feet, Tanner's footfalls thudded to her side. "Did you know that man? Who was he?" he asked, catching his breath.

"I don't know him," Kayla answered, bracing her hands on her knees and drawing in a fresh lung full of air.

"Then why did you chase after the guy?"

She straightened her back and stared into Tanner's inquiring eyes, debating on how much to share with him. "This might sound crazy to you, but I think that was my dad."

Tanner's eyebrow arched, but he didn't laugh. "I don't understand. Why aren't you sure? Has it been a long time since you've seen him?"

"Yes. As a matter of fact, I don't remember my father at all, or know anything about him. My mother and I lived here when I was a child. Something happened, and she took me away to Virginia when I was three." She blurted the information out before thinking, but it was too late to reel the words back in.

Tanner's mind seemed to be working. She figured the journalist in him had a ton of questions, none of which she could—or would answer. She turned and headed for the boardwalk, desperately needing to speak to Kitty.

"Wait, Kayla." Tanner slipped up beside her, and they walked in tandem toward the B&B. "Did your mom and dad divorce when you were small?" he asked.

"Not exactly."

"Oh, I see. Your mother must have run away from him."

Kayla's head jerked toward him. "You don't *see* anything, Tanner. You have no right to judge. Anyway, it's none of your concern."

He held his hands up in a surrender pose. "You're absolutely right. I apologize. Sometimes I can't help myself. I'm like a hound dog, always on the trail sniffing out a good story."

"Well, go sniff somewhere else," she snapped. "You won't find a story here." As soon as the words flew from her mouth, she felt bad. She wasn't a rude person. No matter how nosy he was, Tanner didn't deserve to be treated that way. Anyone in his position would have been curious. After all, she'd brought on the queries herself by exposing a little of her life to him.

She coughed to clear the emotion lodged in her throat. "I'm sorry. I'm a little on edge right now, but that's no excuse. I apologize for jumping on you that way."

"Apology accepted," he said, with a grin.

"Do you always forgive so easily?" she asked.

"Sure. Life is too short to hold grudges."

Kayla thought about that for a moment. "I like your philosophy. I try to have the same attitude. Most of the time I'm successful."

"There's less drama that way." Tanner smiled again and then set his gaze upon the ocean. "Drama's not good for the mind, body, or soul."

Apparently knowing when to stop and keep quiet, he didn't ask any more questions. In fact, with Kayla's mind wandering, the two of them didn't talk again until they reached the bed and breakfast. A nervous looking Kitty met them at the door.

Without waiting until Tanner had excused himself, Kitty grabbed Kayla's hands and exclaimed, "I've been watching for you to return. I have some news, honey. Sonora called me twenty minutes ago. Your grandmother knows your father is in town. She knows you're here, too, and she wants to meet you."

Dizzying dots swam across Kayla's vision. This was unexpected news. "Kitty, I think I just saw my dad. He was outside the casino." After describing him, she said, "Do you think it was him?"

"Yes. I saw him near the casino, too. He's probably taken up residence in the upstairs apartment. That's where he and his father lived when they owned the club, before Matt and your mom married."

Kayla heaved a ragged sigh. Tanner was hearing all this, but she figured it was too late to request him to leave. The cat was already out of the bag. She turned to him and said, "That's where those stairs we saw must have led. Darn! I should have followed my instincts and gone up the stairs and knocked on the door."

"I wouldn't have let you," Tanner said in no uncertain terms.

Taken aback, Kayla felt her ire rise at his nerve. He must have noticed, because he quickly clarified. "He may be your blood, but you told me yourself, you know nothing about him. He could be dangerous."

Her attention traveled back to Kitty. "*You* know him. Do you think he's dangerous?"

Kitty shook her head. "I knew Matt close to thirty years ago. I'm sure he didn't set out to hurt people then, but he did hurt your mother, all the same. Before the trouble began, he appeared to be a decent man. But he fooled us all. And people can change for the worse, Kayla. You need to be wary."

Her words struck a chord. Although Kayla didn't want to believe her own flesh and blood would cause her harm, Matt had cheated on her mother, apparently faked a suicide, and abandoned the two of them. There was no end to what he might do if pushed into a corner.

As an afterthought, Kitty added, "Suzanne is a perfect example of how people can change. I still can't believe she's as sick as you say. My cousin is the last person I'd ever dream would be diagnosed with a mental disorder."

Out of the corner of her eye, Kayla saw Tanner looking at her. *Great.* Now he'd have a dozen more questions about her family. *And* he probably thought she was one in a line of unbalanced people.

Before returning to the subject of her grandma Chandler, she wanted to know about her father's family. "Kitty, is my grandfather Grayson still alive?"

"No." Her mouth drew downward. "He suffered a massive heart attack on the very day Matt's jacket was found washed up on shore. I guess the shock killed him. Sad. He was a nice man."

Kayla's heart sank with the loss of another relative she'd never know. But at least she had Kitty and her grandmother. Sonora wanted to meet her. That was one less hurdle to jump over, since she hadn't known whether she'd be interested in meeting her or not. After all, she hadn't bothered to contact Kayla in twenty-four years.

Suddenly, her shoulders grew stiff with resentment. If Kitty had known where she and Suzanne had been all these years, Sonora must have known, too. She appeared to be a resourceful woman. Somehow, she'd discovered Kayla was in Harmony Beach. Sonora could have contacted her at any time, or at least sent a card on her birthdays. Why hadn't she?

Recalling the venom in which Suzanne spoke of her mother was most likely the answer. Even if Sonora had tried to make contact with Kayla, Suzanne probably would have intercepted any correspondence. Exactly what had her grandmother done all those years ago? What action had been so terrible that her daughter chose to shut her out of their lives for good?

Kayla allowed her shoulders to relax. What did it matter, anyway? The only important thing was that she was here now in Harmony Beach, and her grandmother wanted to meet her. She looked at her watch. It was only four o'clock. Anxious to meet Sonora, she enthusiastically asked Kitty, "When can I go to Seacliff House?"

"About that…"

"You're not going to talk me out of it," Kayla warned. "How did she find out I was here? Did you tell her?"

Kitty kneaded her hands together. "I'm afraid so. When she told me she knew Matt was in town, I sort of blurted out that you were here, too. I'm sorry."

"Don't be. I came to Maryland to meet her."

"It's not a good idea," Kitty said. "If you see your grandmother—"

Kayla interrupted her. "*When* I see my grandmother."

"When," Kitty relented, "you'll soon find out she is a devious woman. She has her ways of finding out things. She has spies and henchmen who carry out her wishes and commands. How do you think she discovered Matt was here?"

Kayla cocked a grin at Tanner, who had been silently witnessing the exchange. "Spies and henchmen? Isn't that a little melodramatic, Kitty?"

Kitty wagged her head. "Believe me, I'm being kind. But if you're determined to spend any time with her, you can be your own judge. You appear to be an intelligent young lady with a good head on your shoulders. It won't take you long to peg Sonora."

"I do intend on spending time with her, starting as soon as I freshen up. Will you tell me how to get to Seacliff House, Kitty? Tanner pointed it out to me when we were on the boardwalk. It looks to be isolated high above the cliffs. Can I reach the house by car?"

"Of course you can. It's a steep, winding road, but this time of year, the house is easily accessible. Wintertime is another story. I'll draw you a map, if you're determined to go."

"I am. Thank you." Kayla read the uncertainty on Kitty's face. She grasped her hands and squeezed. "I'm a grown woman who can take care of herself. I'll be fine. She's my grandma, for goodness sakes. Not a fire-breathing dragon."

"That description is not so far from the truth," Kitty groaned.

"Don't worry about Kayla, Mrs. Chandler.

I'll make sure she's safe."

Both women looked at Tanner. He'd been quiet this whole time. "What's that supposed to mean?" Kayla asked.

He smiled. "It means I'm going with you."

She chuckled. "Oh, no, you're not. This has nothing to do with you. This is a personal matter."

"I understand," he said. "But Sonora Chandler's family is prominent around here. Her ancestor, Maude Tillman, practically turned this once-lonely stretch of beach into a multi-million dollar resort single-handedly. I'd love to meet your grandmother and learn more about her relatives and how this town became what it is today."

"In other words, you want a story." Kayla fisted her hands upon her hips. When he shrugged, she couldn't help but notice how broad his shoulders were.

"I'm just a guy who thirsts for knowledge."

Kitty patted Tanner on the arm. "I think it's a great idea for you to go along. You can be Kayla's bodyguard. I haven't been up to Seacliff House for years, but Sonora used to have some real thugs working for her."

"This is ridiculous," Kayla moaned. "I don't need a bodyguard, and I certainly don't need Tanner tagging along."

"I promise not to get in your way," he said, crossing his heart with a finger. "If you and your grandma want to discuss something personal, I'll step outside. I promise. Please?" he added, curling his lower lip into a pout and making his eyes go puppy-dog soft.

Kayla couldn't help but smile. "If I let you go, how am I going to introduce you?"

"As a friend.   Isn't that what we're becoming?"

Her lips pursed.   She'd probably regret this decision.   But Tanner Bishop, she was discovering, was not a man easily dissuaded.

Chapter Seven

After driving through an open gate flanked by brick pedestals with lion statues on top, Kayla parked her car in front of the house. She and Tanner got out and looked around.

In the center of the circular driveway was a lawn of manicured grass. Early summer flowers poked their heads up from between blades. The blooms were colorful, but the feature that drew Kayla's attention was the magnificent sandstone fountain in the middle of the grass. The beautiful design was elaborate, with its bottom half shaped like a huge Greek urn, and the top part sculpted into five fish that looked to be leaping out of the urn. Water trickled from their open mouths. Kayla wondered if the fountain had been carved out of the stone from the cliffs.

"After you," Tanner said, gesturing her toward a swinging gate and wrought iron fence that separated the driveway from the front garden. A long sidewalk made of stone pavers cut through the yard, leading to the front door of the Gothic-style home.

"It's more foreboding in person than from a distance, isn't it?" he said.

"Imagine living here in winter," Kayla replied. "It would be so isolated. It's hard to believe my mother grew up here. I had no idea."

Before she stepped through the gate, her ears pricked at the sound of ocean waves breaking and pounding upon the rocks below the cliff. She craned her neck over her shoulder. The edge of the cliff wasn't far from the house. This rocky piece of real estate would be perilous for a sleepwalker.

"I feel like we've been thrust into a gothic novel," she said, silently admitting she was glad Tanner was with her. Her nerves jumped under her skin.

As they strolled along the path to the door, her gaze perused the exterior of the house. With its wrap-around porch, steeply pitched roof, pointed arched windows, board and batten siding, widow's walk, and a tall lighthouse-like tower jutting out from one side of the house on the second level, the place reminded her of the haunted houses she'd seen in horror movies.

Seeming to read her mind, Tanner smiled and said, "Do you think this place could be haunted?"

"Don't be silly." She playfully slapped his arm and told herself that was nonsense. At the same time, she found herself trailing behind and letting him lead the way up the steps.

When her feet touched the porch, something caught her attention from the corner of her eye. A curtain moved slightly in one window, and she knew someone had seen them approach. Before Tanner could ring the doorbell, an elderly woman opened the door and stood staring at them, her expression anything but welcoming. She wore a straight black dress that hung like a sack on her bone-thin body. Her gray hair was pulled into a bun at her nape, and her deep-set eyes were as vacant as a doll's.

Adrenaline rushed through Kayla's veins. Was this her grandmother? If so, she was nothing like she'd imagined. Kitty had described her as forbidding, but she'd said nothing about spooky.

"Miss Grayson here to see—"

The woman cut Tanner off and drilled Kayla with an intense gaze. "I know who she is. But who are you?" She stubbed a bony finger in his chest.

Kayla gleaned the hint of a French accent.

Tanner cleared his throat. "My name is Tanner Bishop, Mrs. Chandler. It's a pleasure to meet you." He held out his hand to shake.

She ignored it. "I'm not Mrs. Chandler," the woman snapped. "Come in. You've kept her waiting."

When she turned and stepped further into the dimly lit foyer, Kayla and Tanner's gazes met. Intensity radiated from his eyes. He winked, and she let out a sigh of relief. He closed the door behind them. Then Kayla felt his hand reach for hers and he squeezed, as if assuring her everything was going to be all right. She squeezed back and felt a flash as potent as an electrical current move through her.

"Don't just stand there," the woman said, waving them forward. They walked into a narrow hall, with a steep staircase running up along the wall to their right. "Sit in here," she said. "I'll tell the missus that you're here." She gestured them into the room on the left, opposite the stairs. They entered an old-fashioned parlor that might have come straight out of the Victorian era.

Soft rosy shades, lace curtains at the tall windows, and green ferns in brass containers gave the room a dreamy ambiance. At any other time, Kayla might have delighted in the lovely parlor, but now her focus was entirely on meeting her grandmother. She took a seat on a sofa that was cushioned in deep pink satin. Its frame was scalloped walnut. There was nothing soft about the sofa's upholstery. She wondered if Sonora had chosen the furniture or if it had been handed down through generations. Kayla braced herself, suspecting her grandmother was as hard as the horsehair this piece of furniture was probably stuffed with.

Tanner sat beside her and gazed around. His eyes were watchful, and Kayla had the uncomfortable feeling he was looking forward to the upcoming encounter. But why shouldn't he? He was first and foremost a journalist, always sniffing out a story, as he put it. Still, he'd seemed a little too eager to tag along with her today. Why? She remembered him saying he'd come to Harmony Beach to track down a story of personal nature. Did his interest also lie somewhere in or near Seacliff House?

Kayla studied his profile and the granite set of his jaw, wondering.

Tanner turned toward her and caught her staring. "Mrs. Chandler must be a lady who likes to keep people waiting. I expect she likes to make an entrance."

"I've already waited twenty-seven years," Kayla said. "I suppose a few more minutes won't kill me." Inside her chest, her heart hammered. The waiting *was* killing her. Soon, she would meet the formidable woman who had run both Kayla's mother and father away. Was she a monster, or simply a willful woman who insisted on ruling the roost?

Mentally, Kayla was still preparing herself when Sonora finally appeared, entering from the hallway and being pushed in a wheelchair by the woman in black. Kayla shot up from the sofa like a rocket. Tanner followed her example.

As the wheelchair rattled forward, Kayla perused her grandmother. Her long hair was dyed an unnatural ebony color, slicked back from her forehead, and held with tortoise-shell combs. Surprisingly, her face appeared remarkably unwrinkled. Slippers showed from beneath her long gown of navy satin. With puffy sleeves trimmed in black lace, and a ruffle along the bottom hem and accented by black ribbon, her wardrobe appeared to have come straight out of the nineteenth century.

Even from the wheelchair, Kayla could tell Sonora was a petite woman, like Suzanne. But she didn't appear frail. Her chin was pointed, her cheekbones high and pronounced, and her eyes, dark and probing. Her direct gaze didn't waver from Kayla's face.

Her first words were, "Didn't Kitty tell you I'm disabled?"

"No, ma'am," Kayla answered.

"Come here," Sonora ordered in a strong voice once the other woman had parked her in front of the brick fireplace.

Kayla crossed the room to stand before her. Under Sonora's inquisitive gaze, she felt large and inelegant. She suspected her grandmother enjoyed making people feel uncomfortable and suddenly wished she'd heeded Kitty's warning.

"Bend down where I can see you better," Sonora demanded. She pulled a pair of eyeglasses from her breast pocket and slipped them on. Grasping Kayla's chin between her skeletally thin fingers, she tugged Kayla's face this way and that, searching her profile.

Stunned into silence from being manhandled that way, Kayla felt her cheeks burn with humiliation, but she was unable to utter a retort.

"Humph!" Sonora snorted, releasing her chin. "I might have expected as much. You're the spitting image of your father. I never cared two whits for that man."

Feeling no kinship with the woman, Kayla took offense—not only to being negatively compared to her father, but also to the disrespectful manner in which she'd just been treated.

Backing away, she said in a cautionary tone, "I beg your pardon, but you don't know a thing about me. And I don't care for your rough manner. Please don't lay your hands on me that way again, or speak unkindly about my father."

Sonora's painted-on eyebrow cocked. And then she laughed, causing Kayla's annoyance to soar like mercury in a thermometer.

"I see you have some of your mother's spit and vinegar in you. I'm glad to know you got *something* from her."

Kayla straightened her spine. "I wouldn't think it mattered much to you, what I got from my mother."

"Of course it matters." Sonora's gaze narrowed. "Suzanne is a Chandler, which makes you a Chandler."

"My last name is Grayson," Kayla pointed out.

Sonora smiled, but it didn't appear genuine. "So it is. But the Chandler blood runs hot through your veins. There's no escaping that truth."

Something about the way Sonora said it sent chills running down Kayla's arms.

"Who is this?" her grandmother asked, nodding toward Tanner. He stepped forward and extended his hand to shake.

"I'm Tanner Bishop, a friend of your granddaughter's. It's a pleasure to meet you, Mrs. Chandler."

"It is? No one has considered me a pleasure for years, young man. Sit back down the both of you." Her head twisted to meet the solemn gaze of the woman in black. "Martine, push me over to the sofa."

Kayla and Tanner retook their seats. What seemed to Kayla like an afterthought, Sonora finally introduced the other woman.

"This is Martine Allen, my housekeeper. She's been with me for years. That'll be all, Martine. You may go." With the flick of Sonora's dismissive hand, the housekeeper left the room without saying a word.

In a strapping voice, with none of the cracking that sometimes comes with age, Sonora said to Kayla, "Tell me why you're here after all these years. Why didn't your mother come?"

Finally heeding the warnings both her mom and Kitty had given, Kayla decided then and there to stand up to her. If her mother had once managed it, so could she.

"Mom's not feeling well. Her cousin, Kitty, sent her a message asking her to come to Harmony Beach, but it's not possible for my mother to travel. Since there was urgency to Kitty's request, I came instead."

Sonora's scrutiny intensified. "Why can't Suzanne travel?"

Unwilling to admit her mom's weaknesses to her grandmother, Kayla stalled. Beside her, she heard the rise and fall of breath as Tanner, too, waited for an answer. Aware that she was popping her knuckles in her lap, Kayla shoved her hands under her thighs.

"Mom has a disease," she uttered.

"Agoraphobia. She can't leave the house without becoming physically ill."

She looked Sonora in the eyes, and then turned to Tanner. The expression on his face was one of surprise, but also of compassion, for which she felt immense gratitude.

Her grandmother was silent for a moment. Her mouth twitched and it appeared her mind was working. Then she said, "Why did Kitty write to your mother? Was it to tell her Matt has returned to Harmony Beach?"

So, Kitty was not mistaken. Sonora *did* know Kayla's father was here. Kayla nodded, feeling their talk might go somewhere after all. "I think I saw him today myself. Tanner and I were at the old Beach Club and Casino. Someone looking like my father, as described by Kitty, appeared from around the corner. When I approached him, he ran away."

"Humph! Sounds just like Matt Grayson. He always was a coward."

Kayla clenched her fists under her legs. "I wish you'd stop talking about my dad that way. Kitty told me how he treated my mother when I was a child. I can understand why you don't like him. But in defense of the man, he didn't have the slightest idea of who I was today. There wasn't a chance for me to tell him."

Sonora rolled her eyes.

"Has he been here to see you?" Kayla asked.

"No. And he'd better not darken my door, either. That man is not welcome here."

"Then how did you know he's in town?"

"I have my ways, granddaughter."

Kayla thought about that for a moment and remembered Kitty's comment about spies. "Do you know why he'd come back after so many years?"

"Don't know and don't care."

"Good. Then there's no need for a confrontation between the two of you. Kitty is afraid of what might happen if you were to see each other."

Sonora slapped the arm of the wheelchair, causing Kayla to jump. "Kitty's a nincompoop. She scares as easily as a mouse."

Her grandmother certainly didn't censor herself, which Kayla didn't mind. Probably most people her age didn't. She wasn't intimidated by Sonora's brashness, but her grandmother sure was different from her mother, who'd been quiet and proper all of Kayla's life. It was just about as difficult to believe that Suzanne and Sonora were mother and daughter as it was to find commonality between herself and her mom.

"I like Kitty," Kayla said, in defense of the woman who'd been nothing but kind to her so far.

"You don't know her like I do," Sonora said.

"I don't know her at all. I only found out about her, my father, and *you*, yesterday."

"How much do you know about the past?" Sonora asked, leaning forward.

"Almost nothing."

"And that's the way it's going to stay. For now, anyway." Sonora flicked her hand at Tanner. "Come over here and give me a push, young man. I'll give you two the grand tour of the house now."

Tanner jumped up from the sofa, too eager for Kayla's liking. She opened her mouth to protest. They could see the house later. There were a million questions she wanted to ask her grandmother about her mother, father,

and what had happened here all those years
ago. But, apparently, they would have to
wait. Sonora's lips pressed together, and her
gaze grew into pinpoints, daring Kayla to
object.

Chapter Eight

As Kayla rose from the sofa and followed Tanner and the wheelchair into the hallway, she thought it odd that her grandmother hadn't asked anything about *her* life yet. Didn't the woman care about how she'd grown up? Where she'd gone to school? What she did for a living? And why didn't she want to know more about her own daughter?

With each year that had passed with no communication between them, had Sonora's heart grown so cold that she'd become completely detached from Suzanne? Perhaps Suzanne's leaving and staying away was a hurt that had been too hard to bear and too great to forgive.

Kayla wanted to give her grandmother the benefit of the doubt, and hoped she'd warm up in time. She glanced around the parlor before exiting. The furnishings were probably the same as those that decorated the house a century ago. The room held nothing contemporary, and there were no family photos anywhere in sight. Sad. Kayla was reminded of that old saying—out of sight, out of mind.

"Roll me to the end of the hall," Sonora ordered Tanner. "Come here, Kayla. I want to show you something."

Although she didn't care to be bossed around, Kayla bit her tongue and did as requested. She passed another room on the left that was obviously a formal dining room. At the end of the dim hallway, she was aware of a portrait on the wall above her grandmother's head, lost in murky light. It was an oil painting of a woman, encased in an ornate gold frame.

"Turn on the hall light," Sonora

commanded Tanner, pointing with a long finger to a switch on the wall. When he flicked the switch and the hallway was bathed in light, Kayla's attention caught Sonora's.

"This is Maude Tillman, an ancestor who is part of your heritage," Sonora said, with pride.

Kayla eyed Tanner, having remembered the research he'd done on the Tillman family. At the time, she hadn't put two and two together— that she was related to Maude Tillman. She stared at the painting and into the eyes of a woman no less daunting than her grandmother. Wearing wire-rimmed glasses and a dress with a high collar and an ivory broach at her neck, her brown hair was pushed off her high forehead and parted down the middle, swept into a knot at the back of her head. The intense gaze of the portrait seemed to challenge her.

"Maude built Seacliff House in 1896," Sonora said. "She was fifty-two years old and already a very rich woman by that time. At the back of the house is the kitchen. I doubt you're interested in it. The upstairs bedrooms are much more fascinating. The rooms haven't changed much since Maude's days. Perhaps you'd like to see them."

"Why?" The house would be intriguing any other time, but Kayla was annoyed with Sonora. She wanted answers to questions about her own past, not to be deluged with stories about dead ancestors.

"*Why*?" Sonora's eyes flashed. "Because you belong to this house as much as I do. Part of you is Tillman, whether you accept that fact or not. A Tillman built this house, and the Tillmans have always lived here. I was a Tillman before I married. Perhaps I'll leave Seacliff House to you when I die."

That unexpected revelation shocked Kayla. The last thing she wanted right then was to think about being left this monstrosity or to have much else to do with the woman who lived here. No wonder her mother had walked out never to return. Sonora Chandler was a bitter, albeit funny woman. She *had* to be joking about leaving Kayla this house. They were total strangers.

Deciding to tweak her attitude, Kayla stepped in front of Sonora's wheelchair and changed the tone of her voice.

"Grandmother…" The word tasted like metal in her mouth. "Please tell me what happened to my father, and why my mother left Harmony Beach and Seacliff House. I won't go upstairs or spend another minute here unless you share the true story. I've lived twenty-seven years in the dark. I need to know."

She felt Tanner's comforting hand on her shoulder. When she turned her head and gazed into his face, he nodded, giving her the encouragement she desperately needed. But her questions were too personal to speak about in front of him. "Would you mind?" she asked, remembering he'd promised to give her privacy if she wanted to be alone with her grandmother.

"Not at all."

Once Tanner stepped outside the door, a loud noise whooshed from Sonora's mouth, like a horse blowing out air. "There isn't much to tell. Your mother met Matt Grayson, a man I disapproved of, and they eloped. You were born nine months later. When you were three years old, I caught Matt cheating. I suspected it hadn't been the first time. When I told your mother what I'd seen, she didn't want to believe me. She told me later that she confronted Matt and he left the house. Then his jacket was found washed up on the beach below the cliffs. We all assumed he'd drowned himself, out of guilt."

This was the third time Kayla had heard that story. "But he didn't drown himself, did he?"

Sonora snorted. "Apparently not."

"Where do you think he's been all these years?" Kayla asked.

"How would I know?" Sonora shrugged her bony shoulders.

Unfortunately, her grandmother had not revealed anything Kitty hadn't already told her. "If my father cheated, and Mom kicked him out and then thought he'd died, why did she take me and leave Harmony Beach? What would be the purpose of moving us? And why hasn't she spoken to you all these years? Why didn't she want me to know about my family here?"

Kayla's blood surged through her like a speeding train. She'd grown up aware of her mother's secrets and was tired of them. "For once, can someone be honest with me?" Tears threatened to burst from her eyes. Her shoulders grew stiff with unexpected rage.

It seemed an eternity before Sonora answered. When she did, her attitude was blasé. "Suzanne was as stubborn as a goat, Kayla. She and I often butted heads. She got this crazy notion into her mind that I had something to do with Matt's disappearance. Then when his jacket was discovered, she imagined I'd somehow goaded him into committing suicide." She chuckled. "As if I were *that* powerful." Her cold hand reached out and stroked Kayla's arm, sending shivers rippling down Kayla's back.

"The truth is, your mother took you and left because she couldn't face the truth. When she learned her husband had slept with other women, she felt humiliated and disgraced. She knew people would judge her, which would reflect poorly on me. She was, after all, a Chandler, and a Tillman by blood. For those of us fortunate enough to have been born into such a prestigious family, we owe it to the memories of our ancestors to uphold a spotless reputation. The best thing for everyone involved was for Suzanne to leave and try to forget all about Matt Grayson and Seacliff House."

Stunned, Kayla eased away from Sonora's touch. The twist in the story made sense, sort of. Her head swam with visions of growing up with her mother, who'd increasingly become more introverted as the years went by. Were her panic attacks and agoraphobia all a result of years of loneliness, sadness, and her own guilt? Kayla didn't know what to think.

"Does that answer your questions?" Sonora asked.

"For now, I guess." She stepped into the hallway and to the screen door and called outside to Tanner, who was pacing up and down the walk. "You can come back in now."

"Did you get some answers?" he whispered.

Kayla shrugged her shoulders, and they entered the parlor together. A sudden longing washed over her. She wanted nothing more than to get back to the B&B and fall into bed and sleep. "We should be going," she told Sonora. "We've kept you long enough, and it's been a tiring day for me. Kitty is expecting me for dinner."

"Would you like to see the upstairs before you go?" Her grandmother's eyes twinkled with an eerie delight.

Kayla met Tanner's willing gaze. This might be his only chance to see Seacliff House, and he was definitely interested in the place. It was written all over his face. Kayla acquiesced. "All right. If it doesn't take long."

"Go to the top of the stairs and see if any of the rooms speak to you. Perhaps you'll sense what's up there."

Kayla didn't like the sound of that. Her head snapped toward Sonora. "Sense what? What are you talking about?"

"History, child. It leaves its mark. Remember, you are a Tillman. The house recognizes you."

Kayla met Tanner's inquisitive gaze. His head tilted. The small smile parting his lips matched what she thought: her grandmother might be cuckoo.

"Don't turn on any lights," Sonora warned, as Kayla and Tanner started up the steep flight of stairs. "Electricity will ruin the atmosphere. There's still a hint of sun shining through the windows. But if you need more light, there are candles you may use."

Sonora had certainly set the stage for a weird experience, but Kayla refused to be spooked. She *did* want to see where her mother had grown up. Her hand slid slowly along the polished wood banister. She was grateful for Tanner's footsteps behind her, especially when a shadow darted across the path at the top of the stairs. With her breath lodged in her throat, her head swiveled over the rail to meet Sonora's steady gaze.

"Where is your housekeeper, Martine?" Kayla asked.

"Most likely, she's in the kitchen. I'm not sure." Sonora's fake eyebrow lifted, as if she knew a secret and enjoyed the teasing.

Kayla's gaze moved from Sonora to Tanner and back again. "I have one more question. Was Martine working for you when my mother lived at Seacliff House?"

"Yes. Martine and her husband, Dave, have been with me since the late 1950s. He was my handyman."

Mmmm. Martine and Dave were two more people from her mother's past whom Kayla was unaware of until today. The whole situation was overwhelming. Another question popped into her mind. "Is Martine French?"

"She's French Canadian. Why do you ask?"

Tanner probably wondered, too. Kayla felt his fingers in her back, nudging her.

"I noticed her accent and find it hard to believe that my mom had a whole other life here in Maryland that I knew nothing about until now. I'm curious about the people who knew her. And those she grew up around."

"Martine won't answer any of your questions," Sonora stated, gruffly. "So don't bother to ask."

"Why is that?" Annoyance ignited at Sonora's brusque tone and shot through Kayla's nerve endings.

"Because Martine does what I tell her, and she has no business talking about my family's personal affairs."

Kayla swallowed a response and turned away from Sonora's abrasive voice. She stepped into the dim hallway at the top of the landing. The draperies were drawn in the hall window, so candles were going to be needed after all. Sitting on a small table at the head of the stairs were some candlesticks stuck in old-fashioned tin holders and a matchbox. Tanner struck a match to two of the candles and handed one to Kayla. Moving shadows danced across the walls as the flames flickered.

"What are we doing up here?" she whispered to him, as she gazed at the closed doors running down the hall.

"According to your grandmother, we're sensing history."

Kayla let out a sigh. "Well, let's sense it and get out of here. Seacliff House isn't what I expected. It's creepy."

Tanner muffled a laugh and placed his hand on the doorknob of the door closest to them. When they stepped inside, Kayla's gaze fell upon the brick fireplace and then wandered to the four-poster bed and a large wardrobe, both beautiful antiques. A porcelain washbasin and pitcher sat on an oak dry sink with hand towels folded neatly next to them. A bar of unused soap rested in a glass dish. The room smelled of lavender. The floors were hardwood, the walls were papered in a floral print, and the bed was covered in what appeared to be a hand-crocheted spread. It was a lovely room.

Kayla strolled around inside, wondering what it was her grandmother thought she would sense. She opened the wardrobe to find it empty. Obviously, this room was unoccupied.

"Do you feel anything in here?" Tanner asked.

"Nope. Do you?"

"Not a thing. Let's try another room."

The next room they entered was decorated with similar furnishings, including a fireplace. Again, the bedroom seemed not to be inhabited.

"I wonder which one is my grandmother's bedroom. And which was my mother's."

"There must be more rooms on the main level. I didn't notice an elevator downstairs. Mrs. Chandler couldn't get up here in the wheelchair."

"That's true. I'm guessing Martine and her husband live here, too."

"There might be quarters for the servants behind the house," Tanner said. "Back in the eighteen hundreds, rich folks wouldn't have their help living under the same roof. They would have built a separate dwelling or two away from the main house."

The idea of her family coming from money and having servants was such a foreign concept. Kayla and her mom had barely scraped by all their lives. It was only recently they'd become more financially comfortable, due to a raise at work and the good sales she was making on her books.

"You sound like you know a lot about the customs of that time period," she said to Tanner.

"I read a lot. And I'm a journalist. Remember? I thirst for knowledge."

She smiled. "I recall that from our earlier conversation."

"If it wasn't getting dark out, I'd like to explore the grounds outside," he said. "Maybe next time."

Would there be a next time? Kayla didn't know. Even if there turned out to be, there was no reason Tanner had to tag along. "Let's check out the next room," she said, stepping back into the hallway.

"You didn't sense anything in this room,

either?" Tanner asked, closing the door behind them.

"No. I think my grandmother might be senile."

He cocked a grin and stood in front of the door at the west end of the hall. He placed his hand on the brass knob. Although the knob turned, the door didn't open.

"Is it locked?" Kayla asked. She hoped so. It would mean their futile investigation was over. "Let's go downstairs," she told Tanner. "I'm done playing my grandmother's silly game."

"The door isn't locked." A low voice spoke behind them. Startled, Kayla nearly dropped the candle. She swung around to find Martine watching them from the top of the stairs.

Chapter Nine

"Mrs. Chandler thought you might need some help." Martine's black clothing faded into the gloom of the hallway. On quiet feet, she glided toward them and placed her hand on the knob. With her skeletal shoulder braced against the wood, she gave it a shove, and the door creaked open.

Kayla's heart raced with apprehension. She hesitated before stepping inside. Unlike the other bedrooms, a stale, musty odor saturated the air. She coughed. Martine flicked the switch next to the door, obviously not adhering to Sonora's rule about the use of electricity.

When the room was awash in light, Kayla gulped. The wallpaper in here was not only faded, it was also stained in patches, and large pieces were torn from the wall. The draperies hanging at the windows were thin and tattered, and cobwebs hugged every corner of the room. Decades' worth of dust caked the furniture. When Tanner began strolling around the room, his movements stirred up the dust, causing Kayla to sneeze.

The hair on her neck bristled. A canopied bed stood against one wall. Like the drapes, the canopy had tears and holes in it. One entire piece hung down the side to almost touch the floor. A ladies desk and chair sat in front of another wall. Kayla noticed an inkpot and several sheets of paper, covered in dust, lying on the tabletop. An oval mirror stood in the corner next to an armoire. The floor was covered with a threadbare and discolored Persian rug.

"This room has never been refurbished," Martine said. "It has remained exactly the way it was before the terrible thing happened."

Kayla felt an ache deep in her chest. *What terrible thing? How many tragic things had happened to this family?*

Martine continued. "Mrs. Chandler doesn't like us to come in here. I've never been allowed to clean." Her nose rode high in the air, showing her disapproval. "She keeps the room closed up, perhaps to shut out the echoes of the screams that sounded in here long ago."

"Screams?" Kayla's mouth fell open.

"Whose room is this?" Tanner asked. "And what kind of godforsaken thing occurred in here?"

Martine's gaze flew to Kayla, addressing her with impatient scorn. "Do you sense her?"

"Who?"

"The spirit of your ancestor."

Kayla looked at Tanner, whose eyes were large with fascination. Her gaze moved back to Martine. "No. I don't believe in ghosts."

"Then you're a silly fool."

"I beg your pardon." Kayla's temper sparked again at Martine's name calling. "What happened in here? Is this where history has supposedly left its mark, as my grandmother suggests?"

Martine nodded. "If you listen carefully, you might hear her crying. I've heard her before."

"Who?" Kayla repeated.

Martine weighed her words carefully before answering. "Over one hundred years ago, two men broke into this house. They were former employees of Maude Tillman's. She'd fired both of them days before, for being intoxicated on the job. That particular day,

Maude, her husband, Angus, and their son, Bradley, had gone to town early in the morning. Their daughter, Charlotte, a thirty-year-old spinster, was home, sleeping in this very bed. Those two men came in and raped her. Only the servants were here, but they had little protection. The men had knives. There was nothing anyone could do."

Kayla's gaze cut toward the bed. She squeezed her eyes shut and could almost hear Charlotte's pleading and cries, and feel her pain. Was this what her grandmother had meant about sensing history?

Martine continued in a whisper. "Nine months later, Charlotte died giving birth to a baby boy, right here in this very bed where she'd been violated."

Kayla's fist flew to her mouth. "How awful! Poor Charlotte. What happened to the baby?"

"Apparently, the servants disposed of the body."

Kayla gasped. "The body? Do you mean…?"

"Not in that way," Martine said. "A couple from another town agreed to take the infant. After all, its father was an unknown rapist. It's doubtful Maude would have chosen to raise the bastard as her own."

Tanner piped in with his opinion. "That's harsh. You would have thought Mr. and Mrs. Tillman would have wanted something left of their daughter."

"Not Maude," Martine said. "There are plenty of stories about how hard she was."

Kayla couldn't listen to anymore. She bolted past Martine to escape the oppressing room. She'd had enough tragedy, both ancient and recent. More than anything, she wanted to leave this house and get back to Kitty's, where it was bright and cheerful. But before she reached the staircase, a couple of burning questions stopped her.

"Which of these rooms was my mother's?" she asked Martine.

She pointed to the first room they'd entered. "This one with the four-poster bed. It didn't look the same back then, of course. Mrs. Chandler had the room redecorated when your mother left Seacliff House."

"And which room is my grandmother's?" Kayla inquired.

Martine's lips puckered. "When she and Mr. Chandler were married, their room was the one at the other end of the hallway." Martine tipped her head in that direction. "It remains locked. No one is allowed inside. It's been that way since Mr. Chandler went away. Mrs. Chandler has made her quarters on the main level for many years."

"I see." Kayla welcomed the information. Since Martine was talking and there may not be another chance to get her alone, Kayla decided to ask what had put her grandmother into the wheelchair. After all, Sonora had mentioned she was disabled, as opposed to simply being old and unable to stand or walk without assistance.

The question seemed to cause Martine some anguish, based on the vein that popped out on her forehead. "Mrs. Chandler was in an automobile accident in which she injured her spinal cord."

Although the answer was short and curt, Kayla was grateful to know. One more thought rattled around in her head. When she and Tanner had arrived, she'd seen an octagonal structure jutting up on this end of the house. "Can the tower room be reached from

Charlotte's bedroom?" she asked. It may have been her imagination, but she thought she saw a glimmer of panic cross Martine's face.

"Yes, but it's only used for storage now. In fact, it's sealed off. There's nothing up there Mrs. Chandler needs anymore."

"I don't remember seeing a door in the bedroom," Kayla said. Tanner shook his head, indicating he hadn't seen one either. Kayla stared at Martine waiting for a response.

"As I said, it's been sealed. Covered up," she answered in a monotone voice, while glaring at Kayla.

Kayla's body went cold at Martine's sharp scrutiny. She and Sonora were two of a kind. They both were odd and seemed to enjoy trying to intimidate Kayla. She was done playing games. She reached for the banister and fled down the staircase.

"Hold up, Kayla." Tanner pushed around Martine and scampered down the steps after her.

She flung the front door open, letting the screen door slam shut behind her, and ran onto the porch and gulped in fresh air. She turned her head toward the cliffs. The sun was setting over the ocean. Like being touched by a painter's brush, the sky was afire with magnificent streaks of yellow, pink and orange.

From behind her inside the house, Kayla heard the wheels of her grandmother's chair rattling across the hallway floor toward the door. She couldn't speak to her right now. She had to get away from this place.

The screen door squeaked open again, and she felt a large hand clasp her shoulder. With tears of frustration pricking her eyes, she whirled and instinctively let her head drop onto Tanner's broad chest. Thank goodness he'd come with her. Although they barely knew each other, he was kind and a comfort.

Reaching for calm, she gazed into his soft eyes and said, "Please take me home."

Tanner wrapped his arm around her and helped her to the car. She fished the keys from her purse and dropped them in his open palm. Before she crawled onto the seat of the passenger side, she lifted her gaze above the car roof and saw Sonora sitting inside the front door in her wheelchair. Neither woman waved.

Tanner closed the car door behind Kayla. Then he started the vehicle and drove through the gate.

When Kayla laid her head back against the seat, she closed her eyes thinking her mom and Kitty had both been right. It had been a big mistake to come here.

* * * *

As Tanner drove, Kayla shared with him the information Mrs. Chandler had given her regarding her father and mother. After that, the ride to the B&B was a quiet one. Not only did he not want to interrupt Kayla from her thoughts, he had some ruminating of his own to do.

Seacliff House was just as he'd imagined it would be. If only he'd been able to see more of the dwelling, and the grounds, too. He tapped his fingers upon the steering wheel. It had taken all his willpower not to ask Mrs. Chandler about Pearl. At her advanced age, would she even remember a girl who had worked for her in the 1950s? She was on the ball, so he assumed so.

He'd even thought of asking Martine about Pearl. From what he gathered, Martine and her husband had already become employed by the Chandlers when Pearl was hired. But the timing hadn't been right to bring it all up, especially after Martine told the gruesome story about the Tillman daughter.

Tanner shook his head, amazed at the similarities. Maude Tillman's daughter had died giving birth to a son conceived in violence in that house. Sixty some years later, Pearl had given birth to a son, abandoned him, and unknowingly fled to the same house. According to Vivien's diary, her brother Vince had raised Pearl's boy. After all, he was the child's natural father. Poor Charlotte's son would never know his true father. Nevertheless, both children had been denied the love and care of their mothers.

Now that he'd finagled his way inside once, Tanner was determined to return to Seacliff House as soon as possible. Learning more about his great grandmother, Pearl, and the mystery of what eventually happened to her, was the reason he was in Harmony Beach. He wasn't about to leave before discovering the whole story.

He pulled Kayla's car into a vacant parking space behind the bed and breakfast and cut off the motor. He glanced at her. She'd fallen asleep in the short drive. Soft and steady breath escaped through her slightly parted lips. She looked like an angel with all that coppery-red hair flowing over her shoulders like a waterfall. Kayla was a pretty girl. The best part about her though was her grit. He liked the way she'd stood her ground with the old woman.

A soft moan tore from her mouth, sending a pleasant sensation rolling through Tanner's torso. The poor thing had been through a lot for one day. He couldn't imagine how she was holding up after all the information that had been thrown at her. Not to mention meeting that dragon of a grandmother and seeing the man she thought was her father.

Cutting another glance at Kayla, his heart went out to her. Confessing to the old lady that her mother had a mental disorder had to be particularly tough. Being dyslexic, he knew firsthand the way a label could affect a person. The mean old bird didn't give off any warm grandmotherly vibes. It must have been difficult for Kayla's mother to grow up with such a chilly woman. In his opinion, Kayla hadn't missed anything, not having had Mrs. Chandler in her life all these years.

As he replayed the episode over in his mind, he found it unusual that he'd been more shocked to hear the news about Kayla's mother than Mrs. Chandler seemed to be. But then, a woman as hard as the stone cliffs outside her door probably didn't show much weakness. Or maybe she just didn't give a damn about her daughter.

Kayla stirred. "We're here," he said, gently jiggling her arm.

Her eyelids fluttered open, and her chest expanded as she stretched her arms behind her head. "Where are we?"

"Back at the B&B."

"Really? Did I fall asleep?"

"There was just enough time for a cat nap. You must be exhausted," he said, watching her try to suppress a yawn.

She sighed. "I was on the road at five o'clock this morning. It was a six-hour drive. Ever since I arrived, there's been one surprise after another. To say I'm beat is putting it mildly."

"Let's get you to your room." Tanner stepped out of the car and came around to her side to assist her out. When her hand slid into his, a spark ignited deep in his belly, and a flash of heat crawled over his neck. They'd only just met, and yet, he knew Kayla was a woman he could care about.

She yawned again. "I'm supposed to have dinner with Kitty tonight, but I think I'll have to bow out. I just want to take a hot bath and go to bed."

"That's reasonable. I'm sure she'll understand."

Once they were inside, Kitty was nowhere to be seen. Table lamps in the parlor were lit to create a warm ambience, and a plate of freshly baked cookies sat on the sidebar in the dining area.

"Those smell great. Want one?" Tanner asked, snatching a couple of cookies from off the plate.

"No thanks." Kayla ambled to her room, located on the other side of the dining room and slipped the door key into the lock. Tanner sidled up behind her and handed her the car keys.

"Thanks for driving me back." She nudged the bedroom door open and turned to face him. "And thank you for going with me to meet my grandmother."

"I kind of invited myself," he reminded her.

She smiled. "That, you did. Still, I'm glad you were there. She's something else, isn't she?"

"Yep. But from what I saw, she didn't

get the best of you. You were polite but still held your ground. After all, your grandmother was the one to extend an invitation to you. She must have expected you'd have questions about your family."

Though obviously tired, Kayla's face lit up. "Thank you, Tanner. I appreciate you saying that. I experienced a few moments of frustration, but hopefully I wasn't rude." She seemed to think about his comment for a moment. Then her mouth turned down. "What about that heartbreaking story Martine told us?" She shook her head. "It seems bad luck has been with my family as far back as anyone can remember."

A painful expression so deep and sorrowful filled her face. No doubt, she believed the bad luck had started many generations ago and continued to haunt her family. Her father had cheated and lied, and left his wife and daughter. Her mother suffered from mental problems. And her grandmother lived in a spooky house where awful things had happened. That was enough bad luck for any one person to deal with.

Tanner had the sudden urge to kiss Kayla and ensure her everything was going to be all right. He sensed she was a resilient woman, but he also detected an innocence about her that made him afraid for her. She didn't need protecting, exactly. But he felt she could use a friend. What kind of friend would he be if he tried to kiss her when she was vulnerable? It was inappropriate.

He leaned toward her, but instead of kissing her, he awkwardly patted her shoulder.

Despite his hard-earned skill of putting words on paper, like a lot of Mainer men, he wasn't the greatest at verbally expressing his emotions. All the same, his words were heartfelt when he said, "Don't worry, Kayla. I think you've probably broken the curse."

She gazed at him with wide and grateful eyes. "Why do you say that? You don't even know me."

He grinned. "I was born with an uncanny intuition about people, and I'm also a great judge of character. And you, Miss Grayson, are a quality person. I'd bet my life on it." He was also thinking she was kind, brave, sweet, and one of the most attractive women he'd met in a long time, but those thoughts he kept to himself.

"Thank you. That's nice of you to say so."

He was about to suggest they get together tomorrow and continue their investigation into Harmony Beach and Seacliff House when Kitty appeared in the doorway separating the hall from the dining room.

"Kayla! Good. You're home." Her sandals slapped against the wood floor as she strode toward them.

Tanner noted Kitty's furrowed brow and wondered what was up. He also heard Kayla expel a sigh of fatigue.

"Did you see Sonora?" Kitty asked her.

"Yes, but I'd like to rest before we talk about that. I'm awfully tired."

Kitty seemed to understand. "Then it was as bad as I suspected. I'm sorry."

"I'll tell you about the visit later. I know I promised to have dinner with you, but…"

Kitty placed her hand on Kayla's arm, interrupting her. "Don't worry about dinner." She nibbled her lower lip. It seemed to Tanner she was contemplating on how best to give Kayla more news. And he was right.

"Matt is here," she said. "And he wants to meet you."

Chapter Ten

Kayla felt she'd ascended into a dream.
Apparently, she was to meet her father a lot
sooner than she expected. Myriad conflicted
emotions flowed through her. How many
surprises could she take in one day?

Her gaze flew to Tanner. His eyes
assessed her with such warmth and concern that
she shuddered under their intensity. Right
before Kitty interrupted them, she'd felt sure
he was about to kiss her. She hadn't come to
Harmony Beach expecting to meet a man, but her
stomach had fluttered at the thought of his
lips on hers. It had been far too long since
she'd had a date, let alone been kissed by a
man as handsome, charming and nice as Tanner.

"How did this happen?" she asked Kitty,
focusing on the unpredicted news and trying to
put Tanner's lips out of her mind.

"I'll tell you in a minute." She stared
at Tanner and cleared her throat to give him a
signal.

Obviously, he got the hint, because he
excused himself and wished Kayla good luck.
"Hope to see you tomorrow."

Trying not to appear too anxious, but
wanting to get to know him better, she said,
"I'm sure we'll run into each other. Good
night. Thanks again for your support today."

"It was my pleasure."

She watched him exit the dining room,
unable to keep from admiring his muscular
physique as he swaggered to the staircase.
After he'd traipsed up the steps, Kitty led
her into the hallway. They stopped at a door
Kayla had thought was a linen closet, and
Kitty's voice dropped to a whisper.

"Matt showed up about thirty minutes ago. He said he saw a young woman outside the casino today, and he *knew* you were his daughter. He felt it in his bones. He said looking into your eyes was like staring at his reflection. He forced me to admit that you are, indeed, his long-lost daughter."

Kayla's eyes widened. "What do you mean he forced you? Did he threaten you, Kitty?"

"No, no, I don't mean that." She wrung her hands together. "As I mentioned earlier, Matt Grayson has always been a persuasive man. It seems nothing has changed."

"Oh." Kayla thought she saw understood Kitty's inference, being reminded again of his prior playboy status. "Why didn't you want to tell him about me?"

"It's not that I didn't want to," Kitty assured. "Seeing Matt standing at my door after all these years unnerved me. That's all."

"I understand. Did he want to know anything about me?" she asked.

"Of course he did. He asked if you're living at Seacliff House, or if you're out on your own. He was surprised to find out that you and Suzanne have been in Virginia all these years."

"Did you explain why I'm here now? That you'd emailed Mom asking her to come because you'd seen him?"

"No, I skipped that part. I told him you were here alone, and that you'd come back for a visit."

"Did he seem disappointed that Mom isn't with me?"

"I'm not sure," Kitty admitted. "I've been shaking like a leaf since he arrived. To be honest, I don't remember much of our brief conversation. Matt always did make me nervous. I had him wait at the door while I called Sonora. She said you'd just left. I offered him coffee here in the dining room and then showed him to my apartment downstairs when I saw your car pull up outside." She held out her trembling hands to prove to Kayla that she was still uneasy.

Kayla had a lot of questions. "Did he want to know anything more about my mother?"

"He asked if I'd stayed in touch with her, whether she'd remarried, and how she was, in general."

"What did you say?"

"I wasn't going to give him the satisfaction of knowing he'd ruined her life and she'd become a virtual prisoner in her own home."

Kayla breathed a sigh of relief. "Thank you, Kitty. Is there anything else?"

"No. That's about it."

Kayla saw that Kitty's face was noticeably pale. "Why are you so afraid of him?" she asked.

"It's not that I fear *him,* exactly. I'm worried about what might happen now that he's here. Nothing good can come of it. He should have stayed dead. Coming back to Harmony Beach is bound to stir up a hornet's nest of trouble."

"I still don't understand," Kayla said. "Who could possibly care what happened twenty-four years ago? I doubt anyone even remembers that my dad cheated on my mother and then faked his own death."

"Don't fool yourself. This town thrives on gossip," Kitty said. "Plenty of people remember. Your grandmother is one. Besides, infidelity was not the only thing your father was mixed up in."

That got Kayla's attention. "What else was he involved in? Illegal things?"

Kitty snapped her mouth shut. "I've said too much already."

Kayla's stomach churned with nausea. She wanted to scream, *you people never say anything!*

Kitty opened the door they stood in front of. "My apartment is downstairs. He's waiting for you." Her lips parted into a weak smile. "It's best you ask him any questions you want answered."

I will, Kayla thought, as she descended the carpeted stairs into the basement. At the bottom, she turned the corner and entered a large open room, which appeared to be a combination living, dining and kitchen area. Sitting on the sofa was the same man she'd seen at the casino. His pale melancholy eyes delved into her.

Kayla tilted her chin defensively and stared back. "Hello," she said, approaching and hating the way nervousness made her voice lift an octave.

He didn't answer, but seemed to study her as though she were something to dissect.

She tried again. "I'm Kayla, and you're my father. Aren't you?"

His lips moved faintly above his beard. She tried to conjure up a scrap of memory from when he'd been in her life as a child. There'd been nothing to recall for the past twenty-seven years, and there was still nothing.

When Matt finally spoke, his deep voice startled her. "I chose your name when you were born. Did you know that?"

"No. My mother never mentioned it. She

doesn't speak of the past."

He nodded slowly, as if he understood. "Please, come closer. Have a seat. I won't bite." He gestured toward the chair next to him. When Kayla sat down, he said, "How is Suzanne?"

Kayla's gaze remained glued to his. Inside, her heart galloped. Why did he care? She swallowed a gulp. She'd always abhorred the secrets her mom kept, and decided Matt deserved to know the truth. In reality, it had probably been his deceitful actions that had caused Suzanne's illness, anyway.

"My mother isn't well. She has no friends and no job. I provide financially for the two of us because Mom has a debilitating illness. She never leaves the house anymore. And she has major trust issues. *That's* how she is, *Dad*." She saw him cringe, which gave her a perverse sense of satisfaction.

Conflicting emotions washed over her. The little girl in Kayla wanted to hug Matt, and shout with joy that she'd been reunited with him, while the grownup Kayla, still feeling the sting of abandonment, wanted to slap his face. She lowered her head, gritting her teeth and willing tears not to fall. It was hard not to hold back resentment.

"You must be a good daughter, taking care of your mother the way you do."

Her eyes remained on her lap. "She raised me to be sympathetic to people's plights, including her own."

"She was always a good mother," Matt said, with a hint of nostalgia. "What do you do? For a living, I mean?" he asked, changing the subject.

Her gaze met his, and the pace of her pulse began to decrease. "I work for a

marketing firm. I also write children's
books. I was fortunate to be able to do the
illustrations for one of them. Drawing is my
passion."

"That's nice," he replied, smiling.

An awkward silence hung between them for
a moment. Then she boldly asked, "Why did you
leave us?"

His gaze was sympathetic. "I didn't want
to. You must believe me."

"Why should I? Are you saying someone
twisted your arm?"

"Yes, you could say that's the way it
was."

Kayla crossed her own arms defensively
over her chest. "I suppose you're going to
blame Grandmother Chandler."

Matt's narrowed gaze pinned her to the
chair like a dart. "As a matter of fact, my
leaving you and your mother *was* all of
Sonora's doing. She paid me to fake my death
and skip town. She swore if I ever tried to
contact the two of you, she'd have my head.
There. You wanted the truth. You got it."

Kayla's temper sparked. "Why did you
allow yourself to be intimated by her? Did
you commit other horrible crimes, or
something?"

He answered in a roundabout way. "Wasn't
cheating on your mother and abandoning you by
pretending to be dead enough?"

She reached for calm and was somehow able
to rein in the building anger. Her words were
measured when she replied, "I sure hope you
received a fortune for leaving us. I wouldn't
want to think Mom's suffering came cheap."

Matt slammed his fist on the coffee table
in front of him, causing Kayla to jump. He
raked an unsteady hand through his thick salt

and pepper hair. His outburst shocked and scared her. She cut a glance to the hallway, calculating how many seconds it would take for her to run and scream for help.

"I'm sorry," he apologized a moment later. "I don't mean to take my frustration out on you. I didn't want to leave Harmony Beach. I co-owned a business with my dad, and I loved you and your mother."

"*Really?* You had a strange way of showing it. I was told that you cheated on Mom, more than once." She couldn't keep the venom from leaking into her voice.

Matt sighed. "I deserve anything you want to throw at me. I was a terrible father and a worse husband. You've been better off without me all this time, both of you."

Kayla's heart skipped. Growing up, any father—even a lousy one—would have been better than none. "I never knew anything about you," she said, more quietly. "One time when I was in middle school and feeling especially vulnerable about my gawky teenage looks, I asked Mom if I resembled you. She'd been so upset she dropped a cup of steaming coffee and burnt her hand. I never asked about you again."

Matt shook his head and apologized.

Kayla's emotions were like a roller coaster, up and down. "Where have you been for the past twenty-four years, and why have you come back now?" she asked.

He looked relieved to move onto another topic. "I've been living in Norfolk, Virginia. I bought a bar and grill on the beach."

Kayla's heart skittered to a stop. It was impossible! He'd fled to Virginia, too? This whole time he'd lived only three and a half hours from her? They'd wasted so much time. If only he'd tried to find her. Maybe they could have enjoyed some type of relationship—even a long distance one.

His voice snapped her back from her thoughts.

"I met a woman about ten years ago. Her name is Linda Devlin. It's because of her that I'm here now. She finally convinced me it was time to make peace with my past."

Uncomprehending, Kayla tilted her head. "Who do you have to make peace with in Harmony Beach? I'd think my mother would be first on your apology list. And as you know, she's not here."

"Suzanne's the primary reason I came back. I had no idea she'd taken you and left when you were a little girl until Kitty told me. I thought the two of you were probably living with Sonora all this time."

Kayla didn't know whether to believe him or not. "Did you ever bother to find out?"

"I couldn't. I'd made a deal with Sonora all those years ago. She made me swear never to come back, or try to contact you."

If it hadn't been such a pathetic defense, Kayla would have laughed out loud. "Did my grandmother really hold that much power over you? Come on. Surely, you can come up with a better excuse than that."

"It's true. She threatened to kill me if I ever stepped foot in Harmony Beach again."

Kayla rolled her eyes, but something about the way he said it sent a chill spiraling down her spine. "Then why are you here now? Aren't you still afraid she'll make good on her threat?"

He shook his head. "No. She's an old woman. What can she do? I'm not a young man under her control anymore. Linda has made me realize what I've been missing all this time."

"What's that?"

"A relationship with you. You're my only child, Kayla."

If Matt thought he could wipe out his previous sins with a tender look and sappy sentiment, he was mistaken. She wasn't going to give in that easily. She'd craved a father's love and attention her entire life. But she was a woman now—a strong woman who had survived without him and was as well adjusted as the next person, despite her lack of a father. The bond between her and Suzanne had always been strong, notwithstanding the secrets.

"Linda thought it was time you and I talk," Matt continued. "I was expecting your mom to be around, too. I have a few things I wanted to clear up with her as well." He chewed on his lip and stared at a spot on the wall across the room.

Suddenly, it occurred to Kayla what his true intentions were. Her father had returned to Harmony Beach to ask her mother for a divorce so he could marry this other woman.

Questions swirled through her mind. Had Suzanne ever legally had Matt declared dead? Was it even possible without a body? Kayla had no idea. Suzanne had only dated a few men through the years and none of them seriously. Her illness had been too distracting to keep any relationship going for long, so being single must not have mattered to her. Legally, her parents were probably still married.

"I've figured out your game," Kayla said, standing up. "You can't marry your girlfriend without a divorce from Mom. I suppose Linda is tired of waiting. That's why she urged you to come back and make amends with us. Kitty warned me you've always been a sweet talker. But that's low. Real low."

She narrowed her eyes at him and spun on her heel. Matt jumped up from the sofa and heaved a ragged sigh.

"From all accounts, I'm dead," he said. "I drowned twenty-four years ago. Officially, I don't need a divorce. But I told Linda everything. She's a good woman. She wants me to do the right thing. She wants our marriage to be legal, in every sense of the word."

With her fists clenched at her side, Kayla quietly replied, "I really don't care about you or your girlfriend. You destroyed my mother with your lies and cheating, and I won't let you hurt her anymore. As for me, you've been dead to me my whole life." She turned to leave.

"Wait," Matt said, rushing to her side. He grabbed her hand and stuffed a slip of paper into her palm. "This is my cell phone number. Now that we've met, I really would like to see you again. I didn't come here just to ask Suzanne for a divorce. I've missed having you in my life. I'd be grateful if you'd give me another chance."

Kayla stared into his gray eyes. With a heavy heart, she said, "I don't see the point of any further contact."

He searched her face. "Please call me if you change your mind."

Before she broke down completely, Kayla hurried from the room and ran up the stairs.

Chapter Eleven

Kayla closed the bedroom door behind her and collapsed onto the mattress. She'd talk to Kitty in the morning. Right now, she needed to speak to her mom. But when she dialed the house phone, the nurse answered.

"Hi. This is Kayla. Is my mom available, please?"

She detected a hitch in the nurse's breath on the other end of the line. The woman, who was not a stutterer, fumbled over her response. "Mrs. Grayson...is asleep. Can I...leave...a message?"

Something in the nurse's voice sent up a red flag. "Did something happen? Is Mom all right?" Kayla asked.

There was a brief pause before the nurse replied. "Your mother's fine. She went to bed early. That's all. You have nothing to worry about. I'm sorry if I scared you." Kayla trusted the nurse, the mother of a school friend. She released the breath she'd unconsciously been holding. After all, Suzanne's problem was being unable to leave the house, nothing life threatening.

Suzanne probably wasn't up to hearing a report about her mother, anyway, which was understandable, now that Kayla had met Sonora. And telling her Matt had returned to Harmony Beach to request a divorce might not be the best idea, either. What had Kayla been thinking? The last thing she wanted to do was upset her mom. She was glad her mother was in bed already.

"Please tell her I called and that I'll be driving home tomorrow," she said.

"Tomorrow?" The nurse couldn't disguise her surprise.

Until that moment, Kayla hadn't considered leaving so soon. After all, she'd just arrived. But there didn't seem any point in staying longer. She'd met the family she never knew she had, and frankly, they'd been a disappointment. All, except for Kitty. Despite possessing what seemed to be the Chandler trait for keeping secrets, she was a kind and gracious lady whom Kayla planned to stay in touch with.

"Yes, tomorrow," she replied with conviction. "It'll probably be late before I get home though. Mom doesn't need to wait up."

"I understand," the nurse said. "I'll…I'll tell your mother."

"Thank you. Good night."

Kayla placed her cell phone on the bedside table and curled onto her side. Her head sunk into the downy soft pillow. She was so tired she might go to sleep with her clothes on.

She'd forgotten to close the drapes to the French doors. With her body facing the doors and the porch outside them, she could see the moon glowing dreamily in the sky. Through the door, she heard the ocean waves pounding the surf beyond. Kayla sat up and swung her legs over the side of the bed, listening to their rhythm.

She would miss the sound of those waves, and the serene feeling that accompanied them. But more than the water, Kayla realized she would miss Tanner and his easy smile, and the sweet feelings he aroused in her. Behind his eyes smoldered a man who had awakened a hunger inside her—an ache she hadn't even recognized was there—until now.

* * * *

The next morning, Kayla sat at the small round table on her private section of the porch doodling on a sketchpad and eating the delicious granola and fruit compote Kitty had served for the first course. The secluded area at that end of the house was blocked from the rest of the porch by a wooden tri-fold screen that stood on adjustable metal feet.

Several other guests were at the other end of the porch enjoying their breakfast outside, too. The screen didn't filter out their lively conversation, but at least Kayla didn't have to join in. She didn't feel like socializing, but it was a beautiful morning and she'd wanted to revel in the sunshine, the light breeze, and the gorgeous view of the ocean.

With this being one of Kitty's busiest times of the day, there hadn't been a chance for Kayla to tell her that she was leaving today. There was no rush. It didn't matter when she left or when she arrived home. She wanted to enjoy the ocean a little longer before departing.

Home. Suddenly, the word conjured up the image of a prison. Never had she thought of the small house she and Suzanne lived in on their tree-lined street in that way. But now that she'd been removed from her mom's depressed state and anxious behavior for a little while, it was difficult to think of returning to that atmosphere so quickly. Immediately, Kayla chastised herself for the selfish thought. Still, it wasn't like Suzanne needed someone to watch over her every day. The nurse was there for comfort and friendship, more than anything else.

Kayla gazed at the ocean, and a pang of sadness moved through her. She'd come here to forge a relationship with her father and grandmother, but it was obviously not going to happen.

On the other hand, there was no logical reason for her to go home so soon. Her mother didn't need her, and she'd requested and been granted two weeks of vacation, in case things had gone well here. But they hadn't. Her shoulders drooped, and she sighed heavily. Why postpone the inevitable? It was best to cut her losses and go back to the only life she'd ever known. She could try to forget about the ocean and Tanner by starting another book.

The sound of Tanner's cheerful voice on the other side of the screen grabbed her attention.

"Good morning. How is everyone this morning?"

"Fine," several people replied. "And you?"

"Just great," he answered. "Looks like we can expect another beautiful day."

Kayla heard the legs of his chair scrape against the wood porch floor. She quietly rose from her chair and peeked around the corner of the screen.

He sat at the table closest to her, staring straight ahead toward the boardwalk and the water. Even more rugged looking in the early morning light, her breath caught in her throat and she stared, wondering why she'd never met a man like him back home. The few short-term boyfriends she'd had never would have gone to the lengths he had yesterday to help her out. She'd thought chivalry was dead. Apparently, it wasn't for the man from Maine.

Each time she saw Tanner, she thought him more handsome. His profile appeared carved in granite. Smiling, she reconsidered staying a few more days just so she could look at him.

When his cell phone rang, she knew it wasn't polite to eavesdrop, but she couldn't seem to pry her eyes away. He glanced at the screen and then disconnected the call with the push of a button. Speaking low, but not low enough for Kayla not to hear, Tanner grumbled to himself, "Whitney."

Who was Whitney? Kayla wondered. His sister? A colleague? Or was she a girlfriend? Chances were a good-looking guy like him wouldn't be single. But if he was taken, why had she gotten the distinct impression he'd wanted to kiss her last night? Her chest knotted with mild irritation. Was Tanner a player, just like her dad? She sincerely hoped he was not. She liked him, tattoos and all.

"Scrambled egg casserole and biscuits fresh from the oven." Kitty's jovial voice chirped as she walked through the open French doors carrying a tray.

Surprised at being caught eavesdropping with her ear to the screen, Kayla accidentally bumped it with her shoulder. She teetered, lost her balance, and both she and the screen went down. Kitty screamed. The screen crashed into Tanner's table as Kayla awkwardly careened down the side of it and landed on the floor with a thud. Luckily, the tabletop was wooden so it didn't break, and Tanner was able to push back in time without getting injured.

"Kayla! My gosh. Are you all right?" He flew out of the chair, shoved his hands under her armpits, and unceremoniously hauled her to her feet. His face was etched with concern. Kitty was at her side in a flash with her hand covering her mouth. Two male guests from the other end of the porch rushed forward and lifted the screen off the table and stood it back on its feet.

"Are you hurt?" Kitty wanted to know.

"Only my pride." Kayla felt her face flame with embarrassment. Her hip was sore, but it was no big deal.

"How did that screen fall?" Kitty asked. Apparently, she hadn't noticed Kayla acting like a lovesick teenager and checking out Tanner from the other side of it.

"I stumbled getting out of my chair and bumped it when I stood up," Kayla said, feeling bad for telling a white lie.

Kitty frowned. "I'll have it removed immediately. If it's that wobbly, it's a danger to everyone near it. Are you sure you're okay?"

"I'm fine." Kayla brushed off her shorts and readjusted her tank top that had shimmied up to show a white strip of her belly. When she lifted her gaze, she caught Tanner looking at her stomach before his interested gaze moved down to her bare legs.

Her falling had been his fault for being so handsome. If he didn't look so good, she wouldn't have acted like a fool. But that didn't give him the right to ogle her—even though she secretly was flattered. She jerked her tank top down, cleared her throat, and said, "Thanks for helping me up."

Only then did his gaze return to her face, accompanied by a big grin. "No problem."

"Here's your cell phone, sir," someone said, stepping forward and handing him the device. "It slid under our table."

"Oh, thanks." He pushed a few buttons and announced that it still worked. "It must have flown out of my hands when I scooted back. You and that screen nearly falling in my lap startled me."

"Sorry," Kayla said. "I'm sorry for causing such a disturbance," she told Kitty. "Of course, I'll pay for any damages."

Kitty waved her away. "There doesn't seem to be any damages to worry about. You're all I'm concerned with. Are you sure you're not hurt?"

"I'm sure. I don't even have a scratch."

Kitty nodded. "Good. That was a close one. I'm going to get you another breakfast tray. Your food is probably cold."

"Please don't go to any bother." Kayla had already caused enough trouble. "I'll grab something on the boardwalk before I leave this morning."

"Leave?" Kitty and Tanner questioned in unison.

"Yes. I've decided to drive home today. I found what I came for, but there doesn't seem to be any reason to stick around. I don't know what I expected, but meeting my father and grandmother didn't turn out the way I'd hoped."

Kitty flashed her a look that said, *I told you so.*

"Can we talk about this?" Tanner asked.

Did she imagine the hurt expression on his face?

Kitty excused herself and disappeared around the screen. A moment later, her footsteps could be heard passing through the French doors and into the house.

"Is that your private space?" Tanner stretched his neck around the screen to get a glimpse.

"Yes." She saw a couple of the other

guests watching them. "We can talk over there." They both stepped around the screen, and she offered him a seat at the small table.

"What's that?" he asked, noticing her drawing pad.

"Some ideas I have for my next children's book." She showed him the drawing of a big scary looking mansion that resembled Seacliff House.

"That place looks familiar," he said, smiling. "I didn't know you write children's books. Is your next one going to be a mystery?"

"It's a definite possibility. Seacliff House has inspired me, in the written realm, anyway."

"That's understandable, given its unique ambiance. Have I heard of any of your books?"

"I don't know. Have you?" He seemed genuinely interested, so she rattled off the titles of her two books and their themes. He clapped his hands enthusiastically. "I *have* heard of you! I read the one about the horses to my goddaughter a few weeks ago! April loves that one."

"You're lying."

"I'm not. Swear." Tanner crossed his heart. "What a coincidence."

Kayla couldn't help but be drawn into his smile and infectious personality. If his grin got any bigger, it might slide off his face.

"You're a good story teller," he said.

"Thanks."

"And you did the illustrations, too?"

"Only for the horse book. It was a special allowance by my publisher. Art is my true passion. I've loved to draw ever since I was a young girl. I'm always sketching and doodling. My mother has often told me she doesn't know where my talent comes from. She can't draw a stick person to save her life." She chuckled, once again feeling at ease with Tanner, despite wondering if he pretended to like her because of some ulterior motive. "Of course, Mom never told me if my dad was artistic. I wonder…"

Tanner's smile faded. "Why are you leaving? It seems premature, now that you've met your dad and grandmother. Don't you want to get to know them better? And learn more about Seacliff House?"

She shrugged. "You seem more interested in Seacliff House than I do." Her inquisitive gaze pierced him.

After a moment's hesitation, he said, "You read people well, don't you? I *do* have an interest in the Chandlers and Seacliff House."

"Something other than for a story for your small-town newspaper?"

"Yes."

"What's your interest?"

Before he could answer, Kitty hollered, "Coming through your room." She exited the French doors and appeared on the porch, but there was no breakfast tray in her hands. She gazed between Kayla and Tanner, probably surprised to see them sitting together and deep in conversation. "I'm sorry to interrupt, but you have a phone call, Kayla. You can take it in the kitchen."

"Oh? I can't imagine who would be calling me here. My mom would call my cell phone."

"It's not Suzanne," Kitty said.

Kayla wondered if Matt could be the caller. "Excuse me," she said to Tanner. "I'll be right back."

Kitty led her to the kitchen and pointed out the phone on the wall and then vanished. When Kayla lifted the receiver to her ear, the gruff voice of Sonora assaulted her.

"Kayla, this is Sonora Chandler, your grandmother. I've been thinking about it, and I want you to come to Seacliff House and stay for a few days. We need to get to know each other better."

The invitation, curt as it was, sent a jolt racing through her. Although stunned, she remembered her southern manners. "Thank you, but I've decided to go home today."

"You can't!" Sonora exclaimed.

Kayla inhaled a deep breath, determined not to let Sonora get the best of her. "Maybe I'll come back and visit again another time."

"I want you to visit me *now*," Sonora demanded brusquely.

Kayla clamped her lips shut and silently prayed for self-control before responding. "Have you ever heard the old saying you can catch more flies with honey than vinegar, Grandmother?"

"Of course I have," Sonora snapped.

Kayla replied in a sweet tone equal to the message she intended to convey. "Then perhaps you should try it. It works wonders for a relationship."

The line went silent. If not for hearing soft, raspy breathing in her ear, Kayla would have thought Sonora had hung up. Finally, Sonora said, "I apologize. It's been a long time since I've spoken more than a few words to anyone except my servants."

Hearing Sonora call Martine and Dave her servants made Kayla wince.

"Would you reconsider leaving and come stay with me for a few days? There's a lot I want to tell you about Seacliff House and your ancestors."

Kayla hoped the stories didn't involve more tragedy. "Does that include learning more about my mom and dad? They're the people I'm most interested in."

Again, the line went quiet for a few seconds. Then Sonora acquiesced. "I could probably tell you a few tales about your mother when she was growing up."

That was a good start. Kayla didn't need to think long about the invitation. If Sonora kept her promise, she'd learn more in a couple of days than she had in her entire life. Anyway, there was no use in wasting vacation time. "All right. I'll come, on one condition."

"What's the condition?"

"That you allow my friend to tag along. He's been reading about Harmony Beach and Seacliff House. I think he'd enjoy hearing what you have to say about its history."

"Fine," Sonora snorted. "Bring your friend. I'll expect you by lunch." With that, the phone clicked and went dead.

Chapter Twelve

"Thanks again for inviting me to Seacliff House," Tanner hollered over his shoulder. He hauled his duffle bag from the back seat of his car and dropped it on the ground. He and Kayla had driven separately. She had parked her car beside his. When she popped her trunk lid open, he rushed over and said, "I'll get that," and lifted her luggage out.

"Thanks, Tanner."

"No problem."

"And you're welcome. About the invitation, I mean." She smiled and slammed the trunk lid down.

Tanner looped the strap of his duffle bag over his shoulder and clutched her two suitcases in his hands.

Kayla pushed open the swinging gate and he followed her through. "Why *did* you invite me?" he asked.

Her smile widened. "So you can get the story you came for."

He glanced at the house and couldn't believe his good fortune. He'd anticipated somehow being able to wrangle one more interview out of Sonora Chandler. But spending two or three days in the place where Pearl had worked and mysteriously disappeared from was more than he'd hoped for. If he couldn't dig up some information regarding his great grandmother in that time, he didn't deserve to call himself a journalist. Spending more time with Kayla and getting to know her better was an added bonus.

"Ready to encounter the dragon lady again?" she chuckled.

"Shhh." Tanner placed his finger to his lips. "According to Kitty, your grandmother has spies everywhere. Remember?"

On cue, the front door opened. Wearing the same style of dark clothing as yesterday, Martine stood ramrod straight waiting for their approach.

"Come in," she said, giving them what Tanner's family called "the evil eye" as they entered the house. "I'll show you to your rooms."

As Tanner expected, he and Kayla were taken upstairs and given the two uninhabited bedrooms they'd toured yesterday. Apparently, they had no say as to which room each preferred.

"This is where you'll sleep," Martine told Kayla, opening the door to the room with the four-poster bed.

"Thank you. I was hoping I'd get to stay in my mother's old room."

Martine ignored Kayla's sentimentality. "You'll stay next door," she told Tanner, nodding toward that bedroom.

"Thank you, Martine." His head pivoted toward the door at the end of the hallway, the one where Charlotte Tillman had been abused over a hundred years ago. Would he hear her ghost crying, as Martine had suggested during the tour? He chuckled at the thought. Not believing in ghosts, he suspected Martine was a person who enjoyed playing mind games with people.

He entered what was to be his room and left the door standing open. As he tossed his bag onto the bed, he heard Kayla ask about Sonora.

"Is my grandmother around?"

"She's in her suite on the main level. When you're settled, come down. She'll be waiting." With that, Martine's heels clipped

down the steps. Tanner stepped into the hall
and watched her retreat, imagining she had
eyes in the back of her head. Then he closed
the bedroom door behind him, ready to do some
exploring outside. Kayla's door was open.
She was standing at the window with her back
to him. He knocked on the doorframe, and she
turned.

"Did you look out your window?" she
asked.

"No. I dumped my bag, and was going to
ask if you want to head outside to look
around. I'm anxious to see the grounds."

"Come," she said, motioning him inside.
"We have a lovely view of the gardens on this
side of the house."

Tanner moved to the window and stood
beside Kayla. A fruity scent wafted off her
hair. He inhaled, also enjoying a hint of
perfume.

"Do you think that's where Martine and
her husband stay?" Kayla asked. She pointed at
a small cottage tucked amongst some trees in
the distance.

"That would be my guess." His gaze
scanned the backyard. "I wonder if Mr. Allen
does the gardening." He noted the manicured
lawn and four separate beds of flowers, shaped
into triangles. A wooden gazebo that was
painted white, but was in need of some TLC,
sat in the center of the yard, with the
flowerbeds situated near each corner. A wall
of trimmed hedges bordered the entire yard.

"What do you think those three small
brick buildings are used for?" Kayla asked.

"They're probably the old smoke house and
maybe an outdoor kitchen and a wash house for
doing laundry. The servants would have spent
a great deal of time in those buildings in the

olden days."

"The garden is beautiful, isn't it?" she said, meeting his gaze. Her closeness unnerved him, which amazed him. Normally, he moved slowly when it came to women. That choice had become even more significant since breaking up with Whitney. But once again, he felt the desire to kiss Kayla. Or, at the very least, hold her hand.

"I suppose," he answered, with a shrug and a grin. "If you like flowers and gardens."

She smacked his arm playfully, which she'd developed the habit of doing. "I *do* like them. I might have to sketch this garden later."

"Then let's go outside and get a closer look." He gently tugged on her arm, and felt the fire igniting between them. Was she as attracted to him as he was to her? She hadn't given off any overt signals, but something hinted the feeling was mutual.

Kayla closed the bedroom door and led the way down the staircase. She wore tight shorts, which nicely emphasized her shapely legs and curvy derriere. He couldn't help but smile, imagining his hands settled firmly upon those swaying hips. As soon as they reached the bottom of the stairs, he heard Sonora's harsh voice call from the front parlor, ruining the moment.

"Kayla! I'm in here!"

He saw Kayla roll her eyes, and she whispered, "Looks like we'll have to explore the grounds later. "Hello, Grandmother," she said, stepping into the parlor and greeting Sonora. "Do you remember my friend, Tanner?"

"Of course I do. I'm old, but I still have all my faculties." She thumped a spindly finger against her head.

"Good morning, Mrs. Chandler," he said, reaching out to shake her hand.

Sonora crossed her arms over her bosom and vigorously shook her head. "I don't shake hands, young man. I thought you understood that yesterday. There are germs everywhere. Germs will kill a person, you know. I abhor germs."

"I apologize." Tanner nodded his head and took a seat next to Kayla on the sofa. Sonora's mild outburst made him think about Kayla's mom's agoraphobia and wondered if she came by her disorder naturally. If mental illness was heredity, did that mean Kayla might be prone to some psychological disease? When he looked at Kayla, he could swear she had read his mind. Suddenly, her sunny disposition went flat, and her gaze lowered to her lap.

"Did Martine show you to your rooms?" Sonora asked.

Kayla's head lifted. "Yes, thank you. I'm sure we'll both be quite comfortable."

Sonora's narrowed glare ping-ponged between the two of them. She wagged her finger in front of her face. "There'll be no hanky-panky going on under my roof. Is that understood?"

Tanner held in a laugh. What was she going to do, post a guard outside their doors? He would never dream of violating Sonora's ethical rules in her house. He knew Kayla wouldn't either. When he saw the crimson flowing into Kayla's cheeks, he felt sorry for her. His own Grandma Mary Ann was such a sweet person and would never dream of embarrassing him in front of people the way Sonora embarrassed Kayla.

Before Kayla could utter a retort, Tanner heard a door slam open from the back of the house. Heavy footsteps thudded up the hallway. A man's voice thundered out, calling Sonora's name. And then Martine's voice rose in shrill protest. "Get out!"

The intruder must have pushed past her, for she cried in pain, and Tanner heard a thud as though she'd fallen, or been shoved into the wall. He jumped up from the sofa.

It all happened so suddenly. The heavy footsteps stomped up the hall, and a man flung himself into the parlor doorway. Sonora's head turned toward the door.

The man was old and had thinning white hair and an unruly mustache. His face was red and bloated, and his work clothes were soiled and disheveled. Even with his shirt hanging out, Tanner could tell the man had a beer gut. From the way he tried to steady himself against the doorjamb, it was clear that he was drunk.

Kayla gasped. The man held a gun. Tanner's gaze flew from the intruder to Sonora, who showed no outward sign of fear. Instinctively, he moved in front of Kayla, blocking her body with his, like a shield.

"What do you want, David?" Sonora snapped.

The man rocked on his heels, glaring at her. When Martine stumbled up behind him, Tanner realized this must be Dave Allen, Martine's husband. With a gun in his hand, he obviously meant trouble.

"You're a witch! An evil witch who deserves a taste of her own medicine," Dave slurred. He focused his wild-eyed look on Sonora and then turned it to Tanner and Kayla. "Who are they?" He waved the gun so shakily that Tanner expected a blast to go off any moment. He didn't know if it was better to stand still or to ease Kayla behind the sofa where she could be protected if Dave decided to take pot shots. Any movement could cause the guy to go ballistic.

Sonora trundled closer to him. "Put that thing down before you shoot yourself in the foot," she demanded. For a petite old lady in a wheelchair, she had a lot of courage—as much as anyone Tanner had known, except perhaps his grandpa, who'd been in the military before becoming a commercial fisherman. Suddenly, he gained a newfound respect for her.

"Give that pistol to me," she said, stretching out her arm. "There'll be hell to pay if anyone gets hurt." Her words seemed to strike a chord, for after a couple of long moments, Dave handed over the gun and began to weep.

Grandpa had a small collection, so Tanner knew a little about guns. He could tell the weapon was an antique Smith and Wesson revolver. Its grip was made of rosewood, and the gun had probably been manufactured in the middle 1800s. Sonora checked to see if it was loaded, announced it was not, and then placed it in her lap. "Martine, take your husband home and put him to bed."

"Yes, Mrs. Chandler." Martine, who didn't appear to be physically hurt, flung her arms around the bear of a man and maneuvered him out of the doorway, with a proficiency that reflected she'd done this before. Dave went without a fight. Tanner heard them shuffle down the hall toward the back of the house and then a door slammed.

With his body pressed against Kayla, Tanner felt her raggedly breathe in and out.

He turned and placed his hands on her arms. "Are you all right?"

She nodded, but was clearly shaken.

"What was that about?" he asked Sonora, feeling his own heart still pumping at an accelerated speed.

Her lip curled. "The man is a drunkard. David Allen used to be my handyman and chauffeur, but he hasn't been of much use to me in years. He and Martine live on the property, behind the house in the servants' cottage. If it weren't for Martine, I'd have kicked him to the curb long ago."

Tanner and Kayla exchanged glances. He was right that the cottage was where the couple lived.

"Does the gun belong to him?" Kayla wanted to know. "And why was he threatening you?"

Sonora gazed at the pistol in her lap, and the trace of a smile crossed her lips. "This revolver belonged to Angus Tillman, Maude's husband," she said. "Angus's collection was handed down through the generations. He and Maude owned many pistols, shotguns and rifles. Obviously, David removed this one from my gun cabinet."

"Isn't the cabinet locked?" Kayla asked. "Do you allow him to have a key?"

"Of course the cabinet is locked and all my guns are unloaded. And no, he's not allowed to have a key," Sonora said, with a grimace. "He took the key without permission."

"Is he often drunk?" Tanner asked.

"Yes, he is. And a weepy drunk at that—as you witnessed." Sonora snorted. "He can barely handle the smallest job without falling apart."

The back door opened again, and along with the creak of the hinges came the sound of crying. Sonora rolled her eyes. "That will be Martine. I'd better go check on her." She wheeled herself to the doorway.

"Grandmother," Kayla said, stopping her. "Since you're going to be busy with Martine, do you mind if Tanner and I check out the grounds? From the bedroom, the gardens look so pretty."

Sonora threw one hand into the air. "Go ahead. We'll have lunch in thirty minutes. Be on time."

Tanner checked his watch for the time so they wouldn't be late.

"Will it be safe for us to be outside?" Kayla asked, perhaps having second thoughts. "I mean, with Mr. Allen agitated and upset?"

"Didn't you hear me tell Martine to put him to bed? I expect David's already sleeping it off." With that, Sonora rolled into the hallway and toward the kitchen.

"Let's go," Kayla whispered, pulling Tanner toward the front door. They stepped outside, and she placed her hand at her heart. "I've never experienced anything so frightening before. Did that scare you?" A nervous chuckle accompanied her question.

"Hell, yes. My heart began to race when I saw the pistol in his hand. He could have killed all of us. Sorry for cussing, Kayla," he said, as an afterthought.

"It's okay. I haven't led that sheltered of a life. Believe it or not, I've heard cuss words before."

He smiled. "Your grandmother knew how to take care of him though, didn't she?"

"She's certainly a force to be reckoned with. Dave and Martine seem to jump every time she barks an order."

"After all these years together, I suppose they're used to her ways." They strolled around the corner of the house to the backyard. The next time Tanner glanced at Kayla, she seemed to be deep in thought. "Something else wrong?" he asked.

"I was remembering what Kitty said about my mom being the only person who could ever stand up to my grandmother. If you'd see Mom now, you'd get the impression she was afraid of a mouse."

"I'm sorry," he said, not knowing how else to respond.

When they were about twenty feet from the gazebo, Kayla halted her steps, so Tanner followed suit. Her gaze was riveted to the hexagonal structure.

He noticed the decorative railing, the built-in bench inside, and the broken weather vane on the roof. Some of the roof shingles were missing, and the enamel was chipped. Although the gazebo appeared to be solidly built, the structure had to be decades old. No doubt, the weather and sea salt had done a job on it through the years. The whole thing needed a fresh coat of white paint.

"The rest of the garden has been meticulously taken care of," he said. "I wonder why Sonora hasn't ordered Dave to keep the gazebo looking up to par." Beside him, he heard Kayla inhale a deep breath of air. She grabbed for his hand. Her eyes were enlarged, still staring at the gazebo.

"Perhaps he refuses," she quietly said.

"What do you mean?" Tanner's gaze followed hers.

She pointed, and he saw her hand shake. "Maybe Dave is afraid of the ghost."

Chapter Thirteen

Kayla blinked, knowing she wasn't imagining the man standing next to the gazebo. But because of the gossamer shimmer surrounding him, she also knew he wasn't of this world. He was built slim, wore brown slacks, a white polo shirt and loafers, and was clean-shaven with a crew cut hairstyle. His appearance was youthful, and she guessed him to be not much older than herself. With a square jaw and handsome features, he reminded her of the movie stars from the fifties. A cigarette dangled between his fingers to complete the picture.

The man's lips did not move, either to speak or crack a smile. But Kayla had the strangest feeling he wished to communicate with her. He stared, his vibrant brown eyes penetrating her like laser beams.

When Tanner broke the silence between them, the figure receded like a mirage until he was no longer there. "What did you just say, Kayla?" Tanner asked.

His voice wrenched her free of her trance. "Tell me you saw that man standing there," she said, touching his arm.

"What man?"

"The man beside the gazebo."

Tanner cut a glance toward the structure. "Was it Mr. Allen you saw?"

"No." She shook her head. "This guy was…" She hesitated and then clamped her mouth shut. If she admitted to Tanner she thought she'd seen a ghost, he really *would* think her family was cursed or nuts—with her being the craziest of them all. "Never mind," she said, grasping his hand and dragging him to one of the brick buildings.

He angled his head in question, but didn't ask more. And he didn't wriggle free from her hand, either, even though she gripped it hard.

"We came out here to explore. Let's explore," Kayla said, fighting to keep her voice from cracking. She craned her head over her shoulder for one more look at the gazebo. Thank God, the man was no longer there.

Entering the building first, Tanner released Kayla's hand and ducked so he wouldn't bump his head on the low doorframe. The interior was cool and dark, but light from the doorway was enough for them to see that this had once been the smokehouse.

Kayla glanced around thinking of the animals that had been slaughtered and hung in here so their blood would drain out. Her body was suddenly racked with shivers. "Look at those big hooks on the ceiling."

"They had to be secure enough to hang sides of beef and pork on," Tanner said.

Kayla's gaze drifted to the concrete floor and the bloodstains that splotched it. She pinched her nose with a finger. "It smells like death in here." A flush of heat raced through her body. Visualizing a cow or pig suspended from one of the hooks made her stomach roll. Her hand flew to her stomach, and she stumbled out the door and into the sunshine. Tanner followed.

She braced her hands on her knees and inhaled fresh air. Tanner's hand slid over her shoulders and then stroked her back, to soothe her.

"Are you all right?" he asked.

Kayla wiped her damp brow with her hand. When the nausea passed, she released a long breath and nodded. "The heat and the smell got to me. That's all. And the horrible vision of…"

"I understand," Tanner interjected. "That was a stupid thing for me to say. I apologize." He stared at her with compassion in his eyes. "Please forgive me."

She smiled. "It's all right. You don't need to be forgiven. I suppose it's easy for you to conjure up a story everywhere you go."

"That's one of the pitfalls of being a journalist, I'm afraid. But from now on, I'll keep my gruesome thoughts to myself."

"I'd appreciate that. The fresh air helps. I'm feeling better now. Do you want to look at the other buildings?"

"Yes, but I'll check them out first, to make sure there's nothing nasty inside."

She walked across the lawn on wobbly legs, veering widely when they passed the gazebo.

Tanner peeked inside the door of the next building. "It's the wash house. Are you afraid of cobwebs?"

"Not as long as I don't walk through them. I freak out if that sticky stuff gets in my hair."

He gestured her forward. Inside the room, an old wood stove sat in the corner. Its metal pipe went up through the roof. On top of the stove was a rusty bucket, and two steel tubs were sitting nearby on a counter made of brick. "They must have heated the water on the stove and then poured it into the tubs and scrubbed the clothes," Kayla said.

"The wash house obviously got updated as the years went by," Tanner noted, rapping his knuckles against a wringer washer in the opposite corner. "I'll bet this antique contraption is worth something." He tried out the gears to find that they worked.

"That's pretty neat. I wonder if my grandma bought it. Maybe she had this porcelain sink installed, too. Besides the rust stains, it looks to be in good shape." Kayla moved to the sink and picked up a half-used bar of soap that lay inside. "Someone has been in here recently. The sink is wet and this soap is fairly fresh."

"Maybe Martine still does some of the laundry out here, especially in the summer. She might like using this wringer washer. It appears to be in working condition."

"Seems like a lot of work," Kayla said, letting her imagination roam back to the time when Maude Tillman's servants did all the laundry here. "Perhaps there's a modern washer and dryer somewhere inside Seacliff House. I hope so, for Martine's sake."

She stepped outside, leaving Tanner to continue marveling over the wringer washer. As soon as she exited, the sensation that someone was watching crept across her shoulders. Slowly, she turned her head toward the gazebo. The man had appeared again! With an ethereal wave of his hand, he indicated she should come closer. Kayla gulped.

When he took a step forward, her body went numb, and it felt like her blood had turned to ice. The delicate hairs on the back of her neck stood erect. "Who are you?" she whispered, hoping Tanner didn't hear. The man signaled again. When she shook her head and said, "I'm afraid," the man pursed his lips and disappeared in front of her eyes.

"Who were you speaking to, Kayla?"

Tanner's voice caused her to jump. She whirled and smacked into the solid muscle of his body.

"Whoops. Careful, there," he chuckled, setting her back. He gazed around the yard. "I thought I heard you talking to someone."

"Uh." Her tongue felt tied. Tanner seemed to be an understanding guy, but would he be non-judgmental if she confessed she thought she'd seen a ghost? Before she could utter another word, her gaze was drawn to the side yard. A man stepped around the corner of Seacliff House and strode across the lawn toward them. His head was bent, as if he was deep in thought, and his shoulders looked rigid, like the weight of the world were upon them.

"Who could that be?" Kayla thought aloud. "Hello," she greeted, as he approached.

It was obvious he'd been so lost in thought that he hadn't realized she and Tanner were there until he practically ran into them.

"Oh! I didn't know anyone was in the garden," he said, with his green eyes widening.

His and Kayla's gazes connected. "I'm Kayla Grayson," she said. "Sonora Chandler is my grandmother. And this is my friend, Tanner Bishop. He's a journalist from Maine."

The man shook each of their hands, but his confusion was evident by the wrinkling of his brow. "Please excuse me, Miss Grayson, but I didn't realize Mrs. Chandler had a granddaughter, and that you were visiting."

"I've been away for several years," Kayla replied, not feeling the need to explain further. She perused the stranger's features. He was around her age, not as tall as Tanner, but was just as good looking, only in a different way. Where Tanner had the rugged body of an athlete and a friendly open face, this man was slighter in build. His

expression was much more serious. He wore
jeans and a T-shirt and work boots. His hair
was dark brown and was pulled into a ponytail.
His soft green eyes reflected sadness, or
perhaps, loneliness. She guessed he was a
sensitive man.

"I'm Chris Allen," he said, by way of
introduction.

"Allen?" Tanner inquired. "Are you
related to Dave and Martine?"

A cloud passed over Chris's face. He
nodded. "They're my grandparents. I
understand there was a problem earlier with my
grandpa. I'm really sorry if he frightened
you." Chris looked straight at Kayla when he
spoke.

She felt sorry for him, and wondered how
many times Dave had caused "a problem" here or
in town due to his drinking. "We're okay, but
I won't lie. It was a pretty scary moment
when he came into the parlor waving a gun
around."

"You might want to make sure your
grandfather doesn't get a hold of the key to
Mrs. Chandler's gun cabinet again," Tanner
said. His tone was accusatory, but Kayla
understood why. Dave could have killed all of
them in his drunken stupor, accidentally or
not.

Chris sighed heavily. "I'll make sure of
it, Mr. Bishop. Believe me, a gun is the last
thing my grandfather needs in his hands when
he's intoxicated. Again, I apologize for his
actions, Miss Grayson."

"There's no need, Chris," Kayla said,
tossing him a friendly smile so he wouldn't
feel bad. "And please, call us Kayla and
Tanner. We must all be about the same age."
She glanced at Tanner, who stood as straight

as an arrow, unsmiling.

"Are you going to see your grandpa now?" Kayla asked Chris.

"Yes. My grandma asked me to check on him before I start work in the basement of the big house."

"What kind of work are you doing?"

"I'm installing some water filters. The pipes are ancient. Though the water is drinkable, it has a lot of iron in it. The filters should take care of the problem. It's taken me months to convince Mrs. Chandler the cost would be worth it. She doesn't adapt to change well. I want to get them installed before she changes her mind."

Kayla chuckled. In the short time she'd known Sonora, her stubborn trait had become evident. "Do you help out at the house often?"

Chris nodded. "I've taken over the handyman job from Grandpa. This just helps pay my bills. My real passion is music. I'm a singer and songwriter, and I play guitar."

"Really?" She'd never met a singer/songwriter before. Her gaze met Tanner's, but he didn't seem inclined to join in the conversation.

"I play every Wednesday and Saturday nights at a club on the beach called the Beachcomber. I'm playing tonight. You both ought to come," Chris said, reaching into his back pocket. He handed her a business card that also had his summer schedule printed on the reverse side. "Or if you can't make it tonight, maybe this weekend."

"Thank you for the invitation. That sounds fun." She glanced at Tanner again. His blank face indicated he wasn't interested.

"Well, I'd better get a move on," Chris said. "Nice to have met you both. Maybe I'll see you at the club sometime."

"Maybe." Kayla waved and watched him jog toward the cottage in the trees. "He seems nice," she said, once Chris was out of earshot.

"I guess," Tanner replied, treading toward the house.

Kayla caught up with his long strides. "He's probably embarrassed by the way Dave behaves. And Martine is not a friendly person, either. They're a couple of odd ducks. But Chris seems perfectly normal."

Tanner snorted. "You just met the guy. You can't judge a book by its cover, Kayla. I'm sure you've heard the saying, being a writer and all."

His hackles were definitely up. "Of course I've heard the saying. Is something wrong, Tanner? You seem upset, all of a sudden."

"I'm not upset."

She grabbed his arm to halt his steps and stared into his eyes. "You shouldn't judge Chris based on his grandparents," she reminded.

"That's probably true, but something doesn't feel right about the guy. The acorn might not fall far from the tree."

What had given Tanner that impression about Chris? She'd seen nothing in him that indicated he was anything like Dave or Martine. "Are you jealous because I was friendly to Chris?" she asked.

"No," he chuckled.

But she suspected he was. And that made her smile. She pondered the matter as she watched him disappear around the corner of the house.

Kayla took one more look behind her and

exhaled. There was no one standing next to the gazebo, shimmering or not. Perhaps she'd imagined the man with the crew cut after all. But a niggling feeling inside assured her she hadn't.

She jogged to the front porch and caught up with Tanner just as he put his hand on the doorknob. She placed her palm on his arm and flashed him her most genuine smile. She liked Tanner and wanted him to know there was no competition when it came to him and Chris. His muscles tightened under her touch.

"What about it? Do you want to make plans to go the club with me on Saturday night?" she asked.

"I don't know."

"I'm sure it would be a good time."

"We'll see. I might not even be here by then."

"Oh." Now that she'd decided to stay in Harmony Beach a few more days, she hadn't considered he might leave before her. Disappointed, she said, "I thought you wanted to stay long enough to get your story. He still hadn't shared with her the exact reason he was here and why he was so interested in Seacliff House.

His deep brown eyes delved into her, causing her heart to pick up its pace. "I plan on staying long enough to interview Sonora. The sooner, the better."

Kayla tilted her head in question. "Why do you have to interview my grandmother?"

He removed his hand from the doorknob and lowered his voice. "Because, from all accounts, she was the last person to see my great grandmother alive."

Gooseflesh rose on Kayla's arms. Her gaze narrowed. "What are you talking about?"

Tanner took her hand and led her down the sidewalk to the gate, where they couldn't be overheard by anyone listening inside the house. "I have a connection to Seacliff House, too. My grandpa's name was Arlan Bishop. His mother, Pearl O'Neill, gave birth to him in 1958 when she was eighteen. Then she promptly abandoned him. She was not married to his father, Vince Bishop, who was my great grandfather. According to a diary written by Vince's twin sister, Vivien, Vince wanted to marry Pearl, but she wouldn't have him. Are you following this so far?"

Kayla nodded, and he went on.

"According to Vivien's journals, Pearl left Vince, her baby, and Maine behind. Pearl had a relative—a female cousin—here in Harmony Beach, who assured her there was work to be had. So Pearl came to Maryland. Turns out, she was hired by *your* grandmother to work at Seacliff House. One year later, Pearl had disappeared off the face of the earth. I've come here to find out what happened to her."

Unaware that her mouth had dropped open, Kayla stared at Tanner in shock. When she was finally able to make sense of his tale, she mumbled, "That's incredible."

"What's really incredible is the way you and I met, quite by accident." Tanner ran his fingers up her arm and then palmed her cheek, sending a flash of heat surging through her. "Some coincidence, huh?"

"Yeah." She wondered if it had been coincidence at all, or if he'd somehow known who she was from the beginning. Had he stalked her, waiting for the right moment to make his move, and then befriended her just so he'd have a way to meet Sonora? *No*, she thought. That wasn't possible. *She* hadn't even known she was coming to Harmony Beach until the day before yesterday. Their running into each other had truly been accidental. Granted, it was a small town, but it still seemed like a fluke. His great grandmother had worked as a servant for her grandmother. It boggled her mind.

Suddenly, the implication of something he'd said made her nervous. "Did you say Sonora was the last person to know of Pearl's whereabouts?"

"Yes. According to Pearl's cousin, who was later questioned by Vince, Pearl left Seacliff House to return home to Maine. At least, that's what Sonora had told her."

"What are you saying?"

"When the cousin went to Seacliff House asking for Pearl after having had no contact for several weeks, which was unlike her because the two of them were very close, your grandmother apparently told her that Pearl had become homesick and left in a hurry. But Pearl never made it home to Maine. And the cousin never heard from her again. No one ever heard from her."

Kayla didn't understand. She felt no allegiance to her grandmother, but at the same time, it didn't seem right to accuse her of some sort of cover up that happened long ago and couldn't be proven.

"Maybe Pearl didn't go back to Maine," she thought out loud. "She might have lied and gone somewhere else. Maybe she met another man and ran off with him. She'd deserted one man and her baby already. Back then, I'm sure it was a big scandal when she got pregnant and wouldn't marry the child's father. I doubt she could be trusted to tell the truth, if you don't mind my saying so."

"I don't," Tanner said. "Facts are facts."

Another idea occurred to Kayla. "Perhaps the cousin misunderstood Pearl's plans. Or the information in the diary was wrong."

A muscle ticked along Tanner's jaw. "Or maybe Sonora lied," he said.

They stood looking at each other in silence. When the screen door squeaked open, Kayla turned her head.

Martine shuffled onto the porch with her hands fisted on her hips. "Lunch is served."

Chapter Fourteen

Lunch with Sonora in the formal dining room was not what Kayla expected. After the gun incident with Dave, seeing a ghost at the gazebo, and learning of Tanner's real interest in her grandmother, the last thing Kayla wanted was to hear macabre stories of more ancestors gone mad. The way Sonora gleamed with pride as she told tales of their crazy kin over fresh fruit and chicken salad sandwiches made Kayla question her senility.

"In 1916, Gemma Tillman, heartbroken over a love affair gone bad, digested rat poison and died a terrible death. Just twenty years old, she was the daughter of Bradley. Servants found her body in the outdoor kitchen."

Kayla's fork slipped out of her fingers and clinked loudly on her china plate. Alarmed, she cast a glance at Tanner and internally vowed never to explore that last out building.

"Do be careful, Kayla," Sonora admonished. "China chips easily."

"I'm sorry, Grandmother." With her appetite lost, Kayla didn't bother picking up the fork. Sonora's eyes seemed to twinkle as she continued to regale them with more family stories of insanity and death.

"In 1944, my uncle, Captain Randall Bushnell, a decorated World War II hero, sliced his wrists with a broken whiskey bottle. Poor Uncle Randall was remanded to an asylum, where he lived out his days in a drug-induced stupor. Then, of course, there was Angus Tillman himself, who became deranged after he and Bradley murdered Charlotte's rapists on the beach below the cliffs and thought the ghosts of the men were haunting him."

That comment made Kayla take notice. She wondered if one of those men could be the ghost she'd seen by the gazebo. Then she remembered the clothes and hairstyle weren't right for that era. Perhaps the restless spirit was poor Uncle Randall. She stared at Tanner, wondering what he was thinking. He looked distracted, and hadn't said three words since they sat down. She suspected his mind was on Pearl.

Sure enough, when Sonora paused to sip her iced tea, Tanner cleared his throat. "Mrs. Chandler, do you remember a young woman by the name of Pearl O'Neill who was in your employ back in 1958? She'd come down here from Maine."

Sonora gingerly wiped her mouth with a linen napkin. Kayla thought she saw her grandmother's countenance grow pale, but it was hard to tell with the face powder she wore.

After a few seconds had passed, Sonora said, "I remember Pearl." She pushed her plate to the side and clasped her hands in front of her on top of the table. Her voice was measured. "She worked here as a maid. She wasn't a very good one, either, as I recall." Her painted eyebrow shot up. "Why do you ask?"

"She was my great grandmother."

If Sonora was surprised, she didn't show it. Kayla watched her closely for any sign of emotion and found none.

"How unfortunate for you," Sonora said with a straight face. "That girl didn't have a brain in her head. She depended on her looks to get by in life, which is always a mistake. Pearl was a silly, flighty thing, and even had to be taught to make a bed correctly. She barely lasted a year at Seacliff House."

"What happened to her?" Tanner asked.

"As I recall, she gave notice and went back to Maine. Martine was here then. I remember her mentioning the girl was homesick and cried a lot. When Pearl decided it was best to go home, I provided her with her final wages and sent her on her way."

Remaining silent, Kayla stared at Tanner, who kept his eyes on Sonora. He seemed to be weighing his words before speaking them out loud.

"According to some documents I found in my grandfather's possessions after he'd passed away, Pearl never made it to Maine. That story was also corroborated by her cousin, who worked for another family in Harmony Beach."

Sonora shrugged her bony shoulders and suggested Pearl may have changed her mind. "As I said, she was an impulsive and unreliable girl. Who knows where the wind might have blown her?"

Tanner's cell phone rang just then. He pulled the phone from his pocket and glanced at the screen. He didn't seem pleased. "Will you ladies excuse me?" he asked, not waiting for Sonora to grant him permission to leave the table. Kayla watched him exit the room and heard him step out the front door. With him gone, it seemed a good opportunity for her to ask Sonora some questions about her parents and her grandfather.

"Do you have any photographs of my grandfather?" she began.

Sonora's eyes flashed. "No. I hate the man. Why would I keep any photos of him?"

Her comment sent a jolt through Kayla.

Was Sonora saying she didn't have a single photograph of the man she'd been married to? "I don't know," she stalled. "For posterity, I suppose. Didn't you think Mom or I might be interested, *if* you ever saw us again?" Kayla didn't wait for a response before asking, "What was he like?"

Sonora's steely gaze bore into her, sending a shiver rippling across Kayla's nape. "Elliott Chandler was like your father in more ways than one. He was a liar, a philanderer, and a coward." Bitterness rolled off her tongue as easy as honey.

"I apologize if talking about him brings up bad memories, but it's important to me that I learn a little about my relatives. There's been such a void in my life. Are you claiming my grandpa was unfaithful to you?"

Sonora's nose rode high in the air. She inhaled deeply. "Yes. And I don't claim. The evidence was clear-cut."

If Sonora had behaved the same way back then that she did now, it wasn't surprising to learn that Grandpa Elliott had cheated. But Kayla kept that mean thought to herself. "Why do you say he was a coward?"

"Because he ran out on your mother and me as soon as he found out I was pregnant. Wouldn't you call that cowardly?"

"Yes, I would. Poor Mom. I've grown up thinking she and I had nothing in common, but as it turns out, both our fathers deserted us."

"That's right," Sonora snapped. "I raised Suzanne on my own, and she has raised you alone. We don't need men. Chandler women are as strong as the oak trees that stand on this property."

"You wouldn't think that about my mother

if you'd made any effort to stay in touch with her through the years. Why *didn't* you try to find us? You could have hired a private detective. You certainly have the money, power, and resources to get anything you want accomplished."

"My money and resources are none of your business."

Kayla clenched her fists below the table. "Look, Grandmother. I agreed to stay at Seacliff House for a few days because you promised to give me information. Please try to put yourself in my shoes. I'm not asking for the world."

Sonora glared. "Just so we're clear, I *did* hire a detective, many years ago. It wasn't hard for him to find you and Suzanne. She hadn't run far."

This was not what Kayla expected to hear. Her heart slammed against her chest. "What happened?"

"Your mother wanted nothing to do with me, and she wouldn't allow me to contact you, either."

Kayla questioned whether that was true. Was Sonora lying to keep the upper hand? What if the detective *had* found them? Kayla could hardly believe a controlling woman like her grandmother would be stopped if she really wanted to make peace with her daughter, or have a relationship with her granddaughter. That made Kayla angrier.

"If your detective gave you a report on Mom, then you know she's as fragile as a sapling." Kayla's defenses flew up. Her tone was snotty, and the accusation was disrespectful, but she couldn't stop herself. No matter how bad the blood had been between Sonora and Suzanne all those years ago, if

Sonora had reached out with an olive branch at some point, her mom might have accepted it. Maybe then, things could have been different for all of them.

"I simply don't believe that about Suzanne," Sonora said. "It's nonsense. You must be lying to gain my sympathy."

The blood in Kayla's veins began to boil. "I do not lie! And for *your* information, *this* Chandler woman needed a man. My father. But I wasn't given the chance to have him in my life. You destroyed our family." Her eyes narrowed into accusatory pinpoints.

"Humph." With that, Sonora picked up a gold-plated bell that sat on the table next to her and heartily rang it. Martine quickly rushed through the dining room door.

"Yes, Mrs. Chandler."

"Take me to my room, Martine. I feel a headache coming on."

Martine bent to release the wheelchair breaks.

Kayla wasn't going to let her grandmother get away so quickly. It was useless to ask more about her mother and father right now, but she still had other questions. "If you hated my grandpa so much, why did you keep his name? Why not change your name back to Tillman when he left?"

Martine's body snapped to attention. Kayla swore she saw the blood drain from the woman's cheeks. Sonora, as usual, answered with a short and curt reply.

"The Chandlers were, and still are a prominent family in Harmony Beach. Anyway, questions about my former husband are not ones I agreed to answer." Her head swung to Martine. "Take me to my room."

Martine grasped the handles of the

wheelchair and backed Sonora away from the table and into the hallway. Kayla leaned against the back of her chair and took a deep breath, trying to calm her nerves. A moment later, Martine stormed into the room.

"Stop asking so many questions," she hissed. "Better yet—why don't you just go home where you belong? The past is dead and gone. We don't need the likes of you stirring up trouble." Her menacing glower pinned Kayla to the chair. "Seacliff House has its secrets, and here they'll remain. Do you understand?"

Kayla didn't understand at all, but she nodded anyway. Martine looked angry enough to slap her. When she whirled and stomped out of the room, Kayla sat dumbstruck, stunned by the outburst. The sting of tears pierced her eyes. Her limbs started to shake.

"What just happened?" Tanner entered the room and hurried to Kayla's side. While he scrutinized her, she gazed into his warm eyes and saw concern etched in his gaze.

"They're all nuts," Kayla huffed. "Do you mind if we take a walk? I want to get out of this house."

He scooted her chair out and gave her a hand up. Once outside, they began walking toward the cliffs. Tanner gave her time to compose herself. After she explained the conversation with Sonora and what Martine had said to her, he shook his head, unbelieving.

"Do you want to leave? I can take you back to Kitty's, if you want."

"But that would mean you'd have to leave, too. I couldn't do that to you. You've barely scratched the surface in gathering information about your great grandmother."

"I don't care," he said. "I'm probably not going to get any more out of Mrs.

Chandler, anyway. It doesn't matter if she's your blood relative. I won't let her treat you like one of her servants."

Kayla's heart pounded against her ribs. A man had never come to her rescue before. She stopped them in their tracks and faced him. She kissed him on the cheek, letting her lips linger on his clean-shaven face for a moment.

"What was that for?" Tanner said, smiling, when she stepped back.

"For being a sweet guy. I'm glad you're here, for more than one reason."

"Oh? My charming companionship was not your only motivation for bringing me along?"

She laughed. "It was at the time, but I'll admit, I now have an ulterior motive for keeping you around."

"What's that?"

"It's entirely possible you might have to stop me from strangling the whole lot of them. I might go berserk one night, and generations from now they'll be talking about poor Kayla. She snapped and went on a rampage in Seacliff House and ended up in the loony bin."

He chuckled. "Just one more morbid story to add to your family history."

Her eyebrow arched. Of course Tanner was joking, but he might also be wondering if she'd inherited the crazy gene. At least he was smiling. Whatever had been bothering him earlier seemed to be a non-issue now.

"If you ended up in a nuthouse, that would be a real shame. I'd break you out," he stated.

"You would?"

"Of course. I like you. And from what I hear, loony bins are not nice places."

Kayla's insides lit up like a Christmas

tree. "I like you, too, Tanner."

The crashing of the waves on the shore below the cliff distracted her, transfixing her in a timeless moment. She realized they were standing at the rim. She moved as close to the edge as she felt comfortable and peered over. Even this high up, sea mist dampened her cheeks.

"Do you believe that story about the Tillman men murdering Charlotte's rapists in cold blood down there on the beach?" she asked.

"Yes. They sought revenge for a terrible wrong committed against their loved one. I can't say I wouldn't have done the same thing if I'd been in their shoes."

Kayla realized she should be outraged at such a confession. But she wasn't. Tanner was like a soothing balm for the gaping hole in her heart. He would protect those he loved, which was a reassuring thought. She gazed at his profile and felt her lips spread in silent summons. He liked her, he'd said. But was there someone at home he loved? Again, she wondered who Whitney was.

"Was your news bad?" she asked, changing the subject.

He angled his head, not comprehending.

"Your phone call," she clarified. "Your face dropped when you looked at your screen."

"You're very observant, Kayla." Tanner hesitated, and then, apparently, decided to share the details of the call. "It was a girl I used to date in Maine. Her name is Whitney. We only dated for four months. I broke up with her some time ago, but she's having a hard time letting go and understanding it's over between us."

"Oh." Four months was longer than she'd

ever dated anyone.

"I've been letting her calls go to voice mail and then deleting them. Hopefully, she'll eventually get the message I don't want to talk to her."

"Do you think she's dangerous?"

He shook his head. "I don't think so. Just immature."

"Do you have another girl back in Maine now?"

"No. What about you? Is there a guy in Virginia?" His eyebrow arched in anticipation.

"No. I haven't dated anyone for a while." Warmth spread through Kayla's body. Tanner was single and free, and he was interested in her status. "I'm sorry you're going through that with that girl. But I can understand her not wanting to let you go."

Their fuses latched. Tanner's voice was thick with emotion when he placed his hands on her arms and said, "I really want to kiss you, Kayla."

"Then what are you waiting for?" She closed her eyes. His arms surrounded her, and the solid warmth of his chest pressed against her. The touch of his lips sent a jolt of desire racing through her that ignited every nerve ending in her body.

When her cell phone rang, their mouths parted. Tanner groaned. "I suppose you'll want to answer that. But whoever it is has rotten timing."

She smiled and hesitated before flicking the cell phone out of her pocket. She pressed the answer button. "Hello."

When Tanner started to move away to give her privacy, Kayla boldly wrapped her hand around his waist and tugged him back toward her. She nodded, imploring him to stay. She had nothing to hide. Surprisingly, the cell phone service was good there on top of the cliff.

"Hi, Kitty," she said, hearing her mother's cousin on the line. "What's that? My mom called your B&B? That surprises me. Why didn't she try my cell phone?" She listened to the response. "You say she did? Uh-huh. Yes, perhaps the signal reception wasn't good when she tried before. That's possible up here. Well, I'm glad to know she's doing fine. I was going to call her again today to check on her. Thanks for letting me know." Kayla listened again. "I'm doing okay, but I'm not sure how long I can stay at Seacliff House. You were right about my grandmother. She's not the easiest person to warm up to. I'll be in touch later to inform you of my plans. Thanks for calling."

She clicked off.

"Is your mom okay?" Tanner asked, sweeping her into his arms again.

"Yes. But I'm amazed she called Kitty. As far as I know, they haven't spoken to each other in years—only corresponded by snail mail and email. Then again, my mother has always been very good at keeping secrets." She shrugged her shoulders, not wanting to think about Suzanne, for a change. "Where were we?" she asked, feeling her body hum with longing.

"Right here." Their lips had barely touched when a voice from behind them called out Kayla's name. She felt Tanner's body grow rigid, and they pulled apart for the second time.

"Now what?" she gritted, turning to see Chris striding toward them. Suddenly embarrassed at being caught kissing Tanner, she felt her cheeks warm.

"Kayla," Chris said, as he approached. "Mrs. Chandler asked me to find you." His mouth was drawn into a thin line.

"Is there a problem?"

"You need to come back to the house."

She didn't care for the order, but she knew it had come from Sonora, not him. "I'll be there in a few minutes," she said.

"It won't wait," Chris replied. "There's someone waiting to see you in the parlor."

"Who?"

"A police officer."

Chapter Fifteen

Once the three of them reached the front porch, Kayla glanced at the police car in the drive. Several scenarios skated through her mind, all of them featuring her elderly grandmother.

Strangely, Chris say goodbye quickly and vanished around the corner of the house. Kayla heard voices coming from inside as Tanner opened the screen door. He stepped back and allowed her to enter first.

In the parlor, Sonora sat in her wheelchair with an odd look in her eyes. Martine stood behind her, chewing her lower lip. A female police officer dressed in a blue uniform sat on the hard sofa. She turned her head in Kayla's direction, assessed her quickly, and then stood up.

Sonora made the introductions. "Officer Scott, this is my granddaughter, Kayla Grayson, and her friend, Tanner—what was your last name again, young man?" A smile cracked her powdered face, and her voice was laced with sugar. Kayla fought to keep from rolling her eyes. Obviously, her grandmother was putting on a good show for the policewoman, pretending to be a gracious and feeble-minded hostess.

"Bishop," Tanner said politely.

Kayla knew full well that Sonora remembered his name. Nothing got past her.

"Miss Grayson," Officer Scott began, stepping forward. "I'm afraid I have some bad news."

Kayla knew it couldn't be about her mother or Kitty. She'd just spoken to Kitty. "What kind of bad news?"

"I'm sorry to tell you that Matt Grayson

has been found dead."

Kayla's heart thudded against her breast as the room began to spin. In the recesses of her mind, she barely registered Sonora gasping. She reached an unsteady hand toward the back of a nearby wing chair. Grasping the upholstered fabric, she forced her legs not to buckle under her.

Behind her, she felt Tanner rest his hand on the small of her back. She turned to see his jaw had slackened in alarm, and his eyes were clouded with compassion.

"I understand Mr. Grayson was your father," the policewoman said.

Numbly, Kayla turned her attention back to the officer and nodded, nausea swirling in her stomach. "Yes, but how did you know?"

"We found his wallet in his pants pocket. His address is listed as Norfolk, Virginia. We got in touch with the woman he lives with, and she told us he'd come to Harmony Beach to contact someone here at Seacliff House. When we arrived, Mrs. Chandler said you're the next of kin."

"What happened? Give us the particulars," Sonora interrupted.

Tanner applied more pressure to Kayla's back. His gesture of physical support eased some of the hysteria bubbling in her stomach. She gazed up at him, and he cocked a small smile for reassurance.

"Mr. Grayson's body was found by a fisherman earlier today on the beach below the cliffs. According to the medical examiner, he died sometime between the hours of six a.m. and eleven a.m.," Officer Scott said courteously and softly. Obviously, she was trained to be professional but sympathetic.

"He was found below *our* cliffs?" Sonora

asked.

"Yes. I'm sorry to inform you all that Mr. Grayson died of a gunshot wound to the back of the head. The way his body was wedged between two boulders, it seems the murderer placed him there so he wouldn't wash out to sea."

"What?" Kayla moaned. "My dad was murdered?" A sour taste threatened to work its way up her throat and past her lips.

"I work for a newspaper called The Boothbay Harbor Register in Maine," Tanner interjected. "Do you mind if I ask you a few questions?"

He immediately plunged himself into investigative journalist mode, and for this Kayla was grateful. Having come to recognize his inquisitive nature, she didn't doubt he'd ask the questions that she couldn't, and wouldn't.

"I don't see why a newspaper in Maine would be interested in a local story," the officer said.

"It's not. I'm interested as a friend of Miss Grayson's."

"Please," Kayla whispered to the policewoman, pleading with her eyes. "It's all right with me."

Scott thought a moment and then relented. "Of course, Miss Grayson. I understand. Feel free to ask what you want, Mr. Bishop, and I'll answer what I can."

"Thank you," Tanner said. "Were there any fingerprints found, or marks discovered on the body, besides the gunshot wound?"

Officer Scott shook her head. "No fingerprints. The clothes on the victim were soaked through from the tide. There were no signs of a struggle either, which leads us to believe Mr. Grayson was caught by surprise. He probably never even saw his attacker, since the person or persons came from behind."

"Do you think this was a random attack?" Tanner asked.

"If it was, it was a senseless and brutal crime. As I said, the man's wallet was still in his pocket. That tells us robbery was not the motive. He appears to have been executed. That leads us to believe he was specifically targeted."

"If it had been a crime of passion, his murderer probably would have been facing him when he was shot," Tanner noted. "I've learned a few things working on the police beat, and people who kill during a fit of passion don't sneak up on their victim. Usually, an argument has preceded the crime."

"That's correct. You're thinking like a police officer," Scott said.

"Unfortunately, I covered a couple of murders back home."

Somewhere in her befuddled mind, a thought occurred to Kayla. "It's just like when Angus and Bradley Tillman executed Charlotte's rapists. That was committed on the shore below the cliffs, too."

"What's this about rapists?" Scott asked, narrowing her eyes.

"Just an old family story from over a hundred years ago. Nothing important," Sonora cut in. "You were saying about Matt?"

Fresh panic bloomed in Kayla's chest. The simultaneous visuals of the executions committed by the Tillman men and Matt wedged between the rocks wouldn't leave her mind.

"You don't have to listen to more," Tanner told Kayla. Maybe he'd seen her cringe when Sonora mentioned the old family story.

"Would you like me to take you to your room?"

"No." She'd always been an emotionally strong person and didn't intend on breaking down now. "I want to know what happened."

"All right. But anytime it gets to be too much, you tell me and I'll escort you upstairs."

"Thank you, Tanner, but I'm fine." She squared her shoulders and locked her gaze on Officer Scott so that Tanner would get the picture—she was no wilting rose.

He continued to ask questions of the officer. "What's your theory on why the murderer chose to leave Mr. Grayson's body between the rocks? Why not let him wash out to sea? Wouldn't it make more sense not to leave any evidence?"

"We haven't figured that one out yet."

"Perhaps the murderer was making a point," Sonora piped up, with a smug smile on her face. "He or she may have wanted it known that Matt was actually dead this time." All gazes flew in her direction. She shrugged her shoulders. "Obviously, he faked his death once, over twenty years ago. Everyone in town thought he'd drowned back then. Seems to me it's symbolic—his body being left on the same beach twenty-four years later."

Sudden fury over Sonora's words chased any distraught out of Kayla. She balled up her fists and held them rigidly at her sides. Sonora had paid Matt to fake his death and leave Harmony Beach all those years ago. She had a lot of nerve acting like she'd been duped along with the family and everyone else when she'd known all along Matt wasn't dead.

A sudden chill crept across Kayla's neck. There'd been no love lost between her grandmother and father. *Could Sonora have killed my father*? The thought left her mind as quickly as it had entered. It was not something she wanted to consider. Besides, it seemed too obvious, even given their tumultuous past.

"I read the report from 1988 regarding his suspected drowning," Officer Scott told Sonora. "No body was ever found. I guess we now know why." She redirected her attention to Kayla. "Do you know who would want your father dead?"

In a soft voice, Kayla said, "I didn't know my father. My mother took me away from Maryland when I was three years old. I only met him yesterday."

"I might be able to help with that," Sonora said. "Matt came to see me last night. He asked to borrow some money. It appears he owed several thousand dollars to a local bookie."

Kayla jerked her gaze toward her grandmother. "Why didn't you tell me he'd been here?"

Sonora folded her hands in her lap. "I was going to. The right time hadn't presented itself yet."

"The right time?" Kayla dug her fingernails into her palms. "You could have told me at lunch."

"Did Mr. Grayson give you the name of his bookie?" the officer asked Sonora, while scribbling in a notebook. Her tone was one of annoyance, too. She probably wondered why Sonora was just now telling her about that important detail.

"No. He didn't say, and I wasn't interested. I'm sure Harmony Beach's police department knows all the local hoodlums and will be able to figure out which one was connected to Matt. There was no way in hell I was loaning that man money. He hurt my daughter, and I've never forgiven him."

The policewoman cocked a curious eyebrow. "Where were *you* this morning, Mrs. Chandler, between the hours of six o'clock and noon?"

Sonora's jaw jutted out. "I was right here at Seacliff House the entire time. I rarely leave my home. It's difficult for me to get around." Her hand slapped the arm of the wheelchair to make a point. "My housekeeper, Martine, will vouch for me."

When the officer looked at Martine for confirmation, she nodded once and then lowered her gaze to the floor.

"And my granddaughter and her friend have been here as well," Sonora said, staring at Kayla.

Although she was mad, Kayla decided not to muddy the waters by mentioning that she and Tanner arrived at ten o'clock and couldn't vouch for Sonora's whereabouts in the previous four hours—not until she knew for sure that Sonora was telling the truth about being at home that morning. Her head nodded slightly. Then she looked at Tanner.

He studied her with an intensity that made her squirm inside her clothes. Probably, he didn't understand why she would show any loyalty to her grandmother. Maybe he'd question her about that later, but for now, his mouth remained shut. Anyway, it wasn't his place to differ. This was family business.

Officer Scott snapped her notebook closed. "That's all I have for now. If you think of anything important or need to contact me, here's my number." She handed Kayla a business card with the local police department's address and phone number on it.

"You don't need me to identify my father's body?" Kayla asked quietly.

"No. I won't put you through that since his wallet with I.D. was found in his clothes. We'll also check dental records. They'll confirm his identity."

Kayla nodded. "The woman in Norfolk, Virginia. She and my dad were planning to be married. I assume, when you spoke to her earlier, you told her my father had been killed."

"Yes, she knows." After Officer Scott shook hands with Kayla, Tanner escorted the woman to the front door. He stepped onto the porch with her.

"Will you call us if you make an arrest?" he asked.

"You can count on it." Scott pumped his hand firmly and sauntered down the walk to her car. Tanner returned to the parlor to see Kayla advancing toward her grandmother, with her gray eyes flashing in anger. Once the police car drove off, Kayla lit into Sonora.

"Why were you hiding my father's visit from me?"

"I told you. I hadn't gotten around to mentioning it. I didn't know you'd care so much. He deserted you and your mother. I'd think you'd hate him."

"I don't hate anyone," Kayla snapped. "My mother raised me to be better than that. She taught me to be a caring and considerate person. Obviously, she didn't get her compassion from you. I don't think you give a damn about anyone but yourself."

Tanner grinned, feeling proud of Kayla for showing her backbone.

"How dare you!" Sonora shook a pointy finger at her.

"How dare *you*," Kayla retorted, turning her back on her grandmother. "I've suddenly developed a headache. I'm going to my room."

"Don't walk away like that!" Sonora shouted.

Kayla ignored her. Tanner followed her up the staircase. At the top of the stairs, he was caught off guard when she placed her finger over his lips to hush him and gestured him inside her room.

Once they were behind the closed door, she plopped on the mattress and released a big sigh. After a few moments of deep breathing to calm down, she patted the spot next to her, inviting him to sit.

"Are you okay?" he asked, sitting beside her.

"Yes. I guess so, considering… My grandmother sure has a knack for getting under my skin." She shook her head. "It's so surreal. I feel sad. After all these years, I finally got to meet my dad, and now he's out of my life again. This time it's forever." She gazed into space for a moment. "I don't know what I expected, but our talk yesterday didn't go the way I'd thought it would. I was confused and upset and said some things I now regret. Before we parted, he asked me to contact him again. I told him I'd think about it. I feel terrible I didn't promise to call." Tears pricked at her eyes.

"Your reaction was natural, considering the situation," Tanner assured. "There was no way on earth you would have known this was going to happen. You have nothing to feel guilty about."

"I'm going to have to phone my mom and tell her."

"You can do that later," he said. He

stroked the top of her hand with his
fingertips. She shivered, which brought a slow
smile to his face.

"See what you do to me?" she said softly,
staring into his eyes. "One touch and I'm…"

"Melting like butter?"

She smiled. "That's an accurate
description."

A pleasant sensation rolled through his
torso. He slid his hand underneath her
waterfall of hair and lightly massaged the
back of her neck.

"That feels good," she sighed.

His galloping heart meant he felt
something deep inside. Was it lust, or more?
Unsure of anything except wanting to kiss her
again, he said, "I think this will feel even
better."

He turned her toward him and cupped her
face between his hands. When he touched his
lips to hers, the sweet taste of her mouth,
and the soft press of her breasts against his
chest ignited a firestorm that incinerated
everything but his desire for her. A soft
groan tore from his chest as their kiss
deepened.

She hesitantly broke the kiss. "Sonora
will probably send Martine up here to make
sure no hanky-panky is going on. Then she'll
toss us both out of the house and you'll never
know what happened to your great grandmother.
Besides, it feels wrong to be kissing when we
just found out my father is dead."

Although he didn't want to stop, he knew
Kayla was right. There was no point in
angering Sonora by breaching her rules. And
even though Matt Grayson was a stranger to
Kayla, it was tacky of him to make a pass at
her.

"I don't suppose you'll want to stay at Seacliff House any longer," he said. "Especially since you know Sonora lied to you about Matt, even if it was by omission. Let's go back to Kitty's. I think it would be for the best. I don't want to make you more upset, but I'm not sure you can trust your grandmother."

Kayla slid off the bed and walked to the window and stared out. She inhaled deeply. "Something's bothering me about what she told the police. She said my father came to her to borrow money he owed a local bookie. He's been living in Norfolk, Virginia for many years where he owns a bar on the beach. Why would he owe a *local* bookie money?"

Tanner considered the question. "You're right. That doesn't make sense."

"There's something else. I didn't mention it to you, but Matt told me she'd threatened him."

Tanner sidled next to her at the window. "What kind of threat was it? And when did it take place?"

"When she paid him off all those years ago. He told me Sonora had threatened to kill him if he ever stepped foot in Harmony Beach again." Kayla faced him, her eyes growing moist. "Do you think she made good on her threat today?"

What could he say to make her feel better? He'd thought the same thing. The truth was, he imagined Sonora capable of just about anything. In fact, he believed she was lying about Pearl. His gut told him Sonora Chandler was a woman with dark secrets. He was almost convinced she had something to do with his great grandmother's disappearance fifty years ago. He wouldn't put it past her to have hired someone to whack Matt Grayson. But that wasn't what Kayla needed to hear right now.

"People say a lot of things they don't mean when they're upset and under stress. Your grandmother threatened your father twenty-four years ago because she was furious that he'd cheated on your mother. Sometimes she's rude, and she has the forked tongue of the devil, but it's a far stretch to accuse her of murder."

That reassurance seemed to be what Kayla was looking for. She released a sigh of relief and wedged her head in the crook of his shoulder. Cradled that way, it felt like she belonged there. But his past failed relationships warned him not to put the cart before the horse. He was embroiled in a situation where emotions ran high.

"Thank you, Tanner, for your thoughts and support," Kayla said. "Sonora isn't a very nice person, but she's the only grandmother I have. I owe it to myself to try to break through her icy exterior and figure out a way to bring her and my mother together again—even if it's only through a long distance relationship. If I don't, I'll always regret having the chance and wasting it."

"So, that means you don't want to leave Seacliff House?"

"I'd like to stay another day or two. Maybe you can learn more about Pearl in that time, too."

"Maybe." He wasn't sure how he'd get that accomplished without nosing around Seacliff House and interviewing Martine and Dave. The two of them probably would not be cooperative. But he'd faced more difficult challenges.

Suddenly, he sensed Kayla grow rigid beside him. "What is it?"

She whispered, "He's appeared again."

"Who?" Tanner followed her line of vision out the window and to the garden.

"Do you see him this time?" she whispered. "He's standing next to the gazebo smoking a cigarette."

"See who?" There was no one in the garden.

Kayla stared at Tanner with her mouth gaping. "You really don't see that man with the crew cut? He's staring up at us." She slowly backed away from the window and hid behind the drapes.

Tanner put his face to the glass and peered. "I'm sorry, Kayla, but there's no one there. You must have seen a shadow."

Her eyes were large when their gazes connected. "You're kidding, right? It wasn't a shadow, Tanner. I saw a man. Why am I the only one who can see him?"

She drew the curtain back and peeked out the window one more time and then backed off again. "He's still there."

"*Who*, Kayla?"

"I don't know who he is," she whispered sharply. "But I'm pretty sure of one thing. He's not human."

Tanner didn't understand.

She jiggled his arm, like she was trying to shake sense into him. "That man is a *spirit*, and I think he's trying to communicate with me."

Her eyes assessed him with such concentration the nerve in his jaw began to tick. Was she telling him she believed in ghosts?

Together, they glanced out the window

again. Kayla sighed heavily. "He's gone
now."

Tanner had no idea what to think. As a
sensible man used to dealing with facts in
black and white, he didn't believe in ghosts.
Although he was interested in connections to
his past, like Pearl, spirits walking the
earth amongst the living did not figure in his
way of thinking.

Though she seemed perfectly normal on the
outside, maybe Kayla had issues he wasn't
aware of. Whitney had also seemed ordinary
for the first few months they'd dated. Then
the drama had begun, and he'd seen her true
colors appear. Did he want to invest his time—
and possibly his heart—on someone else who
might turn out to be as unhinged? Tanner's
chest tightened. Coming from a family that
had a few skeletons in the closet was one
thing, but Kayla claiming to see ghosts was
another. It might be a good idea to put some
distance between them. They'd only shared a
couple of kisses. It wasn't too late to put
the brakes on.

"I think I'll go to my room for a while,"
he said. I have a few phone calls to make.
I'll see you at dinner, okay?" He strode to
the door without so much as a goodbye pat on
her shoulder. When he stopped at the
threshold and turned around, Kayla studied
him, her face a mask of confusion. She
probably wondered why he'd grown chilly all of
a sudden. The truth was he'd had enough
female drama in the past few years. Genuinely
caring for Kayla as a person and not wanting
to hurt her, it was best if he didn't lead her
on.

He closed the door behind him and entered
his designated room next door. Feeling like a

jerk, but knowing it was for the best, he flopped onto the bed and scooted against the headboard. With his legs bent, Tanner clasped his hands behind his neck and let his gaze roam around the room. When it landed on his unzipped duffle bag at the end of the bed, he spoke out loud. "I didn't unzip that. I haven't touched my bag since we arrived."

A quick check inside the bag fired his blood. Someone had been in the room and searched through his things.

Chapter Sixteen

Kayla stared at the closed door. It didn't take a brain surgeon to figure out why Tanner had departed so quickly. Obviously, it had been a mistake to tell him she'd seen the spirit. No wonder he practically ran from the room. He probably thought she was as nuts as her deceased relatives. That was probably the last kiss they'd ever share.

"Too bad," she sighed. Getting used to kissing that man would be easy.

She knew she should call home and tell her mom about Matt's death, but her energy was zapped all of a sudden. Suzanne might want to hear the gruesome details, which Kayla wasn't up to explaining. Tomorrow would be soon enough. Hadn't Mom said Matt had been dead to her for years, anyway?

Glancing out the window one more time to find the garden empty, three things skittered through Kayla's mind: Who was the ghost? What did he want with her? And why on earth had she told Tanner about him?

With her shoulders sagging with fatigue, she moved to the porcelain bowl and pitcher on the dry sink and lifted the fragrant soap to her nose. The scent reminded her of spring flowers back home, which reminded her of Mom, the home they shared, and Kayla's predictable life. Until coming to Harmony Beach, she hadn't realized how much she'd needed a change.

Feeling blue, she slipped her sketchpad out of her purse, stretched onto the bed on her stomach, and began doodling. Drawing had always been her refuge. Creating art was a solace in times when life was difficult. As she drew random pictures and started imagining characters for a new story, she found herself dreaming of a new life for herself as well.

The time for moving out of her mother's home and living on her own was long overdue. Meeting Tanner brought that notion home in full force. As if a fragile dam had broken, a pent-up need rushed out. Putting down the pencil and rolling onto her back, Kayla closed her eyes. Her skin prickled as she remembered the way Tanner's lips had molded to hers.

Her mind wandered. She was not that far from thirty. Many of her school friends were married, some with children. She had a good job and a satisfying new career as an author, but dealing with the responsibilities that went along with a parent who had health problems sometimes overshadowed her accomplishments. Often, her dreams of a normal life felt distant and unreachable.

What she really wanted was the same as what her friends had—a loving husband and a family. How would that dream ever become a reality as long as she remained her mother's caretaker?

It seemed fate had stepped in and brought her and Tanner together. He was unlike any man she'd dated. Even with his tattoos, a stalker ex-girlfriend, and a possible jealous streak, he'd captured her interest with that first smile. Who knew what else lurked behind his cheerful façade? Whatever it was, she wanted to find out.

But would their friendship last? Could it turn into something more? Their kisses hinted at romance. She even imagined what a life with him would be like. However, the reality was he was going back to Maine as soon as he dug up the story on his great grandmother. He'd made it clear he planned to return to

Boothbay Harbor and become the editor of the local newspaper in due time.

As for her, she'd be going back to Virginia in a few days, to the mountains and the life she'd known before coming to Maryland. What was the point in trying to start a relationship with Tanner?

That reality caused her mood to dip even lower. Once she returned home, she'd motivate herself to start another book. At least her creative work would help distract her from the memories of Tanner.

The ache she felt in her chest when thinking of having to say goodbye to him turned to a deep, agonizing burn. A tear seeped from the corner of her eye. It seemed impossible in such a short time, but she had to admit she was falling in love with him. She doubted he returned her sentiments. Even if he'd begun to feel a little something for her, blurting out she'd seen a ghost had probably quashed any real interest. From the way he rushed from her room in such a hurry, it was obvious he wanted nothing more to do with one of the crazy Chandler women.

She mashed her fist into the mattress, angry with herself for being so stupid. Why did she think she could trust a guy she barely knew?

The door to Tanner's room opened and then closed. Kayla's head turned and latched onto the back of her door. She listened and waited to hear his knock on the wood, but instead, heavy footfalls treaded down the stairs. Apparently, he wasn't even going to ask if she wanted to accompany him to wherever it was he was off to.

She buried her head in the bedspread and finally let the tears fall. Before long, she'd worn herself out crying. Her lids grew droopy and she drifted to sleep.

* * * *

A loud crack of thunder, accompanied by a bright lightning strike outside the window jolted Kayla awake. Her fingers tingled with numbness from being under her head and in the same position for so long. She rolled onto her back and sat up, blinking. The room was dark. Disoriented and confused as to her surroundings, her heart seized. She wrapped her arms around herself, feeling a cold chill slither over her.

A boom of thunder caused her to jump. Another flash of lightning outside the window lit up the room, jogging her memory. A terrific storm battered Seacliff House. When the next flash illuminated the room, she crawled off the bed, made her way to the wall, and pawed at the light switch. The light didn't come on.

"The power must be out," she groaned. "I wonder what time it is." She dashed to the window. When lightning lit up the sky again, she glanced at her watch. It was eight o'clock! Exhausted, she'd slept for hours and even through dinner. Why hadn't anyone awakened her?

Annoyed at her grandmother for not summoning her to dinner, she was more irritated with Tanner for the same thing—until she remembered why he'd departed so quickly before. Apparently, he had decided to leave her alone to fend for herself.

Frustrated with him for playing games with her heart, she stomped to the door and flung it open. The hallway was pitch black.

She felt her way along the wall and then stretched her hands out in front of her. With cautious steps, she eased her way across the floor until she touched the railing. When she stared over the rail to the foyer below, the house appeared to be clothed in obscurity. There were no movements, no noises. Her grandmother was probably in her bedroom. Most likely, Martine was tucked away with her husband in the cottage weathering out the storm. As for Chris, Kayla had no idea where he lived.

She stood in the hallway alone, with the rest of the house bathed in gloom and seemingly deserted. This scenario was too much like a scary movie. Usually, it was at this precise moment in a slasher movie when the serial killer springs out of the shadows and kills the girl.

Kayla's heart flew into her throat. She reached for composure, telling herself this wasn't a movie and there was no one waiting to murder her.

Human life didn't stir anywhere in Seacliff House, but her ears were assaulted with the sounds of the tumultuous thunder and ragged bolts of lightning creating havoc outside. Rain pounded the roof like nails being driven into wood. To add to her anxiety was the creaking of the old house as wind blew through its cracks and crevices.

She padded to Tanner's room and stood at the door with her fist poised to knock. A question hung in her mind. Why hadn't he checked on her, before dinner or now? Had his chivalrous behavior been an act earlier? Whatever the reason, she didn't want to be alone right now.

Before she knocked, she placed her ear

against the wood and heard nothing. Was he asleep? Seemed impossible. How could anyone sleep through such a racket? There was no light coming from the crack under the doorway, either. Most likely, Tanner hadn't packed a flashlight. Neither had she. Maybe he was sitting in the dark waiting for the storm to pass.

She suddenly remembered the candles on the table located at the top of the stairs. She made her way to the table, felt for the matches and the old fashioned lanterns, and lit a match to a candlewick. The flame caught and licked the air. Weird shadows danced upon the walls like strange misshaped creatures as she shifted the lantern from one hand to the other.

A sequence of thunderclaps boomed so loudly, it felt like the floor underneath Kayla's feet was about to open and swallow her. She let out a whimper and fled to Tanner's door again. Surprisingly, her impatient raps didn't rouse him.

He must be a heavy sleeper, she reasoned. Or he was ignoring her on purpose. That thought made her mad. If it weren't for her, he wouldn't even be at Seacliff House.

"Tanner," she rasped. "Are you awake?"

The squeak of rusty hinges drew her attention. The hairs on the back of her neck bristled. She turned her head slowly and lifted the lantern to eye level. At the end of the hallway, the door to Charlotte Tillman's bedroom crept open. Goosebumps rose on Kayla's flesh. That door had been stuck tight the day Sonora had suggested she and Tanner tour the upstairs. Only Martine's shoulder and obvious know-how had caused the door to give way. Now it stood wide open, its murky interior beckoning, inviting her inside.

Although the room itself had made her feel uncomfortable the other day, and the awful story about Charlotte had distressed her, Kayla felt powerless to resist the room's magnetic pull. As if her body had a mind of its own, she began walking down the hallway at a slow and steady pace. The floorboards groaned under her feet, causing her heart to hammer against her ribs with every step. Thunder rolling over the top of the house sounded like a battalion of military tanks. Kayla glanced up, expecting the ceiling to come crashing down at any moment.

When she reached the bedroom, the strangest sensation flowed through her. Something prodded her forward. An invisible force tugged at her, pulling her inside. With her breath locked deep in her chest, she kept a firm grip on the lantern and stepped into the chamber that had become a creepy memorial to Charlotte.

Kayla slowly pivoted in a circle, swinging the lantern around. From her periphery, she caught a slight movement in the farthest corner of the room. Heart pounding, she watched it for the longest moment before realizing that what she'd spotted was nothing more than the flicker of the candle flame producing a shadow on the wall.

Wholly expecting to see the gazebo ghost standing in the corner, she sighed with relief. But her intrusion had disturbed something else—a mouse. When the rodent ran across her foot, she slapped her free hand over her mouth to keep from shrieking. She stood as still as a statue and watched the mouse scurry over the floor and disappear into a hole in the wall near the baseboard.

Several more long and drawn-out moments passed, in which Kayla felt she was being watched. With her heart beating out of her chest, she slowly backed toward the door. She wasn't brave enough to spend another moment in here.

When the door slammed shut, she jumped and staggered forward. Her fingers flew to her neck when an icy draft blew down her shirt.

Suddenly, the heady smell of flowery perfume tugged at her senses like a memory. The scent was intoxicating—the mingled fragrances of roses, salt and the sea. The smell went straight to her head. Feeling faint, she stumbled and held out her hand in order to steady herself against the nearest object, which was the large armoire. When her hand pressed against the door, she realized it was standing ajar.

After a moment, her dizziness passed. An unexpected, overwhelming desire to look into the armoire swept through her. Kayla opened the door all the way. She held the lantern up and peered inside. It was void of clothes or hangers. Mouse droppings in the bottom were gross evidence that no one had cleaned the room for years.

"Disgusting," she mumbled, recognizing the armoire was just another neglected antique that someone should have taken pains to preserve. What a strange lady her grandmother was to have mandated that this room remain untouched and kept as some sort of macabre shrine.

As Kayla pushed the armoire door closed with her fingertips, the light from her lantern bounced off the top shelf. Something caught her eye. It looked like a large envelope. Praying another rodent or cockroach wouldn't crawl across her fingers, she quickly snatched at the edge of the envelope and pulled it off the shelf, letting it drop to the floor. A puff of dust made her sneeze. Assured there were no cobwebs clinging to the envelope, she gingerly picked it up and blew off the thin coating of dust. There were no writing or markings of any kind on the outside.

What could this be?

Again, the eerie sensation someone watched caused the hair to lift off the back of Kayla's neck. She swept the lantern around the room and saw nothing. Although her limbs were trembling and she wanted to flee, her curiosity was fully piqued. She slid a finger under the envelope flap and particles of dried glue sprinkled onto her hand.

"This must have been sitting on that shelf for years. Maybe decades," she whispered aloud.

She slipped her hand inside the envelope and withdrew a pile of what were obviously homemade cards. As she held the lantern close, Kayla saw that on the front of each one was a drawing of an animal or a flower. A thrill raced up her spine. Who had drawn these pictures? Charlotte Tillman?

No longer concerned about the uncleanliness of the room, Kayla sat down on the thin Persian rug. She placed the lantern beside her and gently shook onto the floor what remained in the envelope. Adrenaline rushed through her body as she perused the cards one by one. There were ten of them. Each drawing or painting was done in either pen and ink or watercolor. Inside each of the cards was a handwritten note—a birthday wish.

"Dearest babe," Kayla read. "Happy

birthday to my precious one-year old child."
The next card was also addressed to *My
Dearest*, and the personal note written in a
beautiful scroll was "for all your wishes to
come true on this your second birthday."

Kayla read each card, with her heart
pounding in her throat. Once again, she
wondered. Who had been the author and
illustrator of these cards?

Also included in the envelope was a stack
of black and white sketches done of a little
girl. The paper they were on was yellowed
with time, but there was no doubt the pictures
were of the same girl at various ages as she'd
grown.

Kayla's head angled in confusion.
Charlotte had given birth to a boy. At least
that's the story Martine had told. Anyway,
whether it was a boy or a girl, Charlotte had
passed away giving birth to her child. If
this artwork was hers, she did it before she
died. But that didn't explain the ten
birthday cards, or who the model for the
sketches had been.

Kayla's heart ricocheted in her chest at
her final discovery—a small booklet bound with
pink ribbon. It was constructed of heavy
paper, almost cardboard like in appearance
with holes punched along the side, in which
the ribbon was woven through. Printed on the
front cover in large letters were the words *MY
ABC's*. Holding her breath, Kayla carefully
flipped through the pages of the book. On
each page was a letter of the alphabet
scrolled in a neat hand, with a drawing of an
object or an animal that corresponded with the
letter—an apple for A, a bear for B, a cat for
C, and so on.

"This is a child's ABC book," she

whispered. But who created it? And for what child was it was made?

Completely spellbound by her discovery, Kayla didn't hear the squeak of the bedroom door when it opened. But when she felt a frosty chill enter the room and creep up her backbone, she craned her head over her shoulder. Her eyes widened at the hulking figure standing in the doorway.

Chapter Seventeen

Kayla heard a click, followed by a beam of light. A flashlight held under the man's chin lit up his face like an eerie glowing jack-o-lantern.

"Boo," Tanner said.

Her teeth, which she hadn't realized she'd been clenching, unclenched. "Tanner, you scared the living hell out of me."

"Sorry." He sauntered into the room, leaving wet footprints in his wake and swinging the flashlight toward the floor where she had the drawings and cards strewn about. "What's all this?"

Kayla scrambled to her knees, scanning his wet clothes, and began gathering up her find. Feeling oddly protective of her discovery, her initial thought was to hide it all from Tanner. She was still aggravated with him.

"First, tell me where you've been, and why you didn't wake me up for dinner. You're completely soaked." She knew her voice cut like a knife, but her nerves were raw.

He apologized while his gaze poured over the sketches still lying on the rug. "I was caught in the rain. Earlier, I knocked, but you didn't answer. After all you've been through I figured you needed your rest. Anyway, there *was* no dinner."

"What do you mean?" She stopped what she was doing and their gazes met. Hearing him say he'd knocked made her feel better.

"Someone came into my room sometime today and searched through my bag. When I went downstairs to confront Sonora about it, she was nowhere to be found. I located Martine in the kitchen, who announced there were cold sandwiches and potato salad in the refrigerator. She said Sonora didn't feel well, so we could help ourselves to the food and Sonora would see us tomorrow morning."

"That's strange," Kayla said. "She seemed fine earlier. Was anything missing from your bag?"

"Not that I could tell. But my stuff had definitely been messed with."

"Why would my grandmother have someone go through your bag?"

He shrugged. "Your guess is as good as mine. But I intend to get to the bottom of it. I don't appreciate people invading my privacy."

"I don't blame you. The culprit must have been Martine or Dave, since my grandmother can't get upstairs in her wheelchair."

"Or that guy, Chris," Tanner said, unsmiling.

Kayla noted the edge in his voice. "Why don't you like Chris? We only spent a few minutes with him. I don't see how you can dislike someone so fast."

"He rubbed me the wrong way. That's all."

His excuse didn't make sense to Kayla. If Tanner was so quick to dismiss people based on first impressions and nothing concrete, he might not be the man she thought he was.

"Anyway," he continued, "I jumped on the opportunity of having a moment alone with Martine and asked if I could talk to her and her husband about what they remember of Pearl."

Despite the excitement Kayla felt about having found the drawings and paintings, she did find herself equally interested in the mystery involving Tanner's great grandmother.

"What did Martine say?"

He shrugged, and Kayla was reminded of how broad his shoulders were. It irked her that she was as fickle as the weather. One moment she was annoyed with him. The next, she felt herself going weak in the knees.

Tanner slicked his wet hair back. "She turned white as a ghost and denied ever knowing anyone named Pearl O'Neill."

"She was lying," Kayla said with conviction. "Grandmother told us Martine and Dave were already working for her when Pearl was hired."

"I know. Either Martine is lying, or your grandmother is. The question is why would either of them lie? If Pearl left on her own accord as Sonora maintains, what's the problem with me asking more questions?"

Kayla didn't have the answer.

"I'll tell you," he said. "Because one or both of them know what happened to my great grandmother, and believe me I'm going to find out how they were involved in her disappearance." His gaze flew to the floor again. "What is all this stuff?" he repeated. He dropped to his knees and touched one of the sketches.

"Don't touch them," Kayla said, gently pushing him away. "These papers are old and delicate, and you're wet. Water stains could ruin them." She inhaled deeply. There was no way she couldn't share her discovery with Tanner now that he'd walked in on her. She carefully displayed the cards, sketches and ABC book on the rug next to the lantern so he could see them clearly. She opened several of the cards and read the messages that were inside.

Tanner's open face could not mask his

enthusiasm. "Wow, these are incredible. Where did you find them?"

"On the shelf inside the armoire. I wonder who the artist was."

"Could they belong to your grandmother?"

"I don't know. I have no idea if she's got artistic talent. If so, my mother didn't inherit any from her."

"Things like that sometimes skip a generation," Tanner pointed out. "If they're Sonora's, why would she leave them in the armoire in this creepy room?"

"She doesn't allow Martine to clean. It's the perfect spot to hide something you don't want found."

"But the door isn't locked. It was hard to open the first time we saw the room, but Martine had no trouble. She can come in and snoop around anytime she wants. There's no way she wouldn't know this envelope was hidden in the armoire."

Kayla agreed. "Perhaps my grandmother stashed it in the armoire many years ago and forgot about it." Another thought occurred to her. "Or, maybe the drawings aren't hers at all. My grandfather Elliott could have been an artist. I don't know a solitary thing about him."

Tanner's mind appeared to be working. "The words in those birthday wishes weren't written by a man. I don't think a man would call a child his dearest. And the handwriting has a feminine slant to it." He nodded his head in the affirmative. "A woman definitely made these cards, and I'd say she was related to the child she created them for. Perhaps she was the mother, or an aunt."

Kayla studied some of the drawings again. She could not picture her hard-nosed

grandmother as ever having been sensitive or
loving enough to have created such heartfelt
pieces. "It might even be possible that one
of my Tillman ancestors did these, like
Charlotte," she said. "I wonder if there's a
way to find out how old this paper is so we
can narrow down the time frame."

"Sure there is," Tanner said. "Haven't
you ever heard of paper forensics and age
dating?"

"No."

"There's a company in Appleton, Wisconsin
that has utilized the capabilities of its
fiber science team to develop a reputation for
paper and document forensics. By using wood
species, pulping chemistry, paper additives
and surface treatments to serve as unique
paper forensic and age dating markers, that
company is able to determine likely age ranges
for paper."

Kayla stared at him with her jaw hanging
open. "What are you, a walking encyclopedia?
How on earth would you know the details of
something like that?"

He flashed her that boyish grin of his,
the one that made her heart flutter. "I *could*
tell you I have the I.Q. score of a genius and
that I just know random stuff like this, but I
doubt you'd fall for it. The truth is I used
to date a girl whose cousin co-founded that
company in Wisconsin. I found it all quite
fascinating and wrote an article for the
paper."

Kayla studied him for a long moment.
Tanner Bishop was full of surprises. She
couldn't help but smile. "Was that girl
Whitney?"

His face screwed up, as if he'd sucked a
lemon down his throat. "No. Let's not talk

about Whitney, okay?"

"What's wrong with her, exactly?" Kayla asked.

"I told you. She's a psycho."

"Mmmm. I might be a psycho, too. After all, I've been seeing a ghost." She watched his reaction carefully.

Tanner smiled sheepishly. "Okay, you got me there. I'm still not sure what to make of that, but I shouldn't have jumped to any conclusion."

Kayla wasn't entirely sure what conclusion he'd jumped to. Probably that she was mental. She *had* seen a ghost—twice. If that made her crazy then so be it. But there was no sense in starting a debate. This new mystery took precedence. She gently returned all the cards, sketches and the booklet to the envelope. As she attempted to stand on her legs that had gone numb, Tanner gave her a hand up.

"How did you know I was in this bedroom?" she asked, suddenly wondering. "Did you hear the door slam?"

"No. Did it slam shut on you?"

"Yes. It scared the dickens out of me. I guess a breeze must have caught it." She glanced around the room, and realized she no longer sensed a presence. "There are probably small cracks in the walls for air to blow through."

"Probably. It's an old house and bound to be drafty."

"If you didn't hear the door close, how'd you know I was in here?" Kayla repeated.

"I came up the stairs and saw the light shining under the door. I couldn't imagine why you'd be in here by yourself, but if it wasn't you, I had to find out where the light came from. Strange, but the door opened easily when I turned the knob."

"That *is* strange," she agreed. "Where have you been?" she asked, changing the subject and hoping to divert questions about what had led her into Charlotte's bedroom. There was no need for him to know that the door had opened on its own and she'd felt drawn to go inside. Nor did he need to know that she'd sensed eyes on her once she was inside the room. Those confessions would make him run again.

"Martine left the kitchen through the back door. When it was obvious she wasn't going to speak to me, I followed her to the cottage in the trees. When I'm sniffing out a story, I'm like a hound dog on a rabbit's trail. If I want something, I don't take no for an answer."

Kayla wondered if his philosophy on women was the same. "Did she let you inside the cottage?"

"No. Martine reached the door a minute before I did and slammed it in my face and locked it. When I peeked into the window next to the door, she glared at me through the glass and threw the curtains together and hollered for me to go away."

"I called back that I was going to learn the truth about Pearl, with or without her help."

Kayla remembered their frightening encounter with Martine's husband. "Weren't you afraid of Dave barging out of the cottage and pulling another gun on you, or beating you up?"

"I didn't figure there was a gun inside. If he owned one himself, he wouldn't have taken that antique pistol from Sonora's gun cabinet. As for beating me up?" He laughed. "I imagine I could hogtie that old drunk with one hand tied behind my back."

Kayla had to snicker. She imagined he could. "So what happened? Did you have a Mexican standoff?"

"Hardly. A breeze turned into howling wind, and the dark sky became an intense storm within a matter of minutes. Right before the rain started, I ran to the washhouse for cover. I've been in there until now. The rain has slacked off some."

For the first time since they'd been talking, Kayla saw Tanner shiver. "You'd better change into dry clothes or you'll catch a cold."

"I think you're right."

Kayla picked up her lantern, and Tanner led the way to the door by following the beam from his flashlight. "Are you taking that with you?" he asked, nodding toward the envelope in her hand.

"It had years of dust on it. Whoever placed it in the armoire has probably long since passed. Even if it belongs to my grandmother, she's probably forgotten all about it. I'll approach her with the illustrations and ask her about them when the time seems right."

Kayla quietly closed the door behind her. "Did you eat anything?" she asked Tanner, feeling her stomach gurgling with hunger pangs.

"No, but I'm starved now. Let me get into dry clothes and we can share a candlelight dinner of sandwiches and potato salad in the kitchen."

"Sounds romantic." Their gazes latched, and Kayla felt her hormones raging with the same wild intensity as the storm outside. She kept her gaze glued to Tanner's, not feeling the least bit ashamed for being bold. "I'll put this envelope in my room and wait for you to knock."

Tanner nodded and slipped inside his room.

Kayla stepped into her bedroom and considered where the best place to hide the envelope would be. If Martine, Dave, or Chris had searched through Tanner's things, they might look through hers, too. Maybe they already had. Oh well. So what if Sonora found out she had the drawings? Kayla planned to ask her about them anyway.

She placed the envelope into the dresser drawer. Then she took a hairbrush out of her purse and ran it through her mane. After cleaning her teeth using water from the pitcher, Kayla dabbed her lips with gloss, then sat on the bed, her stomach fluttering with anticipation, to wait for Tanner.

Chapter Eighteen

Tanner and Kayla sat across from each other at the kitchen island finishing their sandwiches. A single candle flickered between them, setting Kayla's face aglow. In the half an hour they'd spent together, they'd been careful to keep their conversation to a low drone so as not to awaken Sonora, whose quarters, Tanner suspected, were nearby. Still, he'd felt a presence eavesdropping.

No sooner had he swallowed his last bite than power surged through the house like a bear aroused from hibernation, and the kitchen was illuminated with light. At the same time, the rain stopped, as did the howling of the wind. All that remained of the storm was a soft rumble of distant thunder.

While the two of them had whispered shared stories of their childhoods, Tanner had been so engrossed by the southern lilt of Kayla's voice and the way her eyes twinkled above the candle flame, all evidence of the tempest outside had melted into the background.

He'd even told her about being dyslexic. She'd listened carefully as he'd explained the complexities of growing up with a learning disability, and how he'd overcome his difficulties with spelling, writing and reading in order to become a successful journalist. Tears had glistened in Kayla's eyes. She'd placed her hand over his and told him he was an example to anyone facing a trial of their own, and that she was impressed by his courage and determination. That exchange was a pivotal moment. Thunderstruck by how natural it felt to be with her eating cold sandwiches and talking about real life issues,

Tanner was left reeling with a quickening in his chest. He'd never felt so close to a woman.

"The storm has passed," he said, pointing out the obvious.

"So it has." She smiled and then quietly gathered up their plates and rinsed them under the faucet. As she dried the dishes and returned them to the cabinet, Tanner watched her movements with longing. She was a woman with dignity and grace. He knew he'd judged her unfairly before. Although he didn't believe in ghosts and had previously thought anyone who did was a crackpot, in his heart, he knew she wasn't an attention seeker or drama queen. Whatever it was she thought she'd seen in the garden, he owed it to her to listen and be sympathetic. She'd had one shock after another ever since coming to Harmony Beach. The least he could do was give her a supportive shoulder without being judgmental.

Kayla replaced the lid on the container of potato salad and shoved the dish into the refrigerator. When she turned around, he was standing behind her with his arms pulling her into an embrace.

"What are you doing?" Her inquiring eyes searched his face with suspicion. Not blaming her because of his earlier behavior, his fingers sifted through the tangles of her coppery hair and rested on her nape.

"I want to apologize for walking out when you told me you saw a spirit. Although I'm a man who relies on concrete evidence to form my opinions, my gut hints you aren't lying about what you think you saw by the gazebo."

When her hands slowly moved up his arms, his muscles bunched under her touch.

"I don't lie," Kayla said softly. "If we're going to be friends, you need to trust me."

"We barely know each other, but I do trust you." His hands slid down her back to rest at her waist.

"That means a lot to me. And just to set the record straight, this is the first time anything like this has happened to me. I've never had a supernatural experience. It's as strange to me as it sounds to you, but someone from beyond the grave is reaching out to me. For what reason, I don't know."

Tanner tightened his hold around her waist. "We'll figure it out together, if you'll let me help."

"I will. Thank you."

His lips brushed hers lightly. "Do you think there's a chance we might become more than friends?" he asked when they parted.

"Let's take it one day at a time, shall we?"

Before he could respond, the moment was ruined by the sound of someone pounding on the front door. Kayla grew stiff in his arms.

"Who could that be at this time of night?" he wondered.

"Should we wake my grandmother or answer it ourselves?" she asked, following him out of the kitchen and into the dim hall. Without turning the hall lights on, Tanner placed his eye to the peephole in the front door. A woman looking to be in her fifties and wearing a green raincoat stood on the porch. Her complexion was pale, one of her eyes had been blackened, and her dark hair flew untamed about her face. When her fist slammed against the wood again, she dropped her head and began to sob, "Kayla Grayson, I want to talk to you.

Please open this door. I know you're here."

When Tanner glanced at Kayla, her mouth was hanging open. "I think your question was just answered," he said, unbolting the door and easing it halfway open. "Stay behind me. Let me find out who this person is and what she wants."

"Can I help you?" he politely asked the woman, while keeping a firm grip on the handle of the screen door. Although there were no weapons that he could see in the woman's hands, there was no telling what might be hidden in her pockets or under the raincoat.

"Who are you?" the woman asked, raising her head and scanning him up and down. "I want to see Matt's daughter. I know she's in there."

Behind him, Tanner heard Kayla gasp. The woman slurred her words and swayed, causing him to believe she was drunk or high. "It's too late for a social call," he said, scrutinizing her and prepared to slam the door in her face at any sign of danger.

She stomped her foot on the ground like a child. "I don't care what time it is! I have to see her now. It's urgent."

"Must be for you to have come out in a thunderstorm. Who are you? And how do you know about Kayla?"

"I knew her father. I want to see if she looks like him."

Hidden in the shadows beside him, Kayla grabbed Tanner's hand. He could feel anticipation running through her fingers like sparks of electricity. He was just as interested in knowing who this woman was, but not in the condition she was in. "I think you'd better go home and sleep it off. Come back tomorrow if you still want to see Miss

Grayson."He started to close the door, but she stuck her foot inside it.

"I won't come back tomorrow," she gritted between clenched teeth. She glanced around her and spied the two urns that sat on either side of the door. "Let me see her or I'll break a window." Her eyes went wild, and she bent and picked up one of the urns.

When she heaved it over her head using what appeared to be super strength, Tanner burst through the screen door and wrestled the urn from her hands. Kayla stepped out from behind the door at the same time Tanner heard the familiar sound of Sonora's wheelchair trundling up the hall.

"What's going on out here?" Sonora hollered. Kayla pushed open the screen door to allow Sonora to roll onto the porch.

Tanner let the urn drop to the ground with a thump and grabbed the woman's flailing arms.

"Let go of me," she shrieked, twisting like a leaf in the wind. "I'm not going to hurt anyone."

"Calm down and maybe I'll release you," Tanner demanded.

The woman stopped wriggling, so he eased up his grip on her, but he stayed planted at her side in case there was the need to restrain her again.

Her gaze focused solely on Kayla. "It's you, isn't it?" she said quietly. "You look just like him. You're Matt's child, aren't you?"

"Yes," Kayla answered. "Who are you?"

"I'll tell you who she is," Sonora replied. Her razor-sharp scowl could have cut through glass.

Tanner noticed Sonora wore a satin robe

and slippers, but in his opinion, she didn't have the puffy look of someone who'd just been roused from sleep, which made him believe she'd been awake and listening in on his and Kayla's conversation. His gaze dropped to her lap, where the antique pistol lay within the folds of her robe.

Sonora's lip curled. "Kayla, this is Melissa Seeley. She's the tramp I caught sleeping with your father when you were a little girl."

A feather could have knocked Kayla over. She stared at Melissa, not understanding. Up close, it was easy to see the years had not been good to the woman. Maybe she'd been pretty when she was young, but those days were long gone. Kayla stared into her bloodshot eyes and wondered what Matt had seen in her that Suzanne didn't have. Why had he given up his family for this woman?

"Why are you here, and how do you know about me?" she asked.

Melissa gulped and swiped at her damp face where streaks of mascara ran down her cheeks. "I'll explain if you'll give me a chance."

"I'm calling the police," Sonora snapped.

Melissa shot Sonora a look more lethal than poison. "Give me a chance!" Then her weepy gaze returned to Kayla. "I like to go to the Beachcomber on Wednesday nights. I know the singer. His name is Chris. We're friends."

Kayla and Tanner exchanged curious glances. "Go on," Kayla said.

Melissa sniffled. "I saw Matt yesterday, near the old casino. I almost fainted, because I thought I was seeing a walking dead man. Everyone knew Matt had drowned all those

190

years ago. But I was wrong, and so was the town. He's no ghost. It was Matt all right, standing there on the sidewalk in the flesh." She smiled broadly. "It had been twenty-four long years that I've been thinking about Matt. I ran up to him. I said, *Matt, it's me, Melissa*! Her eyes brightened and then dulled.

With her limbs trembling, Kayla listened as Melissa's voice changed and took on the bitter taste of venom.

"He knew who I was. I could tell by the flicker in his gray eyes that he remembered. How could he not? We'd been in love. Matt recognized me, but he wanted nothing to do with me. That bastard! He told me to go away, that he didn't have time for *all this*." Melissa emphasized those last words. "He said there was nothing for us to discuss. What we had ended years ago. He was waiting for his wife. *His wife*! They had some important things to talk about, and he couldn't be seen chatting up the likes of me."

Kayla's mouth dropped open. "His wife? Matt told you he was waiting for his wife?"

Melissa rambled on. "Yeah. *Suzanne Chandler*. That pissed me off."

Kayla cringed at the way Melissa mocked her mother's name.

"There was something important I had to talk about, too," Melissa continued. "Something I'd been keeping a secret my entire adult life." She took a deep breath.

Kayla's heart thudded hard against her ribs, imagining the worst.

"I told him I'd been pregnant with his baby when he drowned. I asked him how he liked that for a surprise." Melissa threw her hands in front of her face and began to wail. "You know what he did? He told me to leave him alone. He didn't care about our child! The creep just turned and walked away. I wanted to slap his face, or kick him in the nuts. I hated him!"

Kayla closed her eyes, feeling she was caught in a nightmare.

"Sounds like a good motive for murder," Sonora said calmly.

Kayla's eyes popped open.

"Murder?" Melissa stopped whining and glanced from Sonora to Kayla and back. "What are you talking about?"

Kayla told her. "My father was found dead on the beach this morning."

"But you probably already know that, don't you?" Sonora questioned.

"No!" Melissa bawled again. She sunk to the porch floor holding her head in her hands.

"Calm down," Tanner interjected, while easing her up by the arm. His gaze swept between Sonora and Melissa. "No one is jumping to any conclusions here. What's your story about Matt Grayson got to do with Chris Allen?" he asked.

Melissa removed her hands from her face. Her breath hitched before she spoke again. "When I told Chris about seeing Matt, he told me his daughter was in town and she was staying at Seacliff House." She looked at Kayla again. "Chris said he'd met you and that you were a nice person. I had to see Matt's child for myself." A tear rolled down her cheek. "You could have been mine and Matt's little girl."

Kayla recoiled, realizing Melissa was disturbed.

"That's enough!" Sonora shouted. "Tanner, call the police. I think they're going to want to talk to this woman about her whereabouts this morning."

Tanner pulled his cell phone out of his pocket. He nodded at Kayla, assuring her that, for once, Sonora made sense.

"No!" Melissa bolted down the stairs and ran to her car with her open raincoat flapping behind her.

"She's drunk," Tanner said, snapping the phone shut. "She could kill someone, or herself. I'll stop her."

"Let her go," Sonora's voice thundered, halting him in his tracks.

"Why are we letting her get away?" Kayla cried. "She might be the one who killed my father."

Sonora waved her hand in the air, and they all watched Melissa speed away with her tires kicking up gravel. "We'll call Officer Scott when we go into the house. If Melissa is Matt's murderer, the police will find her and arrest her. That's their job, not ours."

After watching the taillights of Melissa's car disappear through the gate, Tanner held the door open and Kayla pushed Sonora's wheelchair inside the house. He latched the bolt and then stepped into the parlor to make the call to the police.

Exhausted and confused, Kayla said, "Shall I wheel you into your room, Grandmother?"

"I can do it myself," she answered. "Go to bed and try to get some sleep." In a rare turn of sensitivity, she patted Kayla's hand. "Don't fret over anything Melissa just said. It's a well-known fact she's an alcoholic and lives with a brute for a husband. Didn't you notice her black eye?"

Kayla nodded. "Do you believe what she said about a baby?"

Sonora shrugged. "Who knows?"

"Did you see her pregnant back then? Does she have a child?" Kayla remembered Kitty telling her Sonora had always known everything that went on in Harmony Beach, and still did.

"I'm not aware of any child," Sonora said. "But Melissa got married and left town shortly after the scandal broke. They were gone for many years. She and her husband only returned a couple of years ago when her mother passed away. They took over her T-shirt business on the beach."

"What do you think she meant when she said my dad was waiting to talk to my mother?" Kayla asked. The comment confused her.

"She's inebriated. I wouldn't pay attention to anything she said."

"Officer Scott is going to call on Melissa Seeley," Tanner announced, stepping out of the parlor and interrupting their conversation.

"Thanks for handling that," Kayla said, unable to suppress a yawn. "I guess it's time to call it a night. I just hope I can get my mind to stop racing so I can sleep. A lot has happened in the past two days. I don't know what to make of any of it."

Sonora cleared her throat. "Why don't we spend some time together in the morning, Kayla? I have some things that belonged to your mother I'd like to show you, as well as some old photos you might enjoy. It might help you to relax. Would you like that?"

Despite her fatigue, Kayla couldn't keep the eagerness out of her voice. This was the moment she'd been waiting for. "That would be wonderful, Grandmother. I'll look forward to it."

Sonora's thin lips parted. "After all, that's why you're here, isn't it? To learn about your family?"

"Yes. Thank you for keeping your promise."

Tanner piped up. "I wonder if you might also have a few minutes to spare for me tomorrow, Mrs. Chandler? I won't take up much of your time."

Sonora's eyebrow arched. "I suppose."

"Thank you. Sweet dreams," he said, meeting Kayla's weary gaze. "Ladies, I'll see you both in the morning."

Once he'd walked up the stairs and they heard his bedroom door close, Kayla said good night to her grandmother.

"No hanky-panky," Sonora reminded her, returning to her usual stern manner. "Remember, I have spies everywhere."

Chapter Nineteen

The next morning, Tanner could barely take his eyes off of Kayla as they sat at the dining table eating breakfast. Looking refreshed and serene, she wore a blue halter dress that set off the color of her eyes, and her hair was tied in a ponytail. When she smiled at him from across the table, blood surged through him like a locomotive.

"Is there anything else you need, ma'am?" Martine asked Sonora, clearing their plates.

"That will be all," Sonora replied.

Martine's eyes were rimmed in red and Tanner wondered if she'd been crying or was allergic to something. "Thank you for breakfast," he said as she retreated from the room balancing plates on her arms. "It was delicious."

She craned her neck over her shoulder. "You're welcome."

"Yes, thank you," Kayla parroted.

Tanner pushed back from the table and crossed one leg over the other. "Last night I realized I left my cell phone charger at the B&B. I'm going to drive back to get it, but before I go, is it all right for me to ask you a few questions, Mrs. Chandler?"

"I said it would be. I suppose you want to ask me about Pearl O'Neill."

Relief spread through his body. Although he'd hoped he wouldn't have to strong-arm her, he'd been prepared to do battle in order to get her to talk. "Yes, ma'am."

"Well, fire away. Although I don't know what more I can tell you." Sonora lifted her coffee cup and took a sip.

"Okay. The first thing I'd like to know is if my great grandmother had any friends in

Harmony Beach, aside from her cousin. Or if she dated any men while she was here."

Immediately, Sonora seemed offended. "How would I know? I don't get involved in the social lives of the help. I don't care who they see or where they go on their days off. As long as they do their job at Seacliff House, their personal life is their business. It's always been that way."

Tanner found that hard to believe. From all accounts, Sonora made everything her business. He doubted she'd been any different back in 1958. "Did Pearl tell you anything about her life before coming to Maryland?"

"Such as?"

He'd already decided not to beat around the bush. "Perhaps you knew about the baby she'd left behind in Maine."

Sonora's steely gaze did not waver. "About three months after I'd hired her, I learned she'd given birth to an illegitimate child in Maine and that she'd created a scandal by not marrying the father. Her cousin often came on Pearl's day off so they could spend the day together as Pearl had no car, and she let it slip one day. Obviously, I do not approve of loose women. I wanted to fire Pearl on the spot, but my husband convinced me to not be so hasty. He felt everyone deserved a second chance."

Tanner looked at Kayla, whose eyes brightened at the mention of her grandfather, but she remained quiet.

"So you kept Pearl on, despite your misgivings about her morals?" Tanner asked.

"That's correct," Sonora answered stiffly. "But as I mentioned to you before, the girl lacked more than morals. She knew nothing about polishing silver, doing laundry, or cleaning in general. Martine had to teach her everything."   Someone less observant than Tanner may not have noticed, but a glossy sheen appeared on Sonora's forehead, and he knew she was more than agitated.

"Where did Pearl live when she worked for you? Here in the house?"

Sonora clamped her hands together in front of her on the table. "Of course not. There was a small cottage in the back. We had a bigger staff back then. She shared it with another maid until that girl found employment elsewhere."

"Are you talking about the cottage Mr. and Mrs. Allen live in?"

"No. There was another dwelling. It burned down many years ago."

"I see. And to be clear, it's your understanding that when Pearl left Seacliff House a year after she'd arrived, she was going home to Maine. Is that right?"

"I told you that already."

"So you did. Was her child the reason she was going home?"

"I don't know. I doubt it. Although she knew I was aware of the child, she never spoke of the baby the entire time she worked here. I don't even know if it was a boy or a girl."

"He was a boy," Tanner said. "His name was Arlan, and he grew up to become the best grandpa a boy could have. I miss him a great deal."

"Mmmm. Pearl was a selfish girl, and the poor child was better off without her. Of that I'm sure."

Tanner flinched but chose to bite his tongue. "Did you ever hear rumors about her and any men she might have met in Harmony Beach?"

Sonora's gaze narrowed. "If you're asking me if your great grandmother was a trollop, the answer is yes, Mr. Bishop."

"That's not what I was getting at."

Sonora spoke through tight lips. "I believe in speaking the truth, no matter how hurtful it might be. Based on her loose morals, deserting her baby and its father, and behaving in a less than virtuous manner while at Seacliff House, Pearl O'Neill was a sinful woman. If she never returned to Maine, it would be my guess she ran off with someone as equally sordid as herself. No decent man would have had her. Her lot usually ends up bearing several illegitimate children from different fathers."

"Grandmother! That's a terrible thing to say about Tanner's kin—or *anyone*, for that matter." Kayla's mouth hung open, and her cheeks flushed with shame.

"It's all right, Kayla," Tanner said, keeping his voice sedate. "I expected no less than honesty from Mrs. Chandler. At least, the way she sees it."

"Are we quite finished?" Sonora asked, curtly. "I promised my granddaughter we'd spend time together this morning."

Tanner stood up. "Quite. Thank you for your time." He nodded at Kayla and then sauntered out of the room and stepped through the front door. As he walked down the porch steps, he heard chair legs scrape across the wooden floor from inside. The screen door slapped shut, and Kayla rushed up behind him. She turned him toward her.

"Tanner, I'm sorry. She's one of the rudest people I've known. I hardly know what to say."

He skimmed his hand down her arm. "You

have nothing to apologize for. I entered the conversation knowing how it might turn out. Unfortunately, I didn't gather much information. Sonora really didn't like my great grandmother, did she?"

Kayla shook her head sadly. "I remember the first time you asked her about Pearl. Grandmother mentioned how Pearl had depended on her looks to get ahead. My grandmother might have been jealous of her if Pearl was as pretty as she suggests. Still, that gives her no right to talk as cruelly as she did. After all, Pearl was just a young girl."

"Eighteen or nineteen," Tanner said.

"It seems my grandfather had a heart. He must have realized people make mistakes, but that doesn't make someone a bad person."

"I don't think your grandmother meant to let that slip out about him."

"It appears, after all these years, she still holds a grudge against him for leaving her and my mother."

"I suppose so. It would be a hard thing to forgive. Anyway, don't worry your head over anything your grandmother said to me. Try to enjoy your time with her today."

Kayla rolled her eyes. "I will. Poor Mom. I understand how she developed anxiety issues, but I won't allow Sonora to give me a nervous breakdown."

Standing in the morning light, Kayla looked so pretty and fresh, and vulnerable. The urge to kiss her was overpowering, but Tanner settled for a peck on the cheek. He figured Sonora had probably wheeled herself next to the window and was spying from behind the drapes.

"I'll be back later," he said, subtly inhaling Kayla's sweet perfume. "Is there anything you want me to tell Kitty while I'm there?"

Kayla whispered behind her hand, "Tell her the dragon lady hasn't devoured me yet."

He winked and then jogged to his car and waved goodbye.

Once he reached the B&B, Tanner parked in the one vacant spot behind the house and entered through the back door. The staircase to the second floor was directly inside the door. He placed one foot on the landing and stopped. Female voices drifted out from the kitchen. Although they were not raised, he could tell from their tones that the discussion was heated. One of the voices he recognized as Kitty's. Who would she be arguing with? A customer?

The name of *Matt* caught his attention and caused the hairs on his arms to prickle. Glancing into the dining room to make sure no one was around to catch him eavesdropping, he stood as still as a statue and listened.

"So what if I had a crush on him," Kitty sniveled. "Every woman in Harmony Beach did back then."

"But not every woman threatened to kill him," the other voice reminded her. "Why did you send me the email, begging me to come to Maryland? Were you afraid your feelings for Matt would be resurrected after seeing him? Or were you scared of what harm you might cause him?"

Quicker than the wind changes directions, Kitty's voice grew from timid to brazen. "Are you suggesting I carried through with my threat yesterday?"

"You did disappear early in the morning."

"How would you know? You were asleep in my room. You said the sleeping pills you brought with you knock you out cold for a good ten hours. I know you took one the night before last. I heard you snoring."

"The pill didn't work so well. I heard a car engine start up and looked out the window. I saw you leave."

"So? I often go to the market early in the morning. By all accounts, *you* were probably the last one to see Matt alive. You used my house phone to contact him the night before. You made plans to meet him. Phone records are easy to trace, Suzanne, and you have a strong motive. Maybe Matt's blood is on *your* hands."

Tanner felt his eyes widen. *Suzanne?* Kitty was talking to Kayla's mother! But how was it possible? Kayla had told him she suffered from agoraphobia and never left the house. His mind spun with the repercussions of what he'd overheard. The two women were blaming each other for Matt's death. Could one of them be his murderer?

The conversation went silent, and Tanner wondered if they had sensed him. If he moved or was caught ascending the stairs, they'd know he'd been listening. If either of them was capable of committing murder, his life was in danger.

When Suzanne spoke again, he silently breathed a sigh of relief.

"There's no point in my staying longer. I'll go," she said.

"Oh, no, you don't," Kitty warned. "You're not leaving me with a mess to clean up, the way you did before. If you go now, I'll tell the police you were here. It won't take them long to connect the dots."

"You wouldn't!"

"I would." Kitty sighed heavily.

"Listen. We've got to stick together, Suzanne. We're blood cousins. Kayla is staying at Seacliff House for a few more days. As soon as this thing with Matt blows over, you can go home. Kayla will never have to know you were here."

"You're sure she has no idea I drove in the same day she did?" Suzanne asked.

"I'm sure," Kitty said. "That's why I made you stay away until after she came home and went to bed Tuesday night."

"I still can't believe Matt was here in this house and that he and Kayla actually met. I wonder what she thought of her father."

The front door opened before Kitty could respond. Boisterous chitchat and laughter accompanied several guests coming in from the beach. Tanner seized the opportunity and darted up the stairs. Hurriedly, he unlocked the door to his room and snatched up his cell phone charger that he'd left on the side table.

When he crept down the stairs, he glanced around and could not see nor hear Kitty and Suzanne in the kitchen. Before being discovered, he snuck out the back door and jumped in his car.

Tanner's foot pressed on the gas pedal. The speed of the car matched the accelerated tempo of his pulse as he raced toward Seacliff House. Kayla deserved to know her mother was in Harmony Beach. And he'd have to tell her what he'd overheard, too, even if she ended up hating him for it.

Chapter Twenty

Kayla sat in a wing chair covered in blue velvet with her hands folded in her lap. She could not believe her grandmother had invited her into her private suite. The space was large with a sitting area next to a bay window and an attached bathroom designed to accommodate her wheelchair. The furnishings were antique, and the décor was much the same as the rest of Seacliff House, as if Sonora still lived in the nineteenth century.

Her grandmother rolled toward the hope chest sitting at the end of her spindle bed and opened the lid. "I've kept a few of your mother's things in here for safekeeping."

One by one, Sonora lifted out childhood toys, picture books, and a big stuffed bear with one eye missing, and handed them to Kayla. Kayla couldn't stay seated. She bounded off the chair and dropped to the carpeted floor and sat cross-legged like a child herself. As she examined the treasures that had belonged to her mom, her touch was gentle and bordered on reverence.

"There's a wooden box in the bottom of the chest," Sonora said, pointing. "Lift it out for me."

Kayla did and sat the box on the floor next to her.

"You can open it. Some of Suzanne's things from high school are in there."

It felt like Kayla was about to dive into forbidden territory. Suddenly, her excitement plummeted. More than a sliver of resentment skated through her. There'd been no reason her mother couldn't have told her some things about her school days and friends. Surely, Suzanne's childhood didn't hold secrets the way her adult life had.

"Go ahead," Sonora said, confirming with a firm nod of her head that it was okay to look.

Kayla picked up the first item, a paper booklet with the words *Bye Bye Birdie* printed on the front cover. "What's this?"

Sonora chuckled. "That's the program for the musical the school put on the year your mother was a senior. She played the main girl—the one who wins a date with the rock and roll star."

"You're kidding!" Kayla could not imagine her shy mother acting. "I had no idea." Astounded, she stared at her mother's name in the list of characters.

"Suzanne was quite a ham back then," Sonora said.

"That's hard to imagine. Did you go to see the play?"

"Yes, I did. Suzanne even sang and danced."

Kayla tried to picture her mom on a stage dancing and belting out a song. The image was so unlike the person she knew. "From whom in the family did Mom get her gift for singing and acting?" She held her breath, knowing this might be a controversial question. Kayla had a pretty good feeling Sonora had not passed on any creative genes, so that left her grandfather. She hoped the question would open up a discussion about him.

"Most of the Tillmans were musically inclined," Sonora answered, cleverly skirting the subject of Elliott Chandler.

Kayla let it go. As she examined her mom's athletic awards, report cards, yearbooks, a citizenship medal, dried flowers left over from a prom, photos, and other nostalgic items, she felt sad for the playful, happy girl who had faded into a solemn, adult Suzanne.

"Did your mother ever talk about me?" Sonora asked, out of the blue.

Kayla lifted her gaze from the varsity sports letter she fingered in her hands. Sonora's expression was one of curiosity, but not necessarily one of longing for a daughter she hadn't seen in over twenty years.

"Mom never spoke of the past," Kayla said, heeding her grandmother's policy about honesty. "Do you regret what happened all those years ago that ended with her taking me and leaving Harmony Beach?"

"Life is too short for regrets, Kayla."

"Perhaps. But she was your daughter—your only child. And I was your only grandchild. Couldn't you have done *something* to convince Mom to stay?"

It took a few moments for Sonora to answer. She stared out the window and said, "You can't hold onto someone who never belonged to you in the first place."

Kayla was reminded of a similar saying she'd heard once in regard to a guy who had dumped a girlfriend of hers. But it was a sad state of affairs when you were talking about family.

As she carefully began returning her mom's mementos to the hope chest, she noticed a picture frame on the bottom, lying face down. "What is this a photo of?" Before she had a chance to turn the frame over, Sonora had wheeled toward her with lightning speed and snatched it out of her hand.

"That doesn't belong in there," she groused, mashing the frame into her lap facedown. "The walk down memory lane is over," she announced gruffly.

Kayla rolled her eyes and tried not to laugh. She seemed to have a knack for getting her grandmother riled up—and for the first time, it tickled her. It was better to find humor in Sonora's prickly demeanor as opposed to getting upset, or she'd turn into a big anger ball.

Obviously, the picture frame had triggered Sonora's reaction. She'd behaved almost human up to that point. Kayla closed the lid to the hope chest with her curiosity fully aroused, and the mischief-maker in her made a vow at that moment to somehow find a way to take a look at that photo.

The house phone rang, and a moment later, there was a knock on the door.

"Come in," Sonora called.

"Call for you," Martine said, entering and handing Sonora a portable phone.

"Excuse me, Kayla. That will be all, Martine." Sonora dismissed both of them with a flick of her hand. Kayla left the room first, followed by Martine, who closed the door behind her. When Kayla stepped into the hall, she saw a young man with a ponytail exiting the front door.

"Is that your grandson?" she asked Martine.

"Yes, that's Chris."

Kayla made a beeline for the door.

"Don't be bothering him," Martine called to her back. "He's got work to do."

Ignoring her, Kayla let the screen door slam shut and caught up with him as he traipsed across the lawn toward the fountain. "Hey, Chris!" she hollered.

He turned and waved and sat a large toolbox on the ground and waited for her approach.

"Can I talk to you?" she asked, marching toward him. She was incensed that he'd told the psycho woman, Melissa, who she was and where to find her.

He frowned. He had to notice she wasn't smiling. "Hey, I'm sorry for the loss of your dad," he said, when she drew near. "I had no idea that's why the cop was here when Grandma told me to find you yesterday."

She kept her temper in check. "I understand. I was three when my mom and I moved away from Harmony Beach, so I have no memories of him. I only just met him two days ago."

Chris shook his head in sympathy. "That's a bummer. Have they found his killer yet?"

"Not that we've heard. But since you brought it up, last night we had a strange visitor come to Seacliff House. She's a woman you know. Her name is Melissa Seeley."

He nodded, looking sheepish. "I know her. Can we talk while I work?" he asked, peering over Kayla's shoulder. She craned her neck around and caught a glimpse of a dark-clothed figure standing inside the house door—Martine.

"Sure," she said, letting out a long breath. The next time she turned around, Martine had disappeared.

Chris picked up the toolbox and they walked to the fountain. Kayla noticed it wasn't running.

"I need to take the pump apart and clean it," he said, kneeling to remove a toothbrush, a rag, and a bottle of lime scale remover from the toolbox. He unplugged the pump, took it out of the water, and began cleaning off algae that had wrapped itself around the pump body. "I suppose you're angry that I told Melissa about you," he finally said.

"Yeah, I am. You had no right. That woman needs help. She behaved like a lunatic and said some things that make me wonder about her mental state."

"Such as?"

"I believe she might be capable of committing murder."

Chris ruminated over her comment as he wiped the outside of the pump with the soft cloth. He removed the pump cover and pulled out the impeller. "Melissa's a little messed up because she's an alcoholic, but I don't think she'd hurt anyone. She's in an unhappy marriage."

"So I gathered from the black eye."

"I think she has a lot of regrets."

"I'm not unsympathetic, but if she had anything to do with my father's murder, she's a dangerous woman. I don't want her coming to my grandmother's home causing any more scenes. She might threaten one of us next time."

He nodded. "You're absolutely, right, and I'm sorry I told her about you," Chris said. "It slipped out, and before I knew it, she'd left the Beachcomber. I suppose she was headed here. I never would have said anything if I'd known she was going to contact you. I truly apologize for her scaring you."

Kayla's internal flame began to cool. It seemed Chris was often apologizing for the actions of others. She decided to drop the subject. The police would do their job and, hopefully, Melissa or someone else would be arrested soon. She sat down in the grass and watched Chris's hands move deftly as he poured some of the lime scale remover into a dish and placed the impeller inside. She could visualize those same hands flying across guitar strings.

"This has to soak for a little while," he said.

"How did your show go last night?" she asked, to change the topic.

Their gazes met, and in the sun, his green eyes glittered like emeralds. "It went great. Thanks for asking. Do you think you'll make it Saturday night?"

"I don't know if I'll still be here. If I am, I'll try. I'd like to hear you. What kind of music do you play?"

"Light jazz and some alternative stuff." He dipped the toothbrush into the lime solution and started scrubbing the inside and outside of the pump. "Where's your boyfriend today?" he asked nonchalantly.

Kayla felt her cheeks warm at thinking of Tanner as her boyfriend. "We're not a couple," she clarified. "He's a newspaper reporter from Maine. He had to run an errand in town."

Chris looked like he might ask another question and then decided against it.

"Tanner's great grandmother used to work here at Seacliff House sometime in the late 1950s," Kayla said. "I think it was 1958. He's here to dig up some information about her. Your grandparents knew her. Martine even trained her."

"Oh?"

"Her name was Pearl O'Neill. Did you ever hear either of them talk of her?"

"Nope. But then, my grandparents aren't what you call big conversationalists, especially when it comes to reminiscing about the past."

Kayla noted the sarcasm, slight as it was. His comment about the past was interesting. She got the feeling Chris may have grown up shrouded in secrecy the way she had. The two of them had something in common. "Do you live in the cottage with Martine and Dave?"

"No. My childhood was spent there, but I have my own apartment now. It's located above the Beachcomber." He continued to scrub the pump with the toothbrush as they talked.

"So, your grandparents raised you?" she asked.

"Yeah. My parents were killed together in an automobile accident when I was a baby. Grandpa and Grandma are the only relatives I have."

In their own way, Dave and Martine were as odd as her grandmother. Kayla felt sorry for Chris, but at least he'd had family growing up.

Once he was satisfied that the pump was thoroughly clean, he replaced the impeller and the cover. Then he put the pump back into the water and plugged it in. "There. All done. This fountain will run at its full capacity now. Mrs. Chandler should be happy."

"I'm not sure anything makes her happy," Kayla replied, with a smile.

He chuckled, fully opening his mouth for the first time. She took note of the slight gap between his front teeth, an endearing feature that added to his uniqueness. He snapped the toolbox lid shut and offered his hand to help Kayla up from the grass.

His hand was smooth and supple, except for the tips of his fingers, which were calloused, probably from pressing on guitar strings day in and out. Tanner was built differently—solid and strong, with hands to match.

"Are you going back to the house?" Chris asked.

"Yes. Are you?"

"I'm unloading this toolbox in the basement and then going to check on my grandpa. He's not well."

That was an understatement. Kayla remembered how Dave had barged into the house drunk and waving Sonora's ancestral pistol around in the air. "I hope it's nothing serious," she said politely.

A flash of anxiety crossed Chris's face, and she wondered if Dave had a virus or something worse. "Apparently, he's having chest pains off and on. Grandma calls it angina. She doesn't seem too worried, but if he doesn't look any better than when I arrived earlier, I'm going to call an ambulance whether he likes it or not."

"It's better to be safe than sorry," Kayla pointed out.

Chris nodded in agreement. "I'm going through the back entrance to the basement. See you later."

They said goodbye and Kayla entered the house through the front door.

"Kayla," Sonora called. She sat in her wheelchair at the end of the hall. "Come here. I have some news."

"Yes?"

"The phone call I received was from Officer Scott."

Kayla's heart picked up its pace. "Have they arrested someone?"

"No, but a witness has come forward after reading about Matt's murder in the paper. A woman was walking her dog on the beach early that morning. Apparently, she saw a lady wearing a floppy hat leaving the same vicinity as where Matt's body was found, and she seemed to be in a hurry."

"Did the witness see a face? One she can identify?"

Sonora shook her head. "Unfortunately, she wasn't wearing her glasses and the other woman was about twenty feet away and headed in the opposite direction."

"What color of hair did she see under the hat?"

"If Officer Scott knows, she didn't say."

Kayla's hopes sank. "That doesn't seem like much to go on."

"I agree, but at least it's something. I'm sure the police are doing their best."

Kayla's ears perked at the sound of car tires crunching across the gravel driveway outside. A door slammed and footsteps pounded up the porch steps. She met Tanner at the door ready to tell him about the news. When their gazes met, the inside of her mouth turned as dry as sawdust. His face was drawn and his lips were pinched.

"Is something wrong?" She heard the wheels of Sonora's chair rattle up the hall and stop behind her. Tanner looked like he'd seen a ghost. But he didn't believe in ghosts. So Kayla's next thought was that someone else had died. "What is it?" she prodded.

He glanced between her and Sonora. "Would you excuse us, Mrs. Chandler?" Before she could protest, he gently took Kayla by the arm and escorted her outside and down the walk. He cleared his throat. "I don't know how to tell you this, except to blurt it out."

"Then please do it. You're making me

nervous."

"All right. Your mother is in Harmony Beach. From what I can deduce, she drove herself. She's been staying at Kitty's since Tuesday night."

An icy feeling slid up Kayla's arms. "How could that be? She doesn't leave the house."

"She did this time, Kayla. And that's not all."

Kayla felt lightheaded. She tried to swallow past the tightness in her throat. *What more could there be?*

"I eavesdropped on a conversation between her and Kitty. The two of them seemed to be accusing each other of murdering Matt."

Those were the last words Kayla heard before she felt herself falling and her world go black.

Chapter Twenty-One

When Kayla awoke, the first thing she saw was Tanner's rugged face hovering over her. "What happened?" she asked.

"You fainted."

His caramel-colored eyes held her in an iron grip. She felt his warm hand cupping her arm and remembered what he'd said before she'd felt herself sinking into darkness. "I have to see Mom, right now," she insisted, while struggling to sit up.

"Let's make sure you're okay first," Tanner replied, gently helping her from the ground.

Lightheaded, Kayla leaned against him, grateful for his broad chest and strong arms—one of which was now securely wrapped around her waist. "I've never fainted before."

"I caught you before you hit the ground, but maybe we should still call a doctor."

"You caught me?" She smiled, and a pleasant sensation rolled through her torso at picturing his chivalrous act. "Thank you. I'm glad you have good reflexes."

"Me, too. What about that doctor?"

She smoothed her clothes down and shook off her unsteadiness. "There's no need. I'm fine now. I suppose it was the shock of hearing that Mom drove herself here from Virginia that caused me to faint. Are you sure it was her you heard, Tanner?"

"Kitty called her Suzanne. I don't think there's any doubt."

Kayla shook her head and began walking toward the house. "I'm getting my purse and driving to Kitty's. I have to find out what's going on."

"I'll go with you. I can drive."

"All right."

Sonora was on the porch. Her dark eyes drilled holes into them as they advanced. "What happened? I saw you faint, Kayla."

There was no point in hiding the truth from her. When Kayla explained what Tanner had told her, Sonora seemed genuinely surprised. *Her spies must be losing their touch*, Kayla thought smugly. Her grandmother apparently had no idea that Suzanne was in town until now.

"What are you going to do?" Sonora asked, as Kayla raced up the staircase to get her purse. She stopped at the top.

"I'm going to find out why she followed me here, and why she didn't want me to know."

"I thought you said she never left the house." Sonora raised a suspicious eyebrow.

Anger flared in Kayla's stomach. "Obviously, my mother is still keeping secrets from me." She whirled and stepped into her bedroom to grab her purse. Within moments, she was downstairs again. She touched her grandmother on the shoulder. "See you later."

As she and Tanner stepped out the front door, Sonora called out, "Tell Suzanne I want to see her."

* * * *

Kitty was sitting in the kitchen staring into space when Kayla and Tanner entered the sunny room.

"Where is my mother?" Kayla demanded.

Kitty jumped and placed a hand at her throat. She swung around to face them, her eyes enlarged.

"There's no use in lying," Kayla said. "I know she's here. Tanner overheard the two of you talking."

Kitty's brow furrowed with confusion. "How could that be? He's been with you."

"Never mind that," Kayla said, trying hard to rein in her temper. "Where is she? In your bedroom downstairs?" When Kayla started in that direction, Kitty rose from her chair and toddled toward her. Her arm shot out and a pudgy hand landed on Kayla's arm.

"Let me tell her you're here first. Then you can go down."

Kayla didn't trust either of them. Kitty could have a back door in the basement. Perhaps her mother had already overheard them and was leaving this very minute. "I can find my own way," Kayla said, wrenching free of Kitty's grasp. Tanner followed her down the stairs with Kitty close on his heels.

Suzanne sat on the couch—the same one Matt had sat on two days earlier. "Hello, Kayla," she said softly.

"I tried to stop her," Kitty cried.

Kayla's mouth dropped open. Her hands fisted on her hips. "Mom, what's going on? How did you get to Maryland?"

Suzanne gestured for Kayla to come closer. "Sit down and I'll tell you." Her demeanor was one of calm tranquility, which, for some reason, caused Kayla further agitation. She sunk into one of Kitty's easy chairs and leaned forward, waiting for her mother to talk. Suzanne glanced at Tanner. He remained on the other side of the room standing next to Kitty, who wrung her hands together. "Who's your friend, Kayla?" Suzanne asked.

He didn't wait to be introduced. "I'm Tanner Bishop from Boothbay Harbor, Maine."

"I see. Well, don't just stand there."

Suzanne addressed him in a strong tone, one that Kayla hadn't heard in years. The confidence in her mother's voice reminded her of Sonora.

"Since you're with Kayla, it must mean she trusts you to hear whatever I have to say. You come and sit down, too, Kitty."

Once they were all seated, Kayla repeated, "How did you get here, Mother?"

"I drove myself. I left a few hours after you did on Tuesday."

"But I called that night and the nurse said you were asleep."

"She lied for me. I was already in Harmony Beach by the time you called. I let Kitty know I was in town, and she smuggled me into her room Tuesday night after you'd gone to bed."

Kayla's limbs shook with fury. "I don't understand. Have you been lying to me about the agoraphobia and panic attacks?"

"No," Suzanne replied quickly.

"Then how were you able to leave the house and drive yourself here?"

"It was very difficult, but I forced myself to do it."

"Why?"

Suzanne stared deep into Kayla's eyes. "I was afraid for you."

Kayla was tired of games. "Afraid of what?" she snapped.

"I was afraid of what Matt might say to you, if the two of you met. I didn't want him filling your head full of untruths and lies. He did bad things when we were married, Kayla. I wanted to stop him from seeing you."

Kayla slapped the arms of the chair with her hands. "I'm a grown woman, Mom. You can't protect me for the rest of my life.

Anyway, you're too late. I met my father. He admitted what he did to you all those years ago, and he said he was sorry for making the choices he did. He'd turned his life around and wanted to apologize to me, and also to you."

"Sure," Suzanne said, rolling her eyes.

"It's true! Now he won't ever get the chance, because someone killed him yesterday." She glanced between her mom and Kitty. "But you already know he's dead, don't you?"

Suzanne lowered her gaze. "Yes, we heard."

Kitty loudly sucked air into her throat and then squeezed her eyes shut. Kayla stared at Tanner, who seemed to be biting his tongue. He probably wanted to ask Kitty and Suzanne about the conversation he'd overheard between them and what it had meant.

"Did you talk to my father when you arrived?" Kayla asked Suzanne. When she hesitated, Kayla demanded, "No more lying, Mom. Just tell me. Did you see him before he was murdered?"

Suzanne's face expressed conflicting emotions. It took her a long time to answer, during which it was deathly quiet in the room. Finally, she said, "I spoke to him on the phone, and we arranged to meet. But it never happened. I changed my mind."

Kayla sighed heavily, praying she was telling the truth. Wondering whether her mom might be capable of committing murder made her sick to her stomach.

Before more questions could be asked, they all heard the sound of a bell tinkling from upstairs. Kitty rose from her chair. "Excuse me. That's probably a guest. I'll be back as quick as I can."

In the time Kitty was gone, Kayla stared at her mother, silent, and still flabbergasted at the turn of events. She felt deceived. Suzanne stayed quiet, too. Tanner fidgeted in his chair, looking like he was itching to interrogate Suzanne. Kayla tossed him a warning look to hold his tongue.

When Kitty returned a few moments later, two uniformed police officers followed her down the stairs and into the room. Kayla, Suzanne and Tanner all stood. Kayla's heart began to thud. One of the cops was Officer Scott. She acknowledged Tanner and Kayla in a professional manner, though she must have been surprised to see them there.

"Officer Scott, this is my mother, Suzanne Grayson, from Staunton, Virginia," Kayla said. She pointed at Kitty. "Kitty Chandler is the owner of this B&B and my mother's first cousin."

Officer Scott introduced her partner to all of them and then shook Suzanne's hand.

"Have you come with news of my father's murder?" Kayla asked.

"No, but we're making good headway. We're actually here to ask *you* a few questions, Mrs. Grayson." Scott's gaze penetrated Suzanne like a laser. "Do you mind if we sit?"

"No, please do," Suzanne calmly answered.

Kayla shuddered. *She* was anything but calm. How could her mother act so composed? This couldn't be the same woman she'd seen suffer for years from anxiety and panic attacks. Then Kayla remembered the high school musical program and Sonora saying she'd been an actress during her high school days. Kayla stared at Suzanne, wondering if she knew her at all and feeling distrust slowly seep into her bones, like poison. Was she acting now? Or had she been acting all of Kayla's life?

How had the police even known Suzanne was here in Harmony Beach, let alone at Kitty's? Had Sonora called them? When Kayla's gaze collided with Tanner's, he nodded, seeming to read her mind. Her tenuous disposition dipped further when she caught a subtle glance between her mother and Kitty.

Officer Scott got straight to business. "Mrs. Grayson, we received a phone call late yesterday afternoon from a woman by the name of Melissa Seeley claiming she has personal knowledge that you were planning to meet with Matt Grayson sometime Tuesday. Are you familiar with Melissa Seeley?"

Suzanne's mouth drew tight. "Yes, I know who she is. She's the woman my husband had an affair with twenty-four years ago. Only her name was Melissa White then. I think she was engaged to marry someone named Seeley at the time."

"Dan Seeley."

Suzanne inhaled deeply. "I have no idea how she'd know I was in Harmony Beach. I've lived in Virginia all these years and only just arrived in Maryland. I haven't been anywhere, except here at my cousin's bed and breakfast."

Scott scribbled notes in a notebook. "Have you made any contact at all with Melissa Seeley since you've been in town? By phone or otherwise?"

"No. Why would I? I have no business with her. I just told you I haven't left this B&B."

Kayla was about to mention that Melissa had come to Seacliff House last night when the policewoman said, "Melissa Seeley saw your husband, Matt Grayson, on Tuesday. He told her he was waiting for you—that the two of you were getting together because you had important things to discuss. That could place you as one of the last people to have seen Matt Grayson alive."

Suzanne's face went pale, and her fists clenched and unclenched at her sides.

Scott continued. "To add an unfortunate twist to the tale, Mrs. Seeley has turned up missing. Her husband hasn't seen her since yesterday afternoon, and he suspects there could be foul play involved. He claims a woman calling herself Suzie phoned their house late Tuesday night and made threats over the phone to his wife. He said the woman told Mrs. Seeley to stay away from her husband or else she'd regret it."

"The man is a boldfaced liar!" Suzanne shouted.

Scott ignored the outburst. "Did you go by the name of Suzie when you were young, Mrs. Grayson?"

Suzanne pursed her lips. "No. But even if I *had* been called Suzie at some point, do you think I'd be stupid enough to contact that woman, make a threat, and then tell her my name?"

"Believe me, we've seen people do dumber things than that," the officer said. Her partner nodded and grinned. Officer Scott's face grew somber. "Now, I'll ask you again, Mrs. Grayson. Are you absolutely certain you haven't had any communication with Melissa Seeley? It's not too late to tell the truth."

Kayla realized the conversation had turned grave quickly. She wanted to protect her mother.

"We saw Mrs. Seeley late last night," she blurted. "Tanner, my grandmother, and myself all talked to her. She'd been at the Beachcomber drinking all evening. If you speak to Chris Allen, the handyman who works for my grandmother, he'll confirm seeing her there. He and I talked today, and he told me the woman is an alcoholic." Kayla looked at Tanner. A curious expression filled his face.

"Anyway," she continued, "Mrs. Seeley came to Seacliff House wanting to meet me. She was drunk. After a few minutes, she left and drove away. Anything could have happened to her." Kayla deliberately withheld the part about Melissa claiming to have been pregnant with Matt's baby all those years ago.

When her gaze met Tanner's, she withered under his potent scrutiny. His face wilted with disappointment. Perhaps he didn't agree with her decision to keep that information to herself. But he had the same information and wasn't saying anything, either.

"There you have it," Kitty piped up. "She's probably sleeping off her drunk somewhere."

Officer Scott peered around the room and homed in on a large summer hat sitting on the kitchen table. Her curious gaze clamped on Kitty. "Does that straw hat belong to you?"

All gazes swung toward the kitchen. "Yes," Kitty admitted.

Scott nodded to her partner. "Bag it for evidence."

"Evidence? What for?" Kitty asked. Her voice lifted an octave.

"There's a witness who claims she saw a woman leaving the area where Mr. Grayson's body was found. It was around the time of his death. The woman was wearing a floppy summer hat. Considering the circumstances, it's too big of a coincidence not to consider. Either one of you ladies could have worn that hat to hide your identity when you murdered Matt Grayson."

"No!" Kitty exclaimed.

Suzanne's gaze dropped to the floor. Her shoulders sagged.

Kayla's heart skittered to a stop.

The policewoman's gaze swiveled from Kitty to Suzanne. "Do either of you own a revolver?"

"No," Suzanne said.

Kitty gulped. "I do. It's for protection. There's a lot of drunkenness and debauchery that goes on here at the beach."

"May I see the gun?" Scott requested. "And your license for it?"

Kayla wished she were sitting next to Tanner. She desperately needed to feel the soothing comfort of his hand. Hers were shaking badly. Little by little, the interview had turned into an interrogation, with her mom and Kitty suddenly becoming possible suspects. She wondered if they should ask for a lawyer.

Kitty disappeared into her bedroom and returned holding a gun case with a broken digital locking mechanism. She nervously handed it to Officer Scott's partner. He looked it over and nodded at Scott. Her expression was solemn. "What happened to this lock?" she asked.

"The mechanism broke several months ago. I haven't had time to get it repaired."

"This is the same caliber of gun that was used to shoot Matt Grayson in the head," Scott said. "With this lock malfunctioning, anyone could turn the knob and the door will open on this case. Either of you women could have used the gun. Bag it for fingerprints," she told her partner. "Obviously, we'll find Mrs. Chandler's prints, but will we also find Mrs. Grayson's?" She stared at Suzanne. "I'm giving you another chance to come clean. Is there anything you'd like to say?"

Suzanne shook her head.

"We'll also test the gun to see if it's been recently fired or cleaned," Scott said.

Suzanne sprang up from the chair. "You can't really believe I have a motive for killing Matt, do you? I haven't seen or spoken to him since we separated twenty-four years ago. I moved on with my life. Why would I want to kill him now?"

"And why would I?" Kitty cried. "I hated how he treated Suzanne, but that was all so long ago."

Suzanne glared at her cousin. Her chest began to heave as if she were a volcano about to explode. "Are you going to stand there and lie, Kitty? Even if it's by omission?"

Tears gathered in the corners of Kitty's eyes. "I don't know what you're—"

"Tell the truth!" Suzanne interjected. "You *did* have a motive for wanting Matt dead. Tell them what he did to you."

"Yes, tell us, Mrs. Chandler," Officer Scott prodded.

What was going on here? Kayla thought she might faint again. Then she felt Tanner's body next to hers, his arm drawing her close. She gazed at him when he cleared his throat.

"If you don't," he said, looking at Kitty, "I'll have to inform the officer about the conversation I overheard between you and Mrs. Grayson not more than an hour ago."

Unbelieving the words coming from his

mouth, Kayla glared at Tanner and then stepped out of his embrace. Was he about to get her mom or Kitty arrested for murder?

Chapter Twenty-Two

"What conversation did you overhear?" Officer Scott asked Tanner.

Kayla was so mad she wanted to kick him. But now that he'd opened his mouth, there was no going back.

"I'm sorry, Kayla," he began, searching her face, "but the police need to know everything."

"Go ahead," Scott urged.

"I heard Mrs. Grayson remind Ms. Chandler—Kitty—that she'd threatened to kill Matt Grayson. It seemed Mrs. Grayson was suggesting there was a motive for Kitty wanting Mr. Grayson dead."

The policewoman turned her full attention to Kitty.

Kitty collapsed into the nearest chair, tears pouring from her eyes. Officer Scott knelt in front of her and spoke quietly.

"Get it off your chest, Ms. Chandler. Tell me what Matt Grayson did to you. You'll feel better once it's out in the open. I promise."

Gooseflesh peppered Kayla's skin. Did she want to hear this? *Had* her father been some kind of a monster, as her mother had claimed? Whatever terrible stuff Kitty was about to utter, the secret had apparently bound her and Suzanne together all these years. More secrets, Kayla thought with a bitter taste in her mouth.

"Maybe we should call a lawyer," she blurted, gazing between Kitty and her mother.

"No," Kitty answered. "The officer is right. I *do* need to get this off my chest." Once she stopped sniveling, she sucked in a deep breath and wiped at her eyes. "I knew

Matt before he and Suzanne met. He was such a charming, good-looking man with a fun sense of humor. He had a way with women. Girls were drawn to him like flies to honey, myself included." Her cheeks flamed, and her gaze flew to her lap.

"Go on," Scott said.

"I couldn't tell anyone in my family I was seeing Matt because—well, I was a Chandler and the Chandlers didn't socialize with people like Matt and his dad." She looked at Suzanne with sadness in her eyes. "Suzanne later suffered my aunt's wrath for defying her and marrying Matt—someone Sonora believed was low class."

Kayla's gaze moved to her mother, who remained as still as stone with her eyes glued to Kitty.

"One night, long before Suzanne and Matt got together," Kitty continued, "he and I took a drive down the coast and ended up at a bar in another town where Matt knew there was a poker game going on. From the moment we stepped into the back room of that dive, I felt very uncomfortable. The men scared me. They were all smoking and drinking, and some had tattoos. They weren't the kind of people I associated with."

Kayla glanced at Tanner for a reaction. He didn't seem offended. Obviously, times were different back then.

"I was the only woman in the room," Kitty said. "I told Matt I wanted to go, but he said he wanted to play a few hands and then we'd leave." Kitty's voice grew smaller. "Before long, one of those men suggested a game of strip poker and that I should join them. I didn't know how to play. I didn't like cards, but the dealer dealt me a hand and the game started. The next thing I knew, I'd lost the hand and they said I had to remove a piece of my clothing. I didn't want to, but Matt insisted I play the game. I started to cry and all those dirty men laughed. Even Matt." Kitty's face screwed up at the memory.

"What happened then?" Scott asked.

"I begged Matt to take me out of there. But he said we had to finish the game. And he started to unbutton my blouse." Kitty lowered her gaze and began to weep again. "I was so scared, but there was nothing I could do. I tried to stop him, but he'd had several drinks by then and he grew forceful. The men started chanting, *take it off, take it off*, and Matt laughed and ripped the sleeve. He pulled the blouse off of me. While everyone laughed, I sat there in my bra crying, and he did nothing to help me."

"Did it go further?" the officer asked.

Kitty shook her head. "I didn't let it. I finally came to my senses and jerked my blouse out of Matt's hands and ran for the restroom. A lady inside helped me get dressed and called me a cab. Matt never came to check on me. I left the bar and the cab took me home. Luckily, no one saw me."

"Did you file a complaint on Matt Grayson?"

"No, I didn't. I just wanted to forget what had happened and never lay eyes on him again."

"And you never told anyone about the incident? Not even Mrs. Grayson when she began dating him?"

"I tried once," Kitty said. "Suzanne was so in love, she wouldn't have believed anything anyone told her about Matt. Her mother was already bad-mouthing him. She and

I had been close since we were children. She felt I was the only one she could talk to about how happy she was with Matt. I didn't want to ruffle feathers. I'd hoped he'd changed. And then the two of them eloped."

"I assume there came a time when you finally shared your story with your cousin," Scott said.

"Yes. It was when we all thought Matt had drowned and Suzanne was taking Kayla and leaving Harmony Beach. There was nothing to lose at that point. We both knew Matt had cheated on her numerous times. I told her what happened to me that night." Kitty swallowed hard. "That's when I also told her that if he wasn't already dead, I'd kill him if he ever tried to lay a hand on me again."

Officer Scott, who had been furiously taking notes the whole time Kitty talked, stopped writing. "How did Mrs. Grayson react when you told her?"

"I believed her," Suzanne cut in. "And I told her I was sorry for what she'd gone through. By that time, I knew the kind of man Matt was. Although I had every intention of leaving everyone I knew behind in Harmony Beach, I knew I couldn't say goodbye to Kitty forever. We were more like sisters than cousins. I promised to let her know where Kayla and I settled, and the two of us have stayed in touch ever since."

"Does her version match yours with regard to how that all played out?" Scott asked Kitty. She nodded.

After several moments in which the policewoman contemplated all she'd heard, she closed her notebook. "That'll be all for now, but I'll be contacting you again. Under no circumstances are the two of you to leave

Harmony Beach until I'm in touch again. Is that understood?"

Kitty and Suzanne acknowledged by nodding their heads.

"You're not arresting either of them?" Kayla asked.

"Not at this time, but that doesn't mean I won't be back. Let's go, Willis," she said to her partner. "We can find our way upstairs and let ourselves out," she told Kitty.

The two of them disappeared up the stairs, with Officer Willis carrying the bag with Kitty's hat and gun.

For a moment, Kayla, Tanner, Suzanne and Kitty stood stock still, staring at each other with nobody speaking. Then Kayla and her mother opened their mouths at the same time.

"Kayla, I'm sorry if—"

With her hand in front of her face, Kayla stopped her mother in mid-sentence. "I can't talk to you right now, Mom. I feel deceived and hurt, and confused. I don't know what to believe—about either of you." Her gaze swung between Suzanne and Kitty. "I'm sorry my dad did that to you all those years ago, Kitty, but it wasn't such a terrible crime that he deserved to die for it."

Kitty's mouth turned down. "Kayla, I didn't—"

Kayla felt on the verge of losing it. "And you, Mom," she stormed. "Did you call that woman, Mrs. Seeley, and threaten her? Did you know she'd been pregnant with Dad's child when he supposedly drowned? Perhaps you found out somehow, and that was the needle that broke the camel's back. Did you hurt Melissa Seeley, Mom?" Kayla knew she was spitting out questions without giving Suzanne a chance to answer them. She was behaving like a mad woman, but she couldn't stop herself.

"I won't even dignify that last question with an answer," Suzanne said, with a stony expression.

Blinking back tears, Kayla said, "Tanner, will you take me back to Seacliff House now?"

"Of course." He hooked his arm through hers and nudged her toward the staircase.

Suddenly, Suzanne's steely expression faded. "When will I see you again?" she cried, with a catch in her throat.

"I don't know, Mom. I need time to sort things out." She stopped before ascending the staircase and delivered a final message. "My grandmother wants to see you. And for the record, she's not half as bad as you've made her out to be."

* * * *

Tanner kept one hand on the steering wheel and his other stretched across the seat holding Kayla's hand as he drove to Seacliff House. The tension in the car was thick.

"Your grandmother *is* pretty bad," he said, referring to the last dig she'd gotten in with her mother. He smiled to help ease the strain, and felt his heart jump when she returned his smile.

"I know. I just added that to be mean. I'm pretty upset with my mother right now."

"I understand."

She sighed. "It feels like my tidy little world has been turned upside down. I don't believe Mom could hurt anyone, let alone commit murder. But she's kept so many secrets for so long… I just don't know what to think."

He felt for her. His own family was about as normal as they came, aside from the

scandal Pearl caused in the fifties—and she'd
been an outsider, not a blood relative.

All of his ancestors who had actually
known Pearl were now dead. Although gossip
ran rampant in his small town, and Mainers
tended to bring up past sins when the occasion
called for it, his immediate family had never
experienced any backlash regarding Vince and
Pearl. In fact, Pearl had virtually vanished
from the family history until turning up in
the diaries left behind in Tanner's deceased
grandpa's belongings.

His thoughts drifted to Grandpa Arlan.
Despite having grown up without the kind of
nurturing only a mother can give, he'd become
a good man with a loving heart. Near the end,
Tanner had listened to him tell the same story
over and over in his delirious state. His
grandpa had found comfort in talking about his
father, Vince, who'd been a fisherman and
never remarried after Arlan's mother had died
giving birth to him. At the time, Tanner
hadn't known any differently. It wasn't until
he read the diary entries about Pearl that he
realized Vince had chosen not to tell his son
the truth about Pearl abandoning them.

Tanner remembered his grandpa saying he
and his father had worked side-by-side on the
boat Vince had christened *Pearl*. Grandpa had
been told Pearl was his mother's name, and he
never understood why the name never pleased
Aunt Vivien. She was Vince's sister and a
spinster, who treated Arlan like her own son
and lived with them until her death.

Tanner's mind wandered. It was amazing
to think that by the time Grandpa Arlan was
eighteen, he was married to Grandma Mary Ann
and was a father to Ladd, Tanner's dad. Ladd
had likewise become a father at the age of

eighteen. They became men earlier in those days.

With a sad smile, Tanner thought about the day Grandpa Arlan died. Ladd had been by Arlan's side holding his hand. Father and son had been about as different as night and day in looks, but their personalities meshed, and their bond had been close their entire lives. Ladd had been the first Bishop man to step away from fishing as an occupation—a decision Grandpa Arlan had supported. Ladd's interest had been in architectural engineering, and he'd encouraged Tanner to follow *his* own heart when it came to a career choice.

Tanner had followed his dad's advice and not regretted any of his decisions so far. There were still plenty of goals to be achieved, but he felt life could be even fuller with a special person by his side. He shook his head and chuckled softly. No way had he been responsible enough at eighteen to have gotten married and been a father, like his dad and grandpa. But at twenty-seven, he felt the itch of domesticity scratching at him like a wool sweater.

He glanced at Kayla, who was staring out the window lost in thought, and pictured her walking down the aisle toward him in a lace gown.

As quickly as the image appeared, he reeled it back in. He'd imagined the last few women he'd dated, including Whitney, as potential mates until discovering character flaws that were relationship deal-breakers.

Tanner stole another glance at Kayla. Her family was a hot mess. Her grandmother descended from a long line of unstable people, her father had been a borderline sociopath, and her mother was either mentally ill or not mentally ill, depending on the day, apparently. And she might or might not be a murderer. On top of all that, Kayla confessed to seeing ghosts.

Besides the mysterious disappearance of his great grandmother, there were no other skeletons in his family's closets—like those that continued to tumble out of Kayla's.

Why on earth would he want to get mixed up in all that? He wasn't the white knight type who tended to rescue damsels in distress.

Because she's not like the rest of her family, and I've fallen in love with her, he admitted silently.

He drove through the gate leading to Seacliff House. Once the car was parked, he squeezed Kayla's hand to bolster her courage, and then led her inside.

Sonora waited in the parlor and asked a lot of questions, wanting to know all about Suzanne, which he found curious. She hadn't seemed interested in her daughter at all until now.

Tanner knew Kayla wasn't up to rehashing the whole scene. She explained the reason her mother gave for driving herself to Maryland, but wisely kept mum about the police visit. He suspected the interrogation wouldn't stay a secret for long, anyway. Sonora would somehow find out about it.

"Did you tell Suzanne I want to see her?" Sonora asked Kayla.

"Yes, but she hasn't left Kitty's B&B since she arrived. I think her agoraphobia has kicked in full throttle. I may have to drug her when it's time to return to Virginia."

Quick thinking, Tanner thought, suppressing a smile.

Sonora slapped the arm of her wheelchair. "Then if she can't come to me, I'll go to her. Martine!" she yelled.

Like a phantom, Martine materialized in the hallway. "You called, ma'am?"

"Yes. Tell Dave to bring the van around. We're going to town to see my daughter."

"Your daughter?" Martine's eyes grew large.

When Tanner glanced at Kayla, hers were just as round. "*You're* going to Kitty's to see Mom?"

"Yes. It's been twenty-four years and high-time the two of us got a few things straightened out." Sonora's head swiveled back to Martine. "You're going with me, so change your clothes. You look like a widow in mourning. I hope that husband of yours is sober."

"He's sober, but he's not feeling well," Martine answered, running a blank gaze down the front of her dress.

"Unless he's on his death bed, tell him to get the van and bring it around front." When Martine didn't immediately scurry away, Sonora rolled her eyes and said, "What are you standing there for? Go get Dave!"

"Yes, ma'am." Martine vanished into the kitchen and Tanner heard the back door close. He and Kayla exchanged glances. When Sonora rolled down the hall and disappeared into her bedroom, he offered to get Kayla a glass of water. "You look tired. Come sit in the parlor," he said.

"I'm fine."

She might think she was fine, but he could tell her mind was working like a well-oiled machine. "What are you thinking about?"

"I'd sure like to be a fly on the wall

when Grandmother and Mom see each other for the first time after all these years. I'll bet the fur is going to fly. I almost told Sonora I'd drive her to the B&B. I hate to miss out on the show."

"If you want to go, I'll drive both of you."

She thought a moment and shook her head. "No. I'd rather take advantage of having the house all to ourselves for a little while."

Kayla's smile about knocked him off his feet. There seemed to be a new sparkle in her eyes that set his pulse to racing, and he wondered what she had in mind.A thrill raced up his spine as he imagined the possibilities. "Whatever you say. You're the boss," he joked.

A few moments later, Sonora trundled up the hallway with a handbag in her lap and a shawl around her shoulders. Within ten minutes, a blue van pulled from around back into the driveway.

"Hold the door open for me, young man," Sonora commanded. Tanner did so, and she rolled across the porch and down the ramp that had been built on the side. "Goodbye," she called to Kayla, giving a backwards wave. Dave approached her wheelchair, walking feebly. Martine was sitting in the passenger seat of the van staring straight ahead.

"Dave looks like death warmed over," Tanner whispered to Kayla.

"This morning, Chris told me he's sick. I hope he doesn't get in a wreck. The man looks like he can hardly walk let alone drive."

As soon as Sonora was loaded and the van had driven out of sight, Kayla quickly strode into the house and headed down the hall.

"Where are you going?" Tanner asked,

catching up.

"I told you. I'm taking advantage of some alone time." When her hand landed on the doorknob of Sonora's bedroom, Tanner angled his head. Suddenly, his excitement withered. Disappointment seeped into his bones.

"Are you going into her room without permission?" he asked.

"Yes."

"Why?"

"There's a photo in here I want to see. I just hope she hasn't moved it, or hidden it where I can't find it."

He didn't understand, but Kayla seemed to be on a mission—one that unfortunately didn't involve him in a more intimate way, as he'd hoped.

Following her into the suite, he watched quietly as she opened the lid of a hope chest and dug around inside.

"I'm sure it's not here anymore, but..." Kayla stopped. "I don't believe it," she said, her mouth gaping. "She didn't remove it from the chest. It's still here! I guess she didn't think I'd spy."

"What a mistake on Sonora's part. You *are* her granddaughter," Tanner teased.

"Very funny," Kayla said, smacking his arm. She lifted a picture frame out of the bottom of the hope chest and pressed it against her body.

"Who is it a photo of?" he asked.

"I don't know. Whoever it is, my grandmother didn't want me to see it."

"Which is why you had to find it."

"Exactly. But now I'm nervous."

"Hurry up and look," Tanner urged. "You're making *me* nervous. I'm afraid Sonora will change her mind about visiting your mom and roll in here any second and catch us."

"Okay." Kayla slowly turned the photo around. Her face went white as paste. She stumbled against the footboard of the bed, and Tanner rushed forward, prepared to catch her in his arms again.

Chapter Twenty-Three

Kayla stared into the face of a ghost.

"This is the man I've seen standing next to the gazebo!" she exclaimed. "He's got the same crew cut and slim build. He's wearing similar clothing in this picture to what I've seen him in. And those piercing eyes… They appear to be looking into your soul. That's how I've felt when he stared at me."

"Let me see," Tanner said.

When she turned the picture frame around, she couldn't stop the mild tremor pulsing through her fingers.

"Do you think this woman with him is your grandmother?" Tanner asked. "He has his arm around her, and they're both smiling."

"I'm sure it's her, although she must be fifty years younger. The man has to be my grandfather, Elliott Chandler." Kayla's gaze fused with Tanner's, and her skin prickled with excitement. "The photo was obviously taken in happier times, before he left."

Kayla gazed longingly at the pair. "I wonder if my mother ever saw this photo. Surely, she must have asked Sonora questions about her father. But maybe Sonora shut her out the same way Mom shut *me* out whenever I asked about *my* father." She peered into Tanner's warm eyes. "Why have the women in my family kept so many secrets?"

"I'm sorry, Kayla," he said, wrapping his arm around her. "You may never have an answer to that question. But, hopefully, the cycle has ended with you."

She snuggled into the crook of his arm, feeling like she belonged there. "I know it sounds crazy, but I think my grandfather has been trying to communicate with me. He wants to tell me something. Otherwise, why would he show himself to me? And why would I find this photo? I don't think it's a coincidence. There's something I need to know. I'm sure of it."

All of a sudden, she became aware of the heady scent of Tanner's cologne. He turned her to face him and ran his hand through her mass of hair. When his fingers rested lightly on her nape and he began stroking her neck, his touch sent her into another world. But the magical moment was destroyed when a high-pitched sound pierced their ears.

"What was that?" she asked, glancing around.

Tanner released her and strode to the window. "Must have been the wind whistling through the eaves. It looks like another storm is brewing outside."

"That's weird. There wasn't a cloud in the sky when we came into the house. It's been a picture perfect day so far."

"Not anymore. Come take a look."

There was no need for Kayla to step to the window. From where she stood, she could see the breeze gusting and hear the rattling of panes as the blasts of air hit the house. The delicate hairs on her arms bristled. A feeling similar to bugs crawling over her skin made her shiver. It wasn't only the threat of another storm that caused her unease. The sensation of a spirit presence was profound.

She placed her head in the palms of her hands. "Tanner, something is happening. It feels like someone is talking to me inside my head. It's a man's voice. He wants me to go outside. I'm frightened, but I feel like I need to go. Will you come with me?"

"There's no way you'd stop me."

She carefully returned the picture frame to where she'd found it, closed the lid to the hope chest, and grabbed Tanner's hand. They shut Sonora's door behind them and ran through the kitchen and out the back door. Stopping short on the grass at the foot of the back stairs, Kayla stared ahead in disbelief.

A mini tornado whirled around the perimeter of the gazebo, blowing leaves and flower petals around the yard. Standing inside the gazebo was the man she now knew was Elliott Chandler. Although there'd been nothing on the picture to confirm his identity, she was certain. Something deep inside told her this was her grandfather, and he was sending her a message from beyond the grave.

"Do you see him?" she asked Tanner.

He nodded. "Yes, I do."

Her gaze snapped to him. "You're not just saying that because you want to stay on my good side, are you?"

"No," he assured. "I see a man with a crew cut standing inside that tornado staring at us."

"Thank God." Her voice was thick with emotion, and grateful, because Tanner would no longer think she was crazy. Her gaze then returned to Elliott, and his eyes assessed her with such poignancy, she shuddered under their intensity. The twister rumbled and spun like a top around him.

"What do you want?" she shouted.

Elliott's head lifted toward the sky, and he pointed to a spot in the air. When Kayla followed his gaze, she saw that it was glued to the tower room.

"He wants us to go into that room," she told Tanner.

"Martine said the room is sealed off. No one has been in there for years."

"I don't care what Martine told us." Kayla's heart beat erratically inside her chest. She turned back to her grandfather. "Is there something in that room you want me to find?"

A sad smile quirked the corner of his mouth, and she felt tears stinging her eyes. For some reason, she believed everything she'd been through so far had led to this moment. Good or bad, her life was about to be changed forever.

"Let's go!" She grabbed Tanner's hand and dragged him up the back steps. The moment they stepped inside the door, the whooshing sound of the tornado disappeared. She looked over her shoulder to find the backyard was once again peaceful and quiet. The sun's rays shone through the gazebo opening, and there was no evidence that the spirit of her grandfather had been there.

She ran to the staircase leading to the second floor of the house and ascended them two at a time, with Tanner following close behind.

"Is this all a dream?" he asked, when they reached the landing.

Kayla shook her head and strode down the hall to Charlotte's room. This time, when her hand touched the knob, the door opened with ease.

"We were in this bedroom before, and I didn't see an entrance to the tower," Tanner said.

"Neither did I, but Martine slipped and told me the tower is reached from this room. The door to it must be hidden." She flipped on the light switch.

Tanner moved to the wall that the armoire stood against. "Based on the outside location of the tower, the stairs to it have to be inside this wall."

"What a coincidence that the armoire is where I discovered the birthday cards and drawings," Kayla said, feeling her heart jump. "I didn't think about them and the tower room being connected before."

"I don't think it's a fluke at all," Tanner replied, wrapping his arms around the bulky wardrobe. "If you'll get on the other side, we can try to shimmy this away from the wall."

Although Tanner did most of the work, after much huffing and puffing, they were finally able to scoot the large piece of furniture far enough away from the wall to peek behind it.

"The wallpaper here is different from the rest of the room," Kayla exclaimed. She grinned, knowing they'd hit the jackpot. "Someone, at some time, has wallpapered over the door!"

"Why?" Tanner asked, swiping at the sweat trickling into his eyes.

"That's what we're going to find out."

After several more attempts by Tanner using almost superhuman strength, he got the armoire moved. Unable to rein in her enthusiasm, Kayla threw her arms around his waist, not even caring that his T-shirt was damp with perspiration, and planted a big kiss on his cheek.

"Well, what are you waiting for?" he chuckled, catching his breath. "Start tearing off that wallpaper."

It didn't take but a few frantic rips to get the brittle stuff off. Her eyes lit up when a small door built into the wall appeared in front of them. Then her gaze swung to the padlock on the door. Although it had to be old, surprisingly, it wasn't rusted.

"Why would there be a padlock on a hidden door? Do you think there are valuables up there?" she asked.

Tanner's eyebrows wiggled comically. "Maybe your ancestors, the Tillmans, were friends with some old pirate back in the day, and that's where his booty is stowed."

Kayla smiled, but she didn't think the story of the sealed off tower room would turn out to be that simple. Nothing in her family seemed to be. "Chris keeps his tools in the basement. We should be able to find something down there to use for breaking this padlock."

"I have an idea that will take less time than running to the basement." Tanner left the room and returned a moment later with one of the old-fashioned lanterns from the table in the hallway. Several hard whacks using the bottom of the lantern broke the lock, and the lamp.

"Good job," Kayla said as Tanner set the damaged lantern on the writing desk. She tossed the pieces of the lock aside and turned the knob. "It won't budge."

"Let me try." Tanner moved in front of her and slammed his shoulder against the door once and then twice.

"Don't hurt yourself," she said, wincing.

"Third time's a charm." With that intonation, he shoved again and the door groaned open. "Piece of cake," he said, backing away and rubbing his shoulder.

Kayla smiled, knowing he would probably be sore later. "Thank you."

"You're welcome. Are you ready to see

what's up there?"

She nodded, took a deep breath, and started up the dark, steep, short staircase. The dust and odor that had been trapped inside the narrow space for years made her sneeze.

"Bless you," Tanner said, who was right behind her.

"Ick," she complained, swiping away sticky cobwebs that blocked her path.

When she reached the top of the stairs and entered the room, Kayla dusted off her clothes and gazed around, allowing her eyes to adjust to the dim surroundings. A sliver of light came through one small window, and it had metal bars over it.

Tanner entered and stood beside her. The eerie space felt like a tomb. Only their shallow breaths shattered the deep silence that lay between them.

Kayla's gaze slowly moved around the octagonal-shaped room. It was sparsely furnished with a wooden chair neatly slipped under a table that was pushed against one wall. A simple three-drawer dresser flanked another wall. Tucked in the corner was a single cot with a moth-eaten blanket on top. No rug covered the plywood floor. There wasn't even paint on the walls or any evidence of a heat source. A corroded chamber pot sat on the floor at the foot of the bed.

"What is this place?" she whispered. "More servant's quarters?"

Tanner's shoulders lifted in a shrug. "I don't think so."

Panic quivered in every cell of Kayla's body. She walked to the window and peeked through the slats. "It overlooks the garden, but there's barely enough space between the bars to see through. Just enough to catch a

glimpse of someone who might be on the lawn."
When her finger drifted across the metal, a
terrible sadness came over her. "Whoever
stayed in here was a prisoner," she announced,
not understanding how she knew, but she knew.

"Come take a look at this," Tanner said.
He had the dresser drawers open. "There are
remnants of moth-riddled fabric in them." He
gently removed a delicate piece that had once
been a piece of clothing. Neither of them
speculated on what it meant.

"I'm experiencing a weird sensation,"
Kayla said, feeling like she was being
propelled toward the table and chair. She
pulled out the chair and sat down. Somehow
sensing the thin drawer below the tabletop,
her hand reached underneath. When she slid
the creaking drawer open, Tanner sidled up
behind her.

Together, they took an inventory of pens,
pencils, drawing papers similar to the those
Kayla had found in the armoire, as well as
dried up pots of paints and stiff bristle
paint brushes inside the drawer.

Tanner spoke first, confirming in words
what Kayla was thinking. "The same person who
made those birthday cards and drew the
drawings of the little girl that you found in
the armoire lived in this tower room. Or, at
least she stayed here for some period of
time."

Kayla's hand flew to her mouth to stifle
the taste of bile creeping into her throat.
Without a doubt, she knew Tanner was right.
But who had the person been? She gazed around
the dreary cell one more time. "How do you
know the person was a woman?" she asked
quietly.

"I'm trained to be observant. The

birthday cards and notes you found written to *Dearest* had to have been done by a woman."

"I agree. But who was she, and how was she connected to my grandfather?"

"Your grandfather?" Tanner tilted his head in question.

"He guided me here. He knew the woman. He's been showing himself to me because he wanted me to find this room. He was sad when he stared up and pointed to the tower."

"Perhaps she was a mentally ill relative or someone with an infectious disease," Tanner offered. "Maybe she was just a rebellious niece or cousin who wouldn't settle down. Maybe he regrets what they did to her and wants to be forgiven. Even back in the fifties, it wasn't unheard of for a defiant or outspoken woman to be locked away in a sanitarium for the insane. If there'd been even the hint of a scandal in the family, the Chandlers would have done anything to keep their good reputation from being sullied. It's possible your grandparents devised their own private sanitarium for some period of time."

Kayla mulled that over while feeling her stomach sour at the inhumanity. "Something tells me she was definitely held here against her will. I feel like it was a punishment." She sighed heavily. "Thinking about someone being locked in here alone for even one day makes me so angry—and melancholy. Let's get out of here before I get really depressed."

Feeling her throat constricting, she stumbled down the steps, not caring about the cobwebs plastered to the walls that her hands touched. When she reached the bottom of the staircase and her gaze landed on the plank door, her eyes widened. Just enough sunlight filtered from upstairs into the space for her to see claw marks all over this side of the door. "Tanner!" she screamed.

He was behind her in a flash. "What is it?"

"Look at this. Whoever was locked in the tower room *was* held against her will and tried desperately to get out. Her fingernail marks are dug into this door." Unable to control her emotions, Kayla started to cry, and Tanner quickly maneuvered her through the door and into Charlotte's bedroom.

Once he'd slammed the door shut, she buried her head in his chest and wept. His arms surrounded her, pressing her close to his heart, making her feel safe and protected. Her nerves were shattered. But as she clung to Tanner, Kayla felt the fire igniting between them. She'd heard an intense experience could bring people together. Even if it was inappropriate, she couldn't stop the sensations stirring within her body.

When she settled and stared into his passion-clouded eyes, she imagined those eyes filled with the same hunger and desire that she felt.

"Tanner—"

"Shhh," he interrupted. He tipped her chin up with his finger and covered her lips with his—gentle at first, and then more demanding as she met his passion. A thrill raced up her spine and spirited downward to kindle that internal flame. She was primed and greedy for his touch.

When their lips parted, she whispered, "Don't stop."

Disappointment rushed through her when Tanner set her back. He took some steadying breaths and swallowed past the obvious tightness in his throat.

"Kayla, there's something I want to say. This is probably not the right time or place, but I'm going to say it anyway."

His burning hot gaze seared two holes straight through her. She felt scared. Had her crying jag turned him off? She thought the worst. "What is it, Tanner?"

He cleared his throat and lowered his gaze.

"Please," she urged while forcing him to look at her. "What are you trying to say? You know I'm already stressed out. I'm going to scream if you make me wait a minute longer. Just say whatever is on your mind. I'm a big girl. I can take it."

His gaze met hers, and he grinned like a Cheshire cat, which confused her even more.

"*Tell* me, Tanner," she said between clenched teeth.

He palmed her cheek and blurted, "I'm in love with you."

Chapter Twenty-Four

Kayla stood with her jaw hanging open. "You…you love me?"

"I know it's fast," Tanner said, "but my dad always told me when I met the right girl, I'd know it in here." He tapped his chest where his heart beat.

She smiled. "And you think I'm the right girl?"

His arms spanned her waist, and he kissed the tip of her nose. "Yes, Kayla. I do."

"How can you be sure?"

"I've never felt this way before."

"You hardly know anything about me, and what you do know about my background is not flattering." She rolled her eyes, knowing that was an understatement.

He grinned. "I don't care about any of that. Everyone brings some baggage to a relationship."

"Yes," she interjected, "but my bags are pretty heavy—and, for all you know, I could be on a one-way trip to crazy town."

Tanner chuckled, cupped her face with his hands, and branded her with another kiss. "You're not crazy. You're the most rational woman I've known. And believe me I've had some practice sorting out the sane from the unbalanced." His lips brushed over hers again. "Kayla, you're a beautiful and sexy woman. And I'm certain there's not a sweeter or kinder person on this earth. You're intelligent, thoughtful, and you have a feisty spirit…the list could go on and on. There's nothing about you I don't love. I've fallen quick and hard."

He thought she was beautiful and sexy? Her heart galloped as she dragged a hand

through her hair and nibbled her lip. "You
don't mind my curves?" she asked, losing
herself in the depths of his brown eyes.
"Most guys like skinny girls."

"I'm not one of them." His hands roamed
over her hips and squeezed. "A woman isn't a
woman without curves."

She stared at him with her body humming.
How had she gotten so lucky? Tanner was a
wonderful, witty, strong man—someone she could
easily fall in love with. Perhaps she already
had.

Captivated by the magical moment, it
seemed she'd ascended into a dream. But she
knew even less about him than he did about
her. Even if she had strong feelings, it
wouldn't be wise to rush into a relationship.
Her parents were the perfect example of how
infatuation could go wrong—very wrong. They
had eloped without knowing much about one
another, and look how that had turned out.

"Aren't you going to say anything?"
Tanner's voice jolted her out of her musings.
His forehead lifted in anticipation.
Obviously, he waited to hear the same words
from her mouth that he'd spoken.

"Tanner, I like you very much…"

"I hear a *but* coming." His brows
furrowed.

"This is all so sudden. And with
everything going on… I just need a little time
to take it all in."

"I understand," he said. "I should have
known it was the wrong time and place."

She stroked his arm and shivered with
lust at feeling the hard muscle beneath her
fingers. "It's never the wrong time or place
to express the way you feel. I'm glad you
did. I just think we need to slow down and

take our time."

"When you know you've met the woman you want to spend the rest of your life with, time no longer matters. You want to start the rest of your life right now."

Trying, but failing to armor herself against the pull of his vibrant eyes, she said, "Hold on, Tanner. One minute ago, you told me you love me. Now you say you want to spend the rest of your life with me? Was that a proposal?"

Smiling, he replied, "I guess it was."

"But you live and work in Maine. I live and work in Virginia. That's one of many roadblocks we'll have to maneuver to make this work."

"We can make it happen. I'm willing to try if you are."

This was every woman's fantasy come true. But Kayla was much too practical to let her heart rule her head in a matter of such great importance. When she married, she wanted to be certain she chose the right man—and that there would never be any lies or secrets between them. She couldn't know that for sure until she got to know Tanner better, and meet his family.

Besides, now wasn't the time for romance. Matt's murderer was still out there, her mother could be a suspect, and there was the little matter of learning who had been locked in the tower room, and why. The past couple of days had been overwhelming, and there were no signs of anything letting up.

She squeezed Tanner's hand. "I appreciate you telling me how you feel. It's important to me that you're able to express yourself. I'm very attracted to you, and I do feel a connection with you."

"But…?"

She smiled. "I'm no different from any other woman. When a man asks me to marry him, I want it done the proper way. So…the next time you decide to propose to me, I'd like you to be down on one knee with a ring in your hand. I'm old-fashioned that way."

Tanner's grin practically flew off his face. "I think I can manage that."

Her heart jumped inside her chest knowing she hadn't made him angry, and there was a chance for them, if she let it happen.

"At least you didn't say no right off the bat." His finger made a trail to the pulse-beating hollow of her throat. He leaned in for another kiss, but the moment was ruined by the sound of slamming car doors outside.

"That must be my grandmother with Dave and Martine. What are we going to do about the armoire?" Kayla asked, casting a glance at the exposed door.

"Nothing." Tanner took her hand and led her out of the room. "Sonora has a lot of explaining to do."

They were at the bottom of the stairs when Dave pushed Sonora through the door and into the hall with Martine following behind. Physically, Dave looked far worse than when they'd left earlier. His face was deathly pale and his hands shook. Although he was obviously sick, Kayla still felt uncomfortable being near him. She was glad when he parked Sonora in the parlor then exited the front door without a word or so much as meeting her gaze. Martine nodded her head in a formal greeting and then disappeared down the hall toward the back of the house. Kayla and Tanner entered the parlor.

"How did it go?" Kayla asked immediately.

For once, Sonora didn't have a quick or smart answer. Her hands were folded in her lap, and her dark eyes seemed to focus somewhere over Kayla's shoulder. At last, she answered. "It went as you might imagine."

Kayla had no idea what that meant. She'd imagined several scenarios when it came to her mother and grandmother seeing and speaking to each other after all these years.

"I'm much too tired to go into it right now," Sonora said, wheeling around and trundling toward the hall.

"Wait!" Kayla said, placing a hand on the wheelchair to stop her. "You can't go without telling me how my mom reacted. Was she surprised? Is she still angry with you? Or did the two of you make up and decide to let bygones be bygones?"

"All of the above," Sonora answered, with a sigh. "I've invited her for breakfast tomorrow morning, and she's accepted."

"You're kidding?"

"I don't kid," Sonora said, in her haughty tone.

"I thought Officer Scott said she wasn't allowed to leave the B&B," Tanner noted.

Kayla shot him a look that shouted *way to go.*

"I know about the police visit," Sonora said. "Suzanne told me. I called the police department and spoke with Officer Scott. She's given Suzanne permission to come to Seacliff House, but under no circumstances is Suzanne allowed to leave Harmony Beach. Apparently, both she and Kitty are possible suspects in Matt's death, although neither of those girls have the kind of constitution it takes to commit murder. The police are barking up the wrong tree."

Deep in her heart, Kayla felt the same way. Although revenge was a common motive for committing murder, she simply couldn't imagine her mom being capable of such a crime. She was relieved to hear Sonora confirm her doubts.

The jury was still out on Kitty, since Kayla didn't know her well. Psychology 101 taught that people are adept at burying deep emotions until something triggers a strong reaction and causes a switch to flip. There could be a volcano raging underneath Kitty's friendly exterior that erupted upon seeing Matt again after so many years. He'd humiliated and frightened her so badly in the past. Who knew what she was truly capable of?

And then there was Sonora. Without a watertight alibi and motive in the way of bad blood, she couldn't be excluded from the list of possible suspects.

"Is Kitty driving Mom here in the morning?" Kayla asked, not wanting to imagine any of her relatives capable of such a heinous crime.

"Yes." Sonora wrinkled her nose.

"Why don't you like Kitty, Grandmother?"

"The woman has no backbone."

Kayla wasn't sure about Sonora's assessment. However, rather than express her thoughts aloud, she said instead, "Not everyone can be as strong as you."

"Humph. I need to go to my room now."

Tanner stepped forward. "Before you retire, there are a few questions Kayla and I would like to ask you about the tower room. We found the hidden door, and we've been inside."

Kayla didn't know he'd blurt out the information, rather than ease into it. She saw Sonora's eyes bulge.

"You had no right," Sonora said evenly. "You've desecrated Charlotte's sanctuary."

"We didn't desecrate it," Kayla replied. "We know someone was kept in the tower. Who was it?"

Sonora's hands balled into tight fists. "Who gave you permission to go into Charlotte's room? Was it Martine? I'll have her head."

"It was you, Grandmother," Kayla said, losing patience. "Remember? The first day, you asked me to go upstairs and see if I sensed anything. Well, I *did* sense something today, and that feeling led me back into Charlotte's room." She badly wanted to mention her grandfather Elliott, and how it had been his *ghost* that had actually led her. But something told her to keep that information to herself a while longer.

Tanner spoke up. "We found evidence of women's clothing in the dresser drawers. Did any of your servants reside in the tower room for any period of time? Perhaps someone needed to be confined with an infectious disease."

"We've always had cottages on the property where the servants lived," Sonora answered.

"I understand," Tanner said, "but you told us one of those cottages burned down. Did anyone move into the tower room after that cottage burned?"

"No, and stop asking me questions."

Tanner's voice grew louder. A muscle twitched in his jaw. "Why are there claw marks on the inside of the door, Mrs. Chandler? Who was locked in that room? And why?"

Sonora's eyes flared with fury. "How *dare* you insinuate…" Her lips clamped together, and she nearly ran over Tanner's foot trying to wheel away.

"Was Pearl O'Neill artistic?" he hollered to her back.

The wheelchair halted. Kayla stared at Tanner. His gaze held steadily onto Sonora, and his chest heaved with expectation.

"Did Pearl like to draw and sketch?" he repeated. "We also found paint brushes, pots, and pens in the desk. Kayla discovered homemade birthday cards and drawings on a shelf in the armoire in Charlotte's room. Who created them, Mrs. Chandler?"

Kayla's heart began to pound. She hadn't realized Tanner was going to lay it all out this way. Perhaps he hadn't either, until now. And he'd mentioned Pearl. Slowly, Sonora's wheelchair turned around. She pierced Tanner with a gaze so menacing, it chilled Kayla to the bones.

Sonora's voice was measured when she said, "I could have you both arrested for trespassing and destruction of property."

"Grandmother! You wouldn't!" Kayla cried, unbelieving.

"Do you know if Pearl was an artist?" Tanner asked for the third time.

Sonora's eyes narrowed into slits. "Pearl O'Neill was nothing but a tramp. Whatever it was that happened to her when she left Seacliff House, I'm sure she got what she deserved." With that, she quickly trundled out of the room and down the hall. They heard her bedroom door slam.

Kayla turned Tanner toward her. "Why didn't you tell me when we were in the tower room that you suspected it was your great grandmother who'd been forced to stay there?"

"There's no evidence that Pearl made those cards or drew the drawings. None of them were signed. It's just a hunch, and I wanted to see how Sonora would react."

"Her reaction was pretty strong, which must mean something. But I'm confused about one thing. You told me Pearl left a baby boy in Maine."

"Yes, my grandpa, Arlan."

"Then if she was the artist, why would she draw pictures of a little girl?"

"I don't know," he sighed. "Maybe Pearl *did* leave Seacliff House exactly the way your grandmother said. Hell. There was probably nothing devious going on in this house at all. We could be making something out of nothing."

Kayla pursed her lips. "You don't believe that."

He shook his head. "I've been trying to come up with other scenarios. Maybe a female guest stayed in the tower room one summer and made the art. If Sonora later had the room sealed off, she probably didn't even know the clothing and art supplies had been left behind."

"If that was the case, why doesn't she tell us? Why act like she has something to hide?"

"Maybe at her age, she's embarrassed to admit she can't remember her past visitors. Or she's so used to keeping secrets it's hard to break free of the habit. Anyway, it was worth the increase in my own blood pressure to get a rise out of her."

Kayla sighed. "Are you giving up trying to learn more about your great grandmother?"

"I might have to. I may never know what happened to Pearl. My grandfather had a good

life, despite not knowing his real mother.   I
guess the journalist in me just wanted a good
story to take back to my family."

"You still might have one," Kayla said,
winking and wrapping her arms around his
waist.   "If you don't mind a different female
lead."

Evidently, Tanner understood her meaning,
because he flashed that smile that melted her
and dove in for a long kiss.

Chapter Twenty-Five

The next morning, Kayla crept out of the house without anyone hearing and strolled toward the cliffs. Having tossed and turned all night, there was a lot on her mind. She needed time alone before her mother arrived for breakfast. The salty air and sea breeze would be a welcome distraction from all that she faced—not the least of those being Tanner's admission of love yesterday.

She stood at the cliff's edge staring down onto the sandy beach where her father had been found dead. It was the same beach where Angus and Bradley Tillman had executed Charlotte's rapists a century earlier. Only heaven knew what else had taken place down there through the years leading up to today.

As the waves lapped upon the shores, she thought about tides, knowing they are created because the Earth and moon are attracted to each other, just like magnets. She and Tanner's physical attraction was like that. He tugged at her heart the way the moon pulls at anything on the Earth to bring it closer.

Did she love him? Yes, she did. But anyone could say those three little words. That was the easy part. Relationships took commitment and a lot of effort—effort her father hadn't been willing to put in, apparently. Nor had her grandfather, Elliott, or Tanner's great grandmother, Pearl. Those people had run away when the going got tough. Was Tanner made of the right stuff? Was she? There was some doubt about her, if genetics had anything to do with it. This was the first time she ever questioned the nature versus nurture theory.

Kayla's thoughts drifted to the tower

room and the marks on the door. The nightmares she'd had of a woman crying and frantically clawing at the door had stirred her awake and kept her in a cold sweat half the night. Even now, her skin grew cold, remembering.

She shook the bad memories out of her head and turned when she heard a vehicle approaching the house.

Surprised to see a police car stop in the drive, and expecting there was news about Matt's murder, she hurried toward it. Her surprise increased twofold at seeing her mother exit the passenger side. Officer Scott stepped from the driver's side.

"Mom, what's going on?" Kayla asked. "Hello, Officer Scott."

The policewoman held out her hand to shake. "Good morning, Miss Grayson."

"Hello, darling," Suzanne said, smiling and giving her an enthusiastic hug. "We've brought good news."

"That would be a welcome treat. What is it?"

"I'm no longer a suspect in your father's murder. Neither is Kitty. Officer Scott came to the B&B to tell us personally and then was kind enough to give me a lift here."

Kayla felt her eyes enlarge. She looked toward the policewoman to elaborate.

"We've arrested Dan Seeley for the murders of both Matt Grayson and Melissa Seeley."

Kayla gasped, and a hand flew to her mouth. "Dan Seeley? Isn't he…?"

"He's Melissa's husband," Scott said. "Unfortunately, we found her body last night. Dan has confessed to strangling her and shooting Mr. Grayson. There are no doubts as to his guilt."

"Why?" Kayla asked.

Scott told the story in a nutshell. "Melissa was pregnant twenty-four years ago. She and Dan were dating at the time, so he'd naturally assumed the baby was his. In fact, he never questioned it until a few days ago when one of his buddies saw Melissa talking to Matt Grayson on the boardwalk near the old casino. The buddy overheard Melissa tell Matt she'd always loved him and had been pregnant with his child at the time he disappeared and was presumed drowned. He also heard her say that she'd only married Dan because she didn't know what else to do at the time. She'd lost the baby, and had regretted her marriage ever since. The buddy went straight to Seeley and told him everything, and Dan flew into a rage. He confronted Melissa. When she admitted the truth, he gave her a black eye, tracked down Matt, and shot him that morning on the beach where he was planning on meeting your mother. The next evening, Dan and Melissa got into another heated argument. When he confessed to her that he'd killed Matt in a jealous rage, she threatened to go to the police and he strangled her."

Shock and sorrow burrowed deep into Kayla's bones. Her body felt as hard as granite, until her mom's comforting arm slipped around her waist.

"I'm so sorry about Matt," Suzanne said, resting her head on Kayla's shoulder. "Whatever things your dad did in the past, he didn't deserve to die that way."

"He'd changed, Mom," Kayla sniffed. "He regretted the hurt he caused you. He wanted to tell you himself and ask for your forgiveness. Would you have given it?"

Suzanne petted Kayla's hair and answered

in a roundabout way. "He'll be forgiven of all his sins now."

"I'll be going," Officer Scott interrupted. "Thank you for your cooperation, both of you, during this investigation. You can be assured Mr. Seeley will stand trial and justice will prevail. With his confessing, it's practically an open and shut case."

"Thank you," Kayla said.

The policewoman got into the squad car and left.

"I'm glad that's over." Kayla wiped at her eyes. "Thank God that man confessed. I was so worried what was going to happen."

"You didn't really think I'd killed Matt, did you?" Suzanne asked.

Kayla's gaze dropped to the ground. "Mom, I've been confused the past few days. I honestly didn't know what to think. You're not the same person I left at home, which made me question everything about you. I'm still trying to wrap my mind around the fact that you drove yourself to Maryland. Now you're at Seacliff House about to enter your childhood home after twenty-four years. The memories of growing up here with Sonora, coupled with leaving in such a dramatic way must be overwhelming for you. They are for me."

Suzanne's forehead creased. "Didn't you know Mother came to see me at the B&B last evening?"

"Yes, and when she returned, she mentioned inviting you to breakfast today. I didn't think you'd show up though. I'm glad you came."

She paused before asking the question that was foremost in her mind. "Mom, have you been lying to me all my life about the anxiety attacks? And now about the agoraphobia?"

Suzanne placed her hands firmly on Kayla's arms and stared her in the face. "No, honey. I haven't been lying about that. Like a mother bear protecting her cub, I felt compelled to safeguard you from the lies your father and grandmother might tell you. I knew what the two of them were capable of—or at least, what they were capable of in the past. I forced myself to come back to Harmony Beach so I could be here for you, if you needed me. Trust me, leaving the house and driving all this way alone was the most difficult thing I've done. But I did it for you."

Kayla's accelerated pulse began to decrease. "Thank you, Mom." They hugged, and she smiled, feeling hope for the first time regarding her mother's health. "Do you think this could be the beginning of something good?" She nodded toward Seacliff House.

"I'm optimistic," Suzanne replied, perusing the exterior. "It might take some time, but coming here is the first step. Standing here, I'm having a few flashbacks, remembering the confident young woman I used to be."

Kayla nibbled her lip. "Mom, I don't want to spoil your good mood, but I'm going to be honest and tell you something."

"You know you can say anything to me, Kayla. What is it?"

"The thought crossed my mind more than once that Sonora killed my father. I knew she hated him. I'm glad it wasn't her."

"Me, too. My mother is a lot of things, but a murderer isn't one of them." Suzanne smiled and then lifted her gaze to the tower room.

Kayla felt gooseflesh on her arms. "Mom, were you ever told the story about our ancestor, Charlotte Tillman, and what happened to her in her bedroom in 1896?"

"Oh, yes," Suzanne sighed. "Obviously, someone told you. Martine enjoyed scaring me as a little girl, with her gruesome tales of madness and mayhem that went on in this house."

Kayla's nose wrinkled with disdain for Martine. "That's a horrible thing for an adult to do to a child."

"I got used to stupid stuff like that," Suzanne said, nonchalantly. "As a teenager, I was so anxious to leave Seacliff House and live my own life in a modern, pretty apartment, and someday a house with my perfect family. This place was so big and drafty, and old. My friends all thought the house was haunted." She chuckled. "Can you believe that?"

Although the sun was shining brightly and warming their skins, Kayla's core temperature dropped, and she shivered. She could definitely believe it. She'd wondered the same thing when she'd first laid eyes on the house. Now that she'd seen the ghost of her grandfather, she *knew* the gazebo was haunted. Perhaps even the tower room. Feeling like someone was watching them now, her gaze moved to the tower, but they weren't standing on the side with the window.

"When you were growing up, did you ever hear crying coming from Charlotte's bedroom?" she asked.

Suzanne hesitated and angled her head. "As a matter of fact, I did a few times. I remember having my ear to the door of that room one day when I was about six or seven. The door was always locked, and I wasn't allowed to go near the room. But that particular day, I was alone upstairs and did hear someone crying. When Martine caught me standing at the door listening, I asked her who was crying. She told me it was an angel girl who wanted to play with me, but she couldn't, because she wasn't allowed out of heaven, and that made her sad. That's why she cried." Suzanne's eyes were fixated on the tower room, lost in the memory.

Kayla touched her mother's shoulder and roused her from her thoughts.

"Why do you ask?" Suzanne inquired.

"No reason. Let's go inside. I'm sure Grandmother is awake and Martine is cooking in the kitchen."

"Martine looks so old, "Suzanne said. "And that's saying something, because she always dressed like a ghoul. Dave looked terrible, too, when he unloaded Mother from the van yesterday."

"He's sick." In more ways than one, Kayla wanted to add, but didn't. "Before we go inside, tell me what you think about Grandmother. Is she the same as you remember her?"

Suzanne nodded. "Unfortunately, some things don't change, like her arrogant demeanor. But I'm willing to let go of the past if she is, and try to move forward. I can't promise we'll be spending holidays and vacations as a family, grant you. But I'll try. Baby steps, as they say."

"That's all that can be expected," Kayla assured.

They ascended the porch steps side by side. Before Kayla opened the screen door, Suzanne said, "Is that young man, Tanner, still here?"

"Yes."

Suzanne smiled. "Is he someone special?"

Kayla felt her cheeks grow warm. "I just met him four days ago. We barely know each other."

"I realize that, but I could see the sparkle in your eyes when you looked at him."

"You could?"

"Yes. Was it love at first sight?"

"No." Kayla rolled her eyes, feeling uncomfortable talking about Tanner with her mom.

Suzanne nudged her in the ribs with her elbow. "I think it was for Tanner. I know the look of love when I see it, and he's aglow with it."

"Mom," Kayla whispered, smiling. "Men don't *glow* with love."

"That one does. Has he told you he loves you yet?"

How could she possibly know? Kayla stared at her mother open-mouthed. "Well, since you asked…"

"I knew it!" Suzanne grabbed Kayla and kissed her cheek. "I like him, honey. Tanner might be just the guy you've been waiting your whole life for."

"Did someone call?" Tanner's handsome face materialized in front of the screen door. He grinned.

"How much of our conversation did you hear?" Kayla wanted to know.

"None," he said, opening the door and gesturing them inside. "I heard my name. That's all. Hello, Mrs. Grayson." He shook Suzanne's hand. "Morning, Kayla. You must have gotten up early."

Their gazes fused. "Good morning," she replied, feeling herself grow weak in the knees. "I took a walk to the cliffs and then saw a car pull up to the house. Mom was inside. Where's my grandmother?"

"I think she's in the dining room," Tanner said.

"Let's find her. Mom has some news that she and I want you both to hear."

Sonora sat at the table in her wheelchair. She greeted them and didn't appear too shocked when told Matt's murderer had confessed.

"Isn't that wonderful?" Kayla asked her. "I knew Mom had nothing to do with any of it. You said so yourself, Grandmother. Didn't you?"

Sonora met Suzanne's poignant gaze. "So I did. My daughter has a heart of gold. From the day she was born, she's been incapable of any wrongdoing."

Normally, this statement would have dripped with sarcasm. But something was different about Sonora this morning. The bones in her face looked softer. Her smile seemed genuine. Her tone was gentle.

Suzanne must have noticed a change, too. Kayla saw her mom nod her head and smile at Sonora. She seemed touched, and a little taken aback, at the kind words.

"Sit down, everyone," Sonora said, gesticulating with her arm. "Martine is about ready to serve."

Tanner pulled out a chair for Suzanne. Just as he did the same for Kayla, the back door slammed and Chris's raised voice carried from the kitchen down the hall. Martine screamed and they heard a thud.

"What on earth is going on?" Sonora said.

Tanner jumped up and shoved away from the table. Footsteps pounded up the hall, and Chris's form filled the entrance to the room.

His face was pale. His gaze searched the room and landed on Kayla. She saw his lip quiver when he said, "My grandma's fainted. Can someone help?"

"Of course," Tanner said, moving toward the door.

"Why did she faint?" Sonora asked.

Chris's mouth turned down. "My grandpa just died."

Chapter Twenty-Six

With smelling salts Sonora retrieved from her bathroom, Martine was revived.

"Someone take her into the parlor and lay her on the couch," Sonora ordered.

Tanner lifted a groaning Martine from the floor and carried her to the parlor with Suzanne and Sonora following. Kayla and Chris trailed behind.

"Are you all right?" she asked him, realizing he must have been with his grandpa when he passed.

Chris didn't answer.

"Did you call nine-one-one?" she asked quietly.

"No reason to." His face was oddly blank, and his voice thick. With eyes unfocused and glazed, Kayla figured he was in shock.

She knew they still had to call the non-emergency hospital number and ask for an ambulance. Perhaps Chris would need attention, too. She touched his arm. "Do you think it was a heart attack?"

"I suppose."

"I'm sure my grandmother has a phone book. I'll look up in the number to the hospital and call for you."

"No," he barked. "Not yet." He gazed darkly at her, sending a ripple of shivers down her spine. Suddenly, she wondered if there was something more going on. "There's business to take care of first—something everyone needs to know," Chris said, sauntering ahead.

Kayla entered the parlor with her heart pounding. What could he be talking about?

Martine lay on the couch with her eyes

closed and her head propped against a pillow someone had gotten from a bedroom. Chris's steps echoed across the room as he moved to the couch and sat on the floor. Upon hearing him, Martine opened her eyes and dangled her arm over the side. Chris clutched her hand and held it tight.

No one in the room said a word. Kayla slipped beside Tanner and slid her hand inside his. When he glanced at her, she shrugged her shoulders and tossed him a *something's going on* look. Suzanne sat in a chair next to Sonora. After several long moments, Sonora broke the silence.

"Is David in the cottage?" she asked.

Chris nodded.

"One of us should contact the morgue and call for an ambulance," she said.

"Later," Chris choked. He squeezed his eyes shut to stop the tears. When he laid his head on Martine's arm and wept openly, she stroked the top of his head with her fingers.

"Don't cry," she said, with uncharacteristic tenderness. "It was Grandpa's time. No one lives forever. He's better off now. The demons won't haunt him anymore." She turned her head and drilled Sonora with such an ominous gaze, Kayla shivered.

Chris stopped crying and wiped at his eyes with the back of his hand. "Are you feeling well enough to sit up, Grandma?" he asked, not waiting for Martine to answer. Clearly agitated, he roughly hauled her to an upright position and plopped down beside her. "Everyone, take a seat," he said, motioning with his hand. "My grandpa had some final words that he wanted me to share with all of you."

A collective sigh broke through the wall of tension that had shrouded the room until now.

"Perhaps I should leave," Tanner said. "This is family business."

"No. You stay, too," Chris insisted. "The story I'm about to tell is one you're sure to be interested in."

Tanner lowered himself into the chair next to Kayla. They exchanged curious glances.

Martine put a shaky hand on Chris's knee. "We don't have time for stories, Chris. We need to take care of your grandpa."

He glared at her and then at Sonora. "Grandpa died in my arms. Before he went, there was something he wanted to get off his chest. He said he couldn't go to his grave without the truth being told."

Kayla saw Martine and Sonora share a quick glance. There was fear behind their eyes. Her chest tightened, and a prickly feeling niggled beneath her goose-fleshed skin.

"Here's the story," Chris said, rubbing his hands together and flashing everyone an odd smile. "I'll begin with my mom and dad, who it turns out weren't decent people killed together in a car accident after all. Apparently, my mother was a very young prostitute who gave birth to me in a flophouse and then dumped me on my father's doorstep. But he didn't want me either, since he was a low life bastard. So guess who got stuck raising me?" He stared at Martine.

Her eyes blinked several times. "We didn't think of it that way, Chris. Grandpa and I loved you from the moment we saw you."

"Why should I believe you? You and

grandpa were just a couple of liars. You probably lied about loving me, too." He turned away from her and scanned the others. "The tale the rest of you will be most interested in began in 1958 when a pretty girl by the name of Pearl O'Neill started working for Elliott and Sonora Chandler at Seacliff House."

Kayla heard the hitch in Tanner's breath and felt him tense next to her. He came here for a story, and it sounded like he was about to get a doozy of one.

"When pretty Pearl got knocked up by the master of the house and his wife found out, there was hell to pay." Chris scowled at Sonora, who didn't move a muscle. In fact, it looked like she had stopped breathing.

Kayla's mouth dropped open, as did Suzanne's.

Chris continued. "Infuriated and humiliated by the affair, Mrs. Chandler confronted her husband, flew into a rage when he admitted he was in love with the maid, and killed him with the fireplace poker. Then she made her handyman—my grandpa—bury her husband in the backyard and forced him to build a gazebo over the grave so the body would never be found. No one in the community was surprised when word got out that Elliott Chandler, who was younger than his wife and wild in his ways, had run off, leaving his wife behind and pregnant."

Kayla felt Tanner's hand reach for hers. She saw her mother's face had gone white as flour. Suzanne's mouth was drawn into a tight, thin line. Her gaze didn't waver from Chris's face. Kayla, herself, did not move a muscle and felt the breath leave her lungs.

Chris went on with his lurid tale. "Only

Mrs. Chandler wasn't pregnant. But her maid was, and what was she to do with a young, pregnant maid—her husband's mistress? How was she to punish Pearl and keep the pregnancy a secret? That was a simple fix. She locked the adulterous tramp in the tower room, where Pearl saw no one except the housekeeper."

Chris looked at Martine, whose gaze held steady, despite being betrayed by him. "On Mrs. Chandler's orders, Martine fed the girl well for the next seven months, to keep her plump and healthy. And when Pearl gave birth to a little girl, her daughter was immediately taken from her." His solemn gaze landed on Suzanne. "The baby was named Suzanne, and she became the new Chandler heir. At least Sonora would have something to show for the humiliation she'd suffered by her husband's indiscretion." His gaze moved to Sonora. "Am I telling the story correctly, Mrs. Chandler? Have I gotten all the details straight so far?"

Tears stung Kayla's eyes as the impact of Chris's words hit home in more ways than one.

"Fast forward," Chris said quickly. "Pearl was held prisoner in the tower room for ten years, sometimes able to catch glimpses of her child playing in the garden through the bars of the one small window, but never able to touch or talk to her. The window was yet another way Mrs. Chandler had devised to torment Pearl. Poor Pearl might have gone mad if it hadn't been for Martine, who was not as cruel as it might appear. Through the years, she secretly furnished Pearl with art supplies, to help keep her from going completely insane with loneliness and heartsickness for her child."

Kayla saw Sonora's eyes snap open and her

mouth pucker. Her menacing gaze zeroed in on Martine.

"Pearl sketched pictures of her little girl as she grew," Chris said, "and made her birthday cards for each year they were separated." He stopped and took a breath. "One winter day, Pearl contracted pneumonia and died. Dave, who had always been *so* handy, removed her body from the cold tower room and buried her somewhere on the property in a shallow grave. Then he spent the rest of his life drinking himself into oblivion in a sad attempt to forget the crimes he'd been a party to. End of story." Chris's head lolled onto his chest, as if he were exhausted.

Kayla's heart broke in two as she watched the tears seep from Suzanne's eyes at the realization that Pearl was her true mother, and that Sonora was no blood relation at all. Were they sad tears, or tears of relief? Kayla wasn't sure, but her guess was pretty good. She was experiencing the same emotions of shock and betrayal her mom had to be feeling on a much grander scale.

Through the veil of deceit, Kayla was able to see that the puzzle pieces had finally come together, including whom she'd gotten her artistic talent from. But that knowledge came at a high price.

She slid a sidelong glance at Tanner, whose gaze was on his lap. An intelligent man like him had surely weaved together the bitter truth—that his great grandmother was Kayla's real grandmother. They were related. She felt sick, and covered her mouth with her hand and swallowed the rising bile, forcing it back down her throat.

The room was so quiet that the waves at the bottom of the cliffs lapping upon the shore could be heard through the open windows.

Without looking at Sonora, Tanner raised his head. In a strangled voice, he asked Martine, "Why did you and Dave do it?"

"She forced us," Martine snarled, pointing an accusatory finger at Sonora. "Dave and I came to this country from Canada illegally, and she threatened to have us deported if we didn't do as she said. We were defenseless to go against her."

"Shut up," Sonora growled.

But Martine didn't shut up. She was on a roll and seemed to want to get some things off her chest. Pent up emotions spilled from her like milk out of a pitcher. "Our son got into a lot of trouble when he was growing up. Sonora always made the trouble go away. Then when he was accused of attacking a teenage girl, Sonora paid him to leave town and never come back. She also bribed certain law enforcement personnel to conveniently look the other way. And when Chris's mother came around wanting a second chance with her baby, I couldn't let her take Chris from me. I knew she was still working the streets, so Sonora made sure she disappeared."

"Shut up!" Sonora cried, slapping her hand on the wheelchair arm.

"Can't you see? Dave and I were indebted to her, because we didn't want Chris to learn the truth about his parents. He's a good boy. We could never let him know the kind of people his mother and father were."

Kayla felt sorry for Chris, but the crimes Dave and Martine committed in the fifties and sixties weren't about protecting him. It was disgusting to think they had both agreed to be accomplices to Sonora's reign of terror just to save their own skins.

Martine rose from the couch and stalked toward Sonora. "You murdered Elliott and Pearl. You drove my husband to drink, and both of us to near insanity with all the secrets we've had to keep. Sometimes I swear I've seen Elliott's ghost by the gazebo. I can still hear Pearl crying in the tower room and clawing at the door." Martine gritted her teeth. "It's over, Sonora. Your hold on me and Dave, and your sovereignty over Seacliff House, has come to an end." She bent and slapped Sonora hard across the face.

Kayla and Suzanne gasped. Tanner jumped out of his chair and pulled his cell phone from his pocket. "I couldn't agree more," he said, punching nine-one-one onto the keypad. "Both of you are going to jail."

"It doesn't matter anymore," Martine muttered quietly. She sulked to the couch and lowered herself onto the cushions. Chris stared at her blankly.

"Seacliff House is mine!" Sonora shouted, drawing everyone's attention. "My ancestors built this house. No one will take it away from me. And I'll be damned if anyone tries to remove me from it. I'll die first! No one crosses Sonora Chandler!"

With that declaration, Kayla watched in astonishment as Sonora lurched out of the wheelchair and wrapped one arm around Suzanne's neck. With the other hand, she retrieved Angus Tillman's antique pistol from her dress pocket and aimed it at Suzanne's head.

"Mom!" Kayla screamed. Her heart nearly stopped beating. Suzanne's eyes were enlarged with fear. Kayla's knees buckled.

"Stand up," Sonora ordered Suzanne, while waving the gun around the room. "Put the cell phone down," she commanded Tanner.

He laid the phone on the chair and held his arms up in surrender. "Please put the gun down, Mrs. Chandler. You don't want to hurt anyone, least of all your daughter."

"You just learned Suzanne's not my real daughter. She hasn't even contacted me in twenty-four years. She's as selfish as her father and mother were."

Kayla's gaze darted to Tanner. He looked ready to make a move. He and Chris could easily tackle Sonora and take the gun from her, but Chris looked despondent. As if reading her mind, Tanner barreled forward.

Sonora bellowed, "Stop!" and pointed the gun to the ceiling above his head and shot. When the bullet struck, plaster cracked and fell to the floor. She stared at Tanner, who stood frozen in place. "Get back where you were and don't try anything that stupid again. Next time, I'll aim this weapon at your heart." He backed up slowly and returned to Kayla's side.

On nimble legs and with the kind of strength unusual for an elderly woman, Sonora maneuvered Suzanne out of the room while brandishing the pistol at each person.

"No one is to follow us or I'll kill her," Sonora said, tugging Suzanne out the front door. The screen door banged shut.

Tanner snatched his cell phone from the chair and tossed it to Chris. "Call the police!" Then he dashed for the door. Kayla ran after him and grabbed his arm, wrenching him to a stop.

"You heard Sonora. She said she'll kill Mom if we follow her. She's insane. And she's obviously not disabled. She's lied about everything."

"We can't sit here and do nothing. She's still an old woman. This time I *will* tackle her and pry the gun free."

Trusting Tanner, Kayla nodded and followed him outside. On the lawn, they looked in all directions. "They're headed for the cliffs!" she exclaimed, seeing Sonora dragging Suzanne by the arm with the gun pointed at her.

Tanner took off in a sprint across the grass with Kayla right beside him. Sonora and Suzanne stopped at the edge of the cliffs.

"Don't come any closer or I'll shoot her," Sonora warned. "And then I'll kill both of you."

"We have no weapons," Tanner said. "You couldn't claim self-defense. Anyway, you don't want to kill anyone, Sonora. Let Suzanne go and we can talk about all this."

"There's nothing to talk about," she snapped.

The sound of a police siren pierced the air.

"The police are coming," Tanner said. "It's not too late to do the right thing. Hand over the gun and let Suzanne go."

"No! People have to pay when they do wrong." She shoved the gun further into Suzanne's temple, and Suzanne winced.

"Mom has done nothing wrong," Kayla said, thinking Sonora was the proverbial pot calling the kettle black. "Please, Grandmother," she begged. "Don't hurt her."

"Don't call me Grandmother," Sonora grumbled. "You're not a Chandler. Neither of you are." She pulled on Suzanne's hair and jerked her head toward her. When she stared at her profile, the gun slipped down a bit from Suzanne's head.

Kayla saw Tanner take a slow step forward. Maybe he thought this was finally the chance he needed to take Sonora down. But if he tackled her, the gun might go off, or all three of them could stumble and fall over the cliff.

"I warned you before. Don't try anything tricky," Sonora shouted, noticing Tanner's slight movement. His steps halted.

"Put the gun down, Mrs. Chandler!" a voice yelled from behind them.

Kayla recognized the voice as that of Officer Scott, but she didn't dare look over her shoulder for fear that Sonora would shoot anyone who moved.

"You're surrounded, Mrs. Chandler," Scott said calmly. "Put the gun down and let Mrs. Grayson go, and no one will get hurt." She continued talking in a passive voice. "Miss Grayson, Mr. Bishop, please move to your right. Slowly."

They did as she said, with Sonora watching with eagle's eyes. Kayla stumbled into Tanner's arms and saw that five more uniformed officers were with the policewoman. All of them had Glock automatics aimed at Sonora and Suzanne. Sonora's nostrils flared as her fury-filled eyes darted back and forth.

"Toss the gun on the ground!" Scott demanded.

"Please, Mama," Suzanne whimpered.

Sonora's head snapped toward Suzanne. The word *Mama* seemed to have momentarily forced some sense into her. A sad smile crossed her lips. "I've missed you, my daughter. You should have come sooner. But now that you're here, we can go home together."

"Yes, let's go home," Suzanne said softly.

Sonora glanced over her shoulder and a wicked grin filled her evil face.

Kayla smelled the scent of seaweed and felt the spray of sea salt upon her skin. The waves crashed rhythmically upon the rocks below like a symphony of music. All of a sudden, she realized what was about to happen. When Sonora grabbed Suzanne around the waist and struggled to pull her closer to the cliff's edge, Kayla screamed, "No!"

With a burst of strength, Suzanne shoved out of Sonora's grasp and dove for the ground. Sonora aimed the gun at her.

"Noooooo!" Kayla howled.

The air was riddled with bullets and the sound of gunfire. The pistol slipped from Sonora's hand as she fell backward. Her body formed a spread-eagled silhouette against the blue sky before vanishing over the cliff's edge.

Kayla and Tanner ran to Suzanne. "Are you all right?" Kayla sobbed.

"I'm fine, honey."

Tanner helped Suzanne from the ground, and she and Kayla hugged.

"You were so brave," Kayla said.

Tears streamed down Suzanne's face. She was unable to speak.

Officer Scott joined the three of them. She, Kayla and Tanner looked over the edge. Sonora's crumpled body lay sprawled on the beach below, near the rocks where Matt had been found. Kayla squeezed her eyes shut.

Scott doled out instructions to the other officers, including asking one of the men to take Suzanne to the house. When Suzanne reached for Kayla, Tanner said, "We'll be right there. I'll bring her up in a moment."

After everyone had cleared out, Kayla

opened her eyes and let Tanner's arms envelope her. She pressed her body against his broad chest, and felt his hands move up and down her back, comforting her. She rested her head where his heart pounded, wishing they could stay like that forever. But as soon as she felt the familiar quiver in her stomach, she pushed away and stared into his eyes.

"We can't do this."

The despair in his gaze was enough for her to know he understood what she meant.

Chapter Twenty-Seven

An ambulance was dispatched to carry Dave and Sonora's bodies to the morgue, and the police took Martine to jail. Officer Scott said she'd be in touch to let them know about Martine's court date, if anyone was interested.

Sometime amidst the confusion, Chris slipped away without speaking to anyone. Unsure of what to do next, Tanner made coffee for Kayla and her mother. The three of them sat at the dining room table, exhausted and in disbelief.

"You never had a clue she wasn't your mother?" Kayla asked Suzanne.

Suzanne shook her head. "I always felt we were as different as night and day, but no one imagines their mother isn't actually their mother. Why in a million years would I ever question that?"

"You wouldn't," Kayla admitted.

"It's going to take some time to wrap my head around all this. All those years growing up, I felt I had a name and reputation to live up to. It was drilled into me from an early age that the Tillman side of the family developed Harmony Beach into the resort destination it became. But the Chandler name meant something back then, too."

"Your father may have been a playboy," Kayla said, "but it was Sonora's Tillman ancestors who were nuts. Be thankful we don't have their blood flowing through our veins after all."

Suzanne smiled. "I don't know anything about my real mother. Or my father."

When Tanner told her what he knew about Pearl from reading the diaries of Vivien

Bishop, she sighed. "No wonder I was stubborn and defiant growing up, and Sonora resented me at times. Apparently, I was a lot like Pearl." She stared into space contemplating. "I wonder how my life would have been different if none of this had happened and she'd lived to raise me. I wonder if her and my father would be together today."

"Pearl loved you very much," Kayla said. "We have proof of it in the drawings and cards she made for you. And your father would have loved you, too, had he gotten the chance. At least you know he didn't abandon you."

"Yes," she agreed. Her hand covered Kayla's. "I'm sorry for keeping so many secrets from you all your life. It was wrong of me. I only wanted to protect you, but I should have told you about your father. He did love you when you were a little girl."

"I know," Kayla said. "He told me when we met, and I believe him." She patted her mom's hand. "It's okay, Mom. I forgive you. All I want is for us to move on and enjoy our lives. I hope you'll be able to do that now that you know the truth about your heritage. It's time to chase away the ghosts from your past."

Suzanne smiled. "That might take some time, but I already feel like the weight of years of anxiety has lifted. Today is the start of a new, healthy life without pills and fear. It may sound like a strange thing for me to say in the midst of this bizarre situation, but I do feel like a new woman."

Kayla gripped her hand. A tear spilled down her cheek. "Nothing makes me happier. It doesn't sound strange at all. If I had to go through all of this drama again for you to get to this moment in your life, I would. It would be worth it to see you happy and at peace."

Tanner stared, wondering if she'd let him into her life again, if she had it all to do over.

Kayla scooted out from the table and took her mom's hand. "I have some long overdue birthday cards to give you. And then I've got a photo to show you of your father."

Suzanne hugged her daughter while trying to hold back tears. Tanner knew he'd never again feel Kayla's arms around him. How could he? They were related. Even as second cousins, the blood ties were there. His throat constricted at the thought of never seeing her again. He saw no reason why her and her mother would stay in touch with him and his family.

"You can go upstairs. I'll meet you in your old room," Kayla told Suzanne. "I'll be right there." When her mother was out of earshot, Kayla walked back to the table and said to Tanner, "Mom and I are going to stay here tonight and then head home tomorrow. I think it'd be best if you return to the B&B."

He stood up and nodded. "I'll call Kitty and make sure she hasn't given my room away."

An awkward silence lay between them.

Damn my rotten luck, he thought. *Just when I find the perfect girl, she turns out to be family.*

"There's nothing we can do," she whispered, reading his mind. "We're related. We can't forge a relationship. It's over."

"I know. But maybe we could keep in touch—not romantically, of course, but—"

She raised her hand to stop him. "Why make it harder? It's like ripping off a bandage. The faster it's done, the less it hurts."

He sighed, feeling his shoulders sag with fatigue. "You're right. I'm becoming a pro at picking the wrong girls. I think I'd better buy stock in bandages."

It was a good attempt to lighten the mood, but Kayla didn't look jovial.

"You'll find someone, Tanner," she said. "So will I, eventually." Her eyes glittered with fresh tears, which meant this was as difficult for her as it was for him. She stuck her hand out to shake. "Goodbye, Tanner. I'm sorry for how it turned out for Pearl. Even if you don't know where she's buried, at least you know what happened to her."

"She was your grandmother, too. But unlike me, you've gained and then lost your family all over again."

"Don't worry about me. I'll be all right. Take care. Safe travels back to Maine." She stuck her hand out one more time, since he hadn't shaken it earlier.

Ignoring her hand, Tanner grabbed her and pressed her to him for one last embrace. The scent of her shampoo wafted into his nostrils making him dizzy with longing he knew was wrong. She pulled away, obviously flustered.

"I'm keeping Mom waiting." She headed for the staircase.

"I'll pack my bag and be out of your way."

She nodded and disappeared into the shadows on the landing at the top of the stairs. When he heard her door close, he dashed up the stairs and into his room. He stuffed his meager belongings into the duffle bag and then said goodbye to Seacliff House for the last time.

* * * *

With neither of them having much of an appetite, Kayla and Suzanne were eating a light supper in the kitchen when the telephone rang.

"Who could that be?" Suzanne wondered.

"Should we answer it?" Kayla asked.

"I think so."

Kayla snatched up the receiver. "Hello? This is Kayla Grayson speaking. Yes, my mother Suzanne is here with me. Hold on, please." She handed the receiver to Suzanne. "It's a man claiming to be Sonora's lawyer. He wants to speak to you."

Kayla listened to the one-sided conversation, curious as to how Sonora's lawyer had known they were at Seacliff House and why he'd be calling on the very day his client had died. When the conversation ended a few moments later, Suzanne walked like a zombie to her chair, plopped onto it and said, "You'll never believe what that man just told me."

"What?"

"Mother—err, Sonora had apparently taken me out of her will years ago. But yesterday, after our visit, she went to the lawyer's office and updated it. She left everything to me—Seacliff House, the property, and all of its furnishings, plus money in the bank."

Kayla glanced around, remembering how the house had felt creepy the first day she visited. When Sonora had mentioned perhaps leaving it to her someday, Kayla hadn't wanted anything to do with the place and told her so. She was even less interested in it now. But her mother had been raised here. She had memories.

"What's your feeling about that?" she asked.

Suzanne didn't hesitate. "I don't want it. I grew up here, but I have no bond to the house or anything in it. To be honest, I never felt a connection. I always felt like a stranger living here. Now I know why."

"Grandpa Elliott lived here once," Kayla reminded her.

"Yes, but it didn't belong to him, either. This has always been Sonora's house, inherited down through the generations. Besides, there are only bad memories here now. My poor mother was locked upstairs for ten years. I could never walk past Charlotte's room without thinking of the tower room and how Pearl suffered. And my father, buried beneath the gazebo." She shuddered. "I'll sell the place lock, stock and barrel, but not before reinterring my father in a cemetery with a proper headstone."

"I think that would be nice." Kayla hoped Elliott would then stop haunting the garden and find peace.

"I only wish we knew where my real mother is buried. We could place them side by side to remain together for all eternity."

Kayla smiled. "They loved each other. I think they're already together, Mom."

"You're probably right." She pushed her plate back, and her face sobered. "Speaking of love… I'm so sorry about Tanner. I know you cared for him. It must have been a terrific shock for you to find out you're both related to Pearl. What are the odds of something like that happening?"

"Probably not too great," Kayla groaned.

"I know I shouldn't be asking you such a personal question, but did you…?"

When Suzanne's voice trailed off, Kayla glanced up and understood her meaning perfectly. She felt her face burn with mortification. "No, Mom. Nothing happened between Tanner and me."

Suzanne heaved a sigh. "Thank God."

"Can we please not talk about him? He's gone. We're over. That's that." Kayla placed her head in her hands and felt the tears about to spill. Suzanne rubbed circles over her back with her hand, like she did when Kayla was a little girl and had woken up with a bad dream. "That feels good," Kayla said.

"You're going to be okay, baby," Suzanne assured. "You'll get through this. You're a strong woman. You come from good stock."

Kayla slowly lifted her head and kissed Suzanne's cheek. "I sure did."

That night, she lay in the four-poster bed staring up at the ceiling. Her mom slept beside her. Neither had wanted to be alone tonight.

Kayla's mind wouldn't stop racing. Everything happened for a reason, Mom had always told her. If that were true, why did Tanner come into her life? She saw no good reason why they should have bumped into each other on the boardwalk and quickly fallen in love.

The reason was to become more resilient, Mom said. But Kayla had been strong all her life. It didn't seem fair that she'd finally met the man of her dreams only to discover they were related! Something that off the wall only happened in television movies.

She turned her head and glanced out the window to peer at the moon hanging in the sky.

I wonder if Tanner's looking at the moon right now, too.

As soon as the words entered her mind, Kayla chastised herself and made a vow never to utter his name again. Tomorrow, she and Mom would drive home to Virginia. Mom would begin her new life of freedom. Kayla would go back to work and start another book. The miles of distance between Virginia and Maine would help her to forget him.

Suzanne had changed through this experience, and so had Kayla. But whom was she kidding? She'd changed all right. She'd lost hope that she'd ever love as fiercely as she loved that Mainer man.

She plowed her face into the pillow and softly cried herself to sleep.

Chapter Twenty-Eight

The next morning, Tanner prepared to check out of the B&B. His bags were packed and he'd paid his bill.

"You can't start a long trip on an empty stomach," Kitty said, insisting he have breakfast before going. The delicious aroma of French toast and eggs wafting from her kitchen convinced him she was right.

"Have a seat outside on the porch," Kitty said. "It'll take about ten minutes for me to get a plate ready. A few of my guests have checked out already. The others have eaten. I hope you don't mind having breakfast alone."

"I prefer it today," he answered, stepping onto the porch and feeling the heat of the morning hit his face.

When he'd returned from Seacliff House yesterday, the first thing he'd mentioned to Kitty was that he was glad she hadn't turned out to be a murderer. Then he told her the whole story about what had transpired above the cliffs. Her eyes had watered with sympathy when he explained the family connection between him and Kayla.

He'd thought Kitty was going to faint when she heard Sonora had taken Suzanne hostage and then had been killed by the police. She immediately ran to the phone to call Suzanne. He'd overheard her crying with joy and relief before heading to his room and to bed.

Sleep had been restless, as Kayla had inhabited his dreams. Once, Tanner jolted up in the middle of the night in a cold sweat, feeling for the first time in his adult life the need to talk to someone about his befuddled emotions. There was no way he and

Kayla would see or communicate with each other in the future, but a guy didn't just turn off his feelings overnight. She was a good person he'd grown close to, and he'd miss her friendship.

His dad was his best friend. He'd be able to give clear perspective. But at two in the morning, Dad would probably have a heart attack if the phone rang at that hour, so the call was put off until now.

Tanner took out his cell phone and punched in the home number. Dad answered on the third ring. When Ladd asked how the journey to find Pearl was going, he listened quietly while Tanner told him everything, from the beginning to the end, including how he'd met Kayla and fallen in love.

"If you're in love, why do you sound so down?" Ladd asked.

When Tanner explained, there was a long silence on the other end of the phone.

"Dad, are you still there?"

"I'm here."

"Isn't that a helluva twist?" Tanner chuckled, though his mood was anything but cheerful. "I finally meet the right girl and she turns out to be a long-lost cousin or something. Like the song says, if I didn't have bad luck, I'd have no luck at all."

Ladd didn't laugh. "Son, I have something to tell you. It's about your Grandpa Arlan."

Tanner squared his back and sat up straighter in the chair. Something in his dad's voice warranted his full attention. "What about Grandpa?"

Ladd cleared his throat. "I don't know the correct way to say this, so I'll just blurt it out. Arlan was not your grandfather."

"What?"

"What I mean to say is he wasn't your birth grandfather."

Tanner tilted his head, uncomprehending. "What are you talking about, Dad?"

"Let me start over," Ladd said, obviously rattled. "My dad, your grandpa, Arlan Bishop, was not *my* birth father. That's about as clear as I can say it."

"Huh?" Tanner felt the hair on the back of his neck stiffen.

Ladd inhaled deeply. "When I was four years old, your grandpa married my mother, your Grandma Mary Ann. She was a widow when they met. My real father died when I was an infant. I never knew him. When Dad became Mom's second husband, he adopted me."

With his jaw hanging open, Tanner leaned back in his chair. It took a few moments before he could speak coherently. "You're adopted?"

"Yes, son."

"Why didn't you ever tell me?"

Tanner could picture his dad shrugging. "I didn't ever see the need. I never knew any other father. Dad loved and cared for me as if I were his flesh and blood. We were father and son. Out of respect to him and Mom, I never talked about being adopted. It wasn't an issue for them, and it wasn't one for me, either."

It didn't take but a minute for Tanner to put two and two together. He smiled. "That means, technically, you're no blood relation to Grandpa Arlan or his mother, Pearl O'Neill, and neither am I. Pearl was my great grandmother in name only, not where genetics are concerned."

"If you want to get technical about it—

and I can understand why you do—that's correct. You're not related to Pearl."

Tanner shot out of the chair, sending it clattering to the floor.

"What was that noise?" Ladd asked.

"My heart exploding," Tanner said.

Ladd laughed. "So when do your mother and I get to meet this girl you're so crazy about?"

"As soon as I can find her and tell her the news!"

"Find her? Where's she gone?"

"She may be on the road already, driving to Virginia. That's where she's from."

"If she's on her way to Virginia," Ladd said, "you'd better get off the phone and get into your car and drive like hell."

"I'm going to do just that, Dad. I'll talk to you again soon."

"Okay, son."

A thought occurred to Tanner before he clicked off. "Dad, I apologize for sounding insensitive when I said you're technically no blood to Grandpa. I didn't mean it the way it came out."

"I understand, and no offense taken."

"Thanks." Tanner hung up and immediately dialed Kayla's cell phone number. When it went directly to voice mail, he left a quick message.

"Kayla, this is Tanner. I hope you haven't started for home. Please don't leave Seacliff House yet. I'm on my way, and I have some great news. You're going to want to hear this. It'll change everything between us."

He flung open the screen door and bolted through it at the same time Kitty stepped out of the kitchen with a steaming plate in her hands.

"I'm sorry, Kitty, but I can't stay for breakfast after all."

"Where are you going in such a hurry?" she asked, as he grabbed his bags that were sitting by the back door.

"I've got to find Kayla. I just received some information that could change our lives."

Kitty cocked her head, but he didn't elaborate.

"If she and Suzanne stop by on their way out of town, will you please ask Kayla to call me and to wait?" Tanner asked.

"Sure I will."

Tanner gave her a peck on the cheek and dashed out the back door with the sound of her giggles lilting through the air.

He raced toward Seacliff House while keeping a lookout for Kayla's vehicle on the road. When he drove through the gate and saw her car was gone, he stopped in the driveway and ran up the walk and onto the porch. The front door was locked tight.

"Dammit!" Jogging back to his car, he tried Kayla's cell phone number and reached her voice mail again. Either she wasn't taking his calls or she'd turned off her phone. There was no reason to leave a second message.

He shifted the car into *drive* and sped through the gate and back onto the main road. While driving, he decided to call Kitty's number to see if Kayla and Suzanne were there. Only he realized he didn't have Kitty's number in his contact list.

Tanner let loose a string of curse words as he slapped his hands against the steering wheel. For all he knew, Kayla was far down the highway headed for the mountains. All he could do was return to the B&B to see if she and Suzanne had arrived yet, or if Kitty had heard from them.

His car tires squealed when he whipped into an empty parking space behind Kitty's cottage. He didn't see Kayla's car anywhere. With his hopes sinking lower than the evening sun, he trekked into the house and hollered for Kitty.

"Yes! I'm coming," she said, hustling up the basement stairs as fast as her heavy legs would carry her.

"Have they been here?" he asked, panting. His lungs felt like they were about to explode from the adrenaline rushing through his body.

Kitty frowned. "I'm sorry, Tanner. Suzanne called a few minutes ago and said they were already on the highway headed for home. Kayla was anxious to get a head start before traffic got bad."

"Oh. Did you mention to Suzanne that I needed to speak to Kayla?"

"I did. Suzanne said she didn't see any point in drawing out the pain. She doesn't want her daughter to go through more heartache."

"I suppose that means she isn't going to tell Kayla."

Kitty bowed her head, which he took as an affirmative.

"They're in separate cars, you know," Kitty reminded him. "Even if Suzanne decides to give Kayla your message, it may be a few hours before they stop for a break and she tells her."

A knot twisted in his stomach. There was nothing more he could do. It was too late. Kayla was gone.

"Thanks, Kitty." With his head bent, he walked out the front door and down the porch steps.

"Where are you going?" Kitty called to his back. "I thought you were leaving for Maine today."

"I think I'll sit on the beach for a while. I'm not quite ready to start for home."

"All right. If you want to stay another night, your room is available."

Tanner heard the screen door slap shut behind him. He shuffled to the beach and sunk into the sand. Watching children play in the water and couples walking along the shoreline hand-in-hand caused his heart to squeeze. The familiar sounds of squawking seagulls and waves lapping upon the beach made him long for home. Suddenly, all the events of the past few days came crashing down, and he felt completely exhausted.

With the sea breeze blowing through his hair, he stretched out, clasped his hands behind his head, and closed his eyes.

When he woke some time later, it was to the touch of a gentle hand jiggling his arm. Squinting from the sun, he slowly opened his eyes.

A woman hovered above him. "Wake up, sleepy head."

Tanner wondered if he was dreaming. An angel with long auburn hair and gray eyes smiled at him. "Kayla, is it you?"

"Yes, it's me, silly."

He sprang to his feet with his heart thundering.

"I understand you have some news to tell me," she said, "and it had better be good, since I was already an hour down the road when I turned on my phone and heard your message."

A smile spread across his face. "You

turned around and came back because of the voice mail I left?"

She nodded. "It sounded important."

He reached for her hands and gazed into her expectant eyes. "Kayla, you're not going to believe this, but I spoke to my dad this morning. I told him everything that's happened here. To cut a long story short, my dad is adopted, which means I'm no blood relation to Pearl O'Neill. You and I are not related in any way, shape, or form."

He rubbed his hands along her arms and felt her body trembling.

"You never knew your dad was adopted?" she asked.

"No. The news couldn't have made me happier today."

Color flooded Kayla's face. She stared at him, unable to utter a word. Apparently, this was something she never expected to hear. Once the shock had ebbed, she buried her head in his neck and cried.

"You don't have to cry," he said, stroking her hair. "Everything's good now."

"I know," she sniffed. "These are tears of joy."

He chuckled. "Okay. You had me worried for a minute." He breathed in her sweet scent and then set her back and gently touched his mouth to hers. The taste of her lips was electrifying. His body heated and flamed when she returned the kiss in a way that left no doubt she wanted and desired him.

When their lips parted, he said, "Kayla, I feel like I've found my other half in you. I hope you feel the same way."

She grinned. "I do. I love you, Tanner."

"I love you, too. It's the best feeling

in the world to say those words and mean them."

His gaze meandered over the sand around their feet. When he saw what he was looking for, he snatched it into his fingers and knelt on one knee. With a metal pop-top ring glinting in the sun, he took her hand and said, "Kayla Grayson, will you be my…"

Her eyes grew wide.

"Girlfriend," he finished, slipping the pop-top onto her finger.

She laughed and hugged him tight.

"It's not a diamond, but it represents my commitment to you, right here, right now," he said.

"It's sweet. And just the kind of thing I'd expect you to do."

Their gazes melded. "There are things we'll have to figure out to make this relationship work," she said, in all seriousness.

"I'm not worried," he replied, with confidence. "As long as we have each other, the world is our oyster."

"And there will never be any secrets between us, right?" Kayla asked.

He whisked her into his arms and drew her to his chest, where his heart beat. "No secrets. That's a promise."

"Our lives are about to change," she said softly.

They certainly were. His parents would love Kayla, and along with Suzanne and Kitty, she'd finally have the family she'd longed for all her life.

Tanner claimed her lips again, and in the passionate kiss that sparked between them, the future became as clear as the diamond she'd wear soon enough.

About the Author

Stacey Coverstone is a multi-published author of western romance, romantic suspense, mysteries, and ghost stories. She lives in Maryland with her husband, their dogs and cats, and a paint horse named Bill. They have two grown daughters and a baby granddaughter. When she's not writing, Stacey enjoys traveling, photography, target shooting, scrapbooking, and cheering on her husband in horseback riding events and Cowboy Action shooting competitions.

Please visit her website at:
http://www.staceycoverstone.com

9377197R00167

Printed in Great Britain
by Amazon.co.uk, Ltd.,
Marston Gate.